TERRORIZED IN NEW YORK CITY

William A Chanler

BookLocker

Saint Petersburg, Florida

Published by BookLocker.com, Inc., St. Petersburg, Florida.

Printed on acid-free paper.

The characters and events in this book are fictitious. Any similarity to real persons, living or dead, is coincidental and not intended by the author.

BookLocker.com, Inc.
2021

First Edition

Dedication

This book is written in memory of Mary Shelley whose fertile mind inspired me to write this book.

Chapter 1

Spring is supposed to be a time of renewal, revival, hope, and love. Flowers bloom, wither and die. People are born and die every second of every day. Some deaths are natural, others are not.

On a warming April morning, Mary Godwin jogged up Fifth Avenue, breathing easily, her mind on her boyfriend, Percy Shelley. *This morning was the first time that Percy didn't even try to make me stay in bed with him. He almost seemed relieved when I told him that I had to go for a jog. What's going on? Is he growing bored with me? Am I not adventurous enough in bed? Is that it? Why am I blaming myself anyway?*

Mary had been sleeping over at his apartment for a few months. It wasn't exactly a move-in situation as she only had part of her wardrobe there. Most of her clothes were still at her parents' luxury four-story townhouse on East 64th Street.

At 72nd Street, she turned sharply to her left and entered Central Park. The multi-lane road she jogged on was closed to vehicles because it was Saturday. The foot traffic was still light at 7:49 AM. Bicyclists, walkers, joggers and serious runners training for the New York Marathon all shared the spacious urban park.

Most of the men and a few women looked her over more than once, admiring her shoulder length brown hair, pretty face, and slender body. Mary had caught more than one person checking out her firm butt. She was a little annoyed by it but satisfied, too. Being ogled was noninvasive to her and much more acceptable than having her picture taken by some jerk so that it could be posted on social media.

At the moment, Mary was oblivious to the smiles and leers and everything else around her. Her face had a determined, neutral expression while her mind remained focused on Percy. *When I moved in to his place after announcing out engagement, he couldn't keep his hands and body off me. It was really nice. Did I ever see love in those beautiful dark eyes of his? Or was it only a reflection of the hunger he felt for my body?*

But he proposed to me with that beautiful poem he wrote for the occasion. And he was on his knees. And the candlelight. It was so romantic. Doesn't that prove he loves me? Or did then.

Mary tried to dispel any self-doubt by focusing her green eyes on the constantly moving landscape scene around her and soaking in the sunrays. Calmness, self-confidence, and good humor replaced the brief tug of despair. She wanted to spread her arms like an eagle in acknowledgement of her appreciation of wellbeing but didn't want to risk being mocked or photographed for posterity. Instead, she settled for doing it in her mind and in doing so brightened the world with her captivating smile.

She knew the songwriter her entire life. The Shelleys and Godwins summered in Dark Harbor, an enclave on Islesboro Maine, located in picturesque Penobscot Bay. Their six-year age difference was steep to keep them in separate circles until fairly recently. Now, their friends overlapped. Their paths also crossed at the tennis and yacht clubs as well as the must attend large parties in the wealthy summer community.

Then last summer, Percy made the moves on her. She was initially cautious, not because the age disparity, but due to his reputation as a lady's man. He had swept a number of beautiful women off their feet because of his good looks, old money, and smooth talking. Percy often sweet talked the objects of his desire with impromptu poems.

Mary was not naïve. She knew what to expect from him and decided that one date would be harmless enough. An hour into their picnic on a nearby island, she found herself laying on her back returning his eager advances. It had been a fun date until a jealous intruder cut short their romantic outing.

They continued seeing one another, mostly at his spacious summer house and then last fall in Manhattan. The couple shared a passion for writing and the theater scene. Mary was an investigative journalist at Manhattan Magazine, which was published by her father, William Godwin. Her pet topic was how the city was dealing with the rising Atlantic Ocean. She feared that entire blocks and neighborhoods would eventually have to be permanently abandoned, possibly even in her lifetime.

Percy was a gifted theatrical songwriter. Just yesterday, he promised Mary that a Tony award would adorn the mantel within a year. Most of the songs were written during daily solo jam sessions on the piano in the spacious living room. A few songs for the musical he was working on were complete, copyrighted, and ready to go.

Mary, half way through her run, was unaware of her fiancé's private audition planned for later that day.

Mary jogged past a man standing in the shadow of an elm tree. He intently gazed at his phone. Not noticing him, she was completely unaware of being filmed. The man wore a cap pulled low over his forehead that managed to hide the disturbing expression on his face.

She looks ripe for the picking. Young enough and fine boned, not that I'm that particular. Yeah, she's a keeper. Add her to the friggin' list of contenders. The winner will get special treatment from yours truly. Something permanent. A one-way ticket to hell.

Thinking about what he would do to her excited him even after the young woman had disappeared around a bend in the road. He saved the footage, pocketed the camera, and departed in the opposite direction.

Mary continued on, heading uptown to the Jacqueline Kennedy Onassis Reservoir in the northern quadrant of Central Park. Occasionally glancing at a digital pedometer, she joined a steady stream of runners circling counterclockwise around the scenic body of water. After a lap, she drank deeply at a water fountain and exited the park at East 90th Street.

Her skin glistened with sweat as she slowed to a fast, energetic walk down Fifth Avenue, the long home stretch. Mary was totally unaware that the satisfaction she felt would soon end.

Chapter 2

Mary paused a beat as the doorman opened the front door for her. She greeted him by name with a smile and strode into the ornate lobby and walked toward the elevator.

She was relieved to have the elevator to herself. The dried sweat and body odor made her feel gross. Staying fit and thin did not come easily. She had to work at it, subconsciously urged on by her boyfriend. Percy always favored beautiful, slender women, pushing Mary to eat sparingly and work out every day possible.

The elevator stopped on the 12th floor. The door quietly slid open and Mary stepped out into a private foyer. The front door to the apartment lay directly ahead. She turned the knob to see if the door was locked. Percy occasionally left the apartment unlocked when he went out. Mary thought he was too cavalier about security.

This time, she was quietly displeased that the door was locked because she customarily did not bring keys when going for a jog.

Didn't I leave the door unlocked when I went out two hours ago?

Mary rang the doorbell, slightly peeved to have to do so. Seconds later, she heard the telltale click of the lock being disengaged. The door opened and there stood Percy Shelley, dressed in a silk bathrobe. Mary knew every inch of Percy's body, but still was in awe of his beautiful face. She beheld his disheveled curly brown hair, mesmerizing dark blue eyes, longish nose and inviting mouth that she desired that instant to kiss. *We can talk later.*

"You look hot," Percy said with a wry inviting smile.

"I am," she replied hoarsely, stepping forward and leaning into Percy. She felt him respond as they slowly moved toward their bedroom.

Twenty minutes later, they lay on their sides, facing one another. Mary felt content for the time being. She knew that her lover often enjoyed love talk until they were ready for another go round of lovemaking. Mary occasionally obliged, but only when she had nothing else to do. She did, in fact, have someplace to go.

Mary stared into Percy's sparkling eyes. "You called me your love bird," she said softly, a finger stroking the underside of his elbow. "Does that make you my song bird?"

The songwriter laughed. "Well, I hope so. I am that."

"I like that song you played last night."

"Thanks." His eyes drifted away, his mind seemingly elsewhere. "It's one of my better efforts. I have high hopes for it."

"Where are you?" Mary asked. She read people very well. And she also knew when someone was being deceitful.

Percy frowned. "Why right here, of course."

"Your mind was somewhere elsewhere. I know it."

"Oh, I was thinking about that song you asked me about." Not waiting for a reply, he kissed her passionately. The sudden and unexpected ardor had the desired effect of distracting Mary from the suspicion that he was possibly hiding something from her.

Mary had the willpower to pull back from Percy at the last moment. She pushed him off her and sat up.

Percy glared. "Why did you do that? We're engaged to be married, for God's sake."

"God has nothing to do with my reason. Being engaged does not mean that I have to agree to make love whenever you want."

"Wow! What's come over you, Mary?"

Mary stood, hands on hips, on the opposite side of the king-sized bed from Percy.

"I'm only reacting to you," she declared.

"Me? What are you talking about?"

"Something's different. Something's changed. Don't tell me you don't know it. That would be an insult."

Mary waited for a truthful response. She noticed Percy's expression change from perplexed to guilt to a blank poker face. That was when she decided that it was time to go out. It would give her an opportunity to think some more about their relationship. There was an iconic place that she had not yet visited – the Observatory on top of the Freedom Tower. She had wanted to go with Percy. But she wasn't in the mood to be with him until he came clean with whatever stood between them.

"Listen, I'm going to take a shower, then go out."

He frowned and nodded.

Mary sighed, then headed to the bathroom as Percy stood, watching her.

Clean and dressed, Mary felt somewhat better, but was still agitated by Percy's attitude. She found him seated at the grand piano. He looked up, smiling thinly as she approached him.

"Don't you even care where I'm going?"

"Of course I do," he replied heatedly and a bit defensively. "Where then?"

"The observatory at the Freedom Tower."

"The view is supposed to be really amazing there. Have fun."

Mary held his uncertain gaze, wondering what to say and do. She knew that, left unresolved, their little spat would fester. That was not her style. She preferred to get to the heart of the matter quickly.

Taking the initiative, she moved closer to Shelley. "Do you want to come with me?" she asked softly.

"Honestly, I do. But I have a deadline, I'm afraid. I need to stay here and work. Sorry."

Mary, troubled, watched Shelley avoid her eyes. "See you later," she said morosely. They always kissed and hugged each other whenever parting company, but not then. She abruptly turned around and walked out.

Shelley watched her leave, shook his head, and muttered to himself, "Here goes."

Mary hoped the episode with Percy was only a minor tiff that would be wiped clean that evening. She fully expected they would kiss and make up. Usually strong and radiating abundant positive energy, she decided to enjoy the rest of the day.

Chapter 3

One World Trade Center, proudly known by American patriots and others as the Freedom Tower, stood on the footprint of the twin towers of the World Trade Center. The history of the world was altered when terrorists destroyed the adjoining buildings on September 11, 2001, the day of infamy known as 9/11.

People from all around the globe considered it an honor to go to the National September 11 Memorial, set in the shadow of the tower. Mary took pictures of the two reflecting pools. After pocketing her phone, she read the names of the victims inscribed on the edges of both pools.   The experience both saddened and angered her.

Mary was fiercely proud of the city, blemishes and all. Mary was aware that she stood a few blocks from a street battle between Union Army soldiers and street gangs during the Civil War. The city had seen riots and additional discord during its four-hundred-year history.

Yet her hometown was undoubtedly a world capital; a magnificent business and cultural center.

Mary stood expectantly in line to take the elevator up to One World Observatory. She had seen videos of the ride and couldn't wait to see for herself if it was the amazing experience that it was supposed to be.

Mary stepped into the Skypod that would take her up to the 102nd floor.

The forty-seven second ride was a thrilling experience for people of all ages. It began below ground within the heart of the tallest building in the Western Hemisphere. Then the door shut tight and the computer animated LED program began. She and the other dozen passengers first saw bedrock around them, then as the Skypod quickly cleared ground level they beheld a clear day with a view of a thriving 16th Century Native American village on the west bank of Manhattan. The view of Manhattan changed, showing the evolving history of the island. A few seconds into the experience, she stared down at the Dutch settlement of New Amsterdam at the southern tip of Manhattan.

Mary witnessed the growth of the city, sweeping north, and gradually higher as taller buildings were constructed. She gawked, transfixed, at the panoramic scene. Toward the end of the multidimensional experience, the steel frames of the skyscraping tower rose majestically high above the cityscape. Then, finally, the cab appeared to be surrounded by solid walls as the elevator arrived at the observatory.

Not everybody was mesmerized by the spectacle. One man with a book bag dangling from a shoulder cast a fleeting eye at the other passengers, finally settling on Mary with a look of recognition. Mary was too hypnotized by the thrilling experience to notice the disturbed expression on the man's face.

Disembarking, Mary felt uplifted, yet disappointed. *It was perhaps more than my brain could absorb. I really want to experience the trip in slow motion to see every change in the city's skyline.* Unfortunately, that was not possible. Perhaps she would return again soon, the next time with Percy. He hated fast moving elevators, but perhaps the feast for the eyes would enable him to forget his fear.

The bearded man followed Mary off the elevator. His dark eyes searched for the sign for the men's bathroom. He remained vigilant as the tour group slowly moved forward. The pace made him uneasy. As he stepped past the welcome area, the desired sign loomed ahead on the right side of the corridor. He pushed his way to the right side of the herd, brashly brushing past people before entering the lavatory.

He ignored the polite nod of a fellow bathroom patron and stepped into the wide stall reserved for handicapped people. He rammed the latch on the door closed, put the toilet seat down and lowered the bag on it. The man quickly unzipped his trousers and hung it on the door hook. He removed his briefs and placed them over the trousers. The undergarment fell to the floor almost immediately.

"Ya Ibn el Sharmouta!" he cursed, picking up the underpants. Glaring, he listened for any activity. The bathroom was quiet. "Alḥamdulillāh," he said, patting his heart a few times.

He then removed sheer leggings and set to work shredding them. The narrow strips were folded and stuffed into the bag. He saved the most important task for last. Holding his mouth compressed tightly, he reached down to his shaved thigh with both hands and ripped off a wide strip of tape. He quickly grabbed a 3D printed plastic gun with his other hand. Releasing a gust of sour hot air, he made sure the pistol was operational.

A short time later, the stall door opened and the Arab-speaking man quickly exited the bathroom.

Mary, despite attempts to block him out of her mind, thought about Percy as she toured the crowded observatory. She occasionally stepped over one of the huge windows to take pictures of the panoramic views of New York Harbor, New Jersey, the Hudson River, and the five boroughs of the City of New York. The clear blue sky also permitted her to see Long Island, Westchester County and Connecticut just below the horizon.

She lowered her gaze almost directly down at the ground 1,250 feet below her. Ant-sized people milled around the two rectangular pools.

"Don't touch the window," a woman near Mary pleaded. "If the glass breaks, you'll fall to your death."

Mary tore her eyes away from the mesmerizing spectacle and turned around. An adolescent girl stood nearby, leaning forward against the ultra-clear glass that separated her from oblivion. She stood on a heating panel that circumvented the base of the window. The girl grinned at Mary as if she was her ally. Mary looked at the frantic older woman who seemed afraid to step near the window. *She must be afraid of heights. The elevator ride must have been terrifying for her. She must really love her daughter.*

"Please, Lauren, don't tempt fate."

"Tell my mother there's nothing to worry about," the teenager told Mary.

As Mary opened her mouth to tell the girl that she was being immature and foolish, a male uniformed security person approached. "Please step away from the window."

"It's a free country, isn't it?" the girl replied snidely, craning her head around.

"I'll have to escort you to the elevator if you refuse to cooperate," the man warned.

Mary sized up the security man, an analytical skill she'd been honing since beginning her career as an investigative journalist. He was about thirty-five, slightly overweight, and wore his hair in a military haircut. She observed a walkie-talkie unit secured to his belt, a baton, mace, and a holstered pistol. *Just like NYPD. What could go wrong here? Everyone went through the security checkpoint before boarding the elevators.*

Her sharp eyes noticed a familiar looking man with a black beard staring at the security officer from about twenty feet away. He looked furtively around him, then removed an eyeglass case from a small book bag hanging on a shoulder. The man quickly removed a canister from it, closed the eyeglass case and placed it back in the canvas bag.

Lauren sullenly stepped down from the baseboard radiator. She stepped over to uniformed man. "Hi," she said, smiling provocatively.

"You should listen to your mother," he replied.

"Thanks a lot!"

An alarm went off in Mary's brain as she stared, eyebrows scrunched, at the bearded man. *Something bad is going to happen.* "Officer, look behind you," she said quietly and urgently.

"What?" he said, swiveling his head toward Mary.

The suspicious behaving man moved in quickly, glaring for an instant at Mary. He harshly pushed the mother and daughter out of the way. They crashed to the hard floor.

The shocked guard blinked, a look of evident disbelief on his face because of what was suddenly happening to his normally uneventful day. He reacted too slowly.

The assailant raised the black canister in his right hand, extended the arm, and aimed the nozzle at the security man's eyes. Moving his hand slightly from left to right, a jet of pepper spray struck both orbs in two seconds.

The guard, screaming, clutched his tormented eyes. As if that was not enough, his testicles received a swift brutal kick. The unfortunate man crashed on the floor, his body curled protectively in the fetal position, writhing in agony. His hands helplessly moved back and forth from his eyes to his groin area.

Having subdued the security man so easily, the assailant threw the canister in his shoulder bag, put a hand in his pants pocket, grabbed the homemade pistol, and pulled it out for everybody to see. He victoriously waved it around.

The milling crowd stampeded, many of the women screaming in terror. A few fast-thinking individuals shot videos of the aftermath, training their phones on the injured guard, the attacker, Mary, Lauren and Lauren's stunned mother. Closed-circuit surveillance cameras, monitored by NYPD, also recorded the incident.

"You!" the terrorist shouted at Mary. "I know you, don't I," he said excitedly.

"Me?" Mary answered, trying to sound calm and not to show how terrified she was. *Has he seen my picture on the magazine's website or on social media?*

The terrorist beckoned her to him with a movement of the gun, his eyes quickly glancing everywhere. Then, impatiently, he grabbed her with his free hand. "Turn around now."

Mary hesitated.

He roughly spun her around, pressing her against his stomach and pelvis. He wrapped an arm around her snuggly and paused, slightly out of breath.

"Tell me where I've seen your face or you'll be sent to the hell of all disbelievers!" the terrorist exclaimed angrily.

Mary felt spittle on her face. "Please don't," she replied, her heart racing.

"Do not tell me what to do. You are only a woman."

I'm only a woman? Who is this chauvinist pig?

She gasped when the grip tightened. "All right, I'm sorry if I misspoke." The words came out garbled through the gag over her mouth.

The man stepped over, Ellen in tow, and moved the cloth so Mary could be understood. "Tell me now!"

"Perhaps you've seen me on my magazine's website."

The man probed her face with his eyes before nodding. "You speak the truth. Sit down on the floor over there," he ordered, pointing his head at the radiator panel. "Understand?"

"Yes," Mary replied meekly.

Chapter 4

Mary sat near the window. The red-eyed security man, occasionally groaning, lay on the floor a few feet away. Lauren sat next to Mary. They were all bound and gagged. The girl stared blankly at the floor, seemingly in another world. Ellen, her mother, stood unsteadily in front of the terrorist, involuntarily acting as a human shield. Ellen's eyes were red from crying. They flickered wildly in search of deliverance, for some sign that the nightmare would soon end.

Their shattered phones lay on the floor nearby, all smashed by their kidnapper. Mary occasionally glanced at her device, hoping that the stored data could be salvaged.

The man, who would later be described by law enforcement agencies as a lone wolf, smiled disdainfully at Mary and Lauren, while keeping an arm around Ellen's waist.

Mary regarded him with steely determination. He laughed at her.

"You think you're better than me, don't you! You tell lies just like all the media in this God forsaken country of yours. You are all stupid. America needs to be punished for interfering in the lives of the honorable people who love the great prophet Mohammed."

Mary tried to block out the hateful words of her abductor. She looked away from the man, scanning the ceilings and walls. *There! A surveillance camera! Someone must be monitoring the nightmare. At least I hope so.*

Her eyes noticed something else. A stairwell door was slightly open. *Is it possible? Are the police here?* She peeked at the terrorist. Luckily, he wasn't then watching her at that moment. Mary made a supreme effort not to look jubilant. *I've got to look as desperate as I feel. He must not know what I know or I'll get us all killed.*

Two armored and helmeted cops stood unseen by everyone except Mary, a hundred feet away, watching the lone wolf from a stairwell landing. One spoke quietly on a portable radio attached to the top of his bulletproof vest.

Mary made sure the terrorist wasn't looking her way, then nodded imperceptivity at them. One of the police officers gave her a thumbs up. Mary looked again at the assailant and caught him watching her. Her heart caught in her throat. *Oh no!*

The fanatic spun around quickly, gun pointed straight ahead, forcibly dragging and injuring Ellen.

"You," he shouted at the policemen. "I want one of you devils to walk over to me real slow. No sudden moves or I break this woman's neck." He tightened his grip on Ellen's neck.

She raised her arms weakly in a vain attempt to try to loosen his hold.

"Put your arms down, woman," he warned through clenched teeth.

They dropped weakly to her sides.

Mary tried to speak through her gag. "You're hurting her." The words were barely understandable.

Her abductor laughed in response. He dared not look at her, in case doing so would tempt NYPD to take immediate action.

Ellen emitted gargled sounds through her gasping mouth.

He stared wickedly at the indecisive police officers.

"If you want her dead, stay where you are. It means nothing to me. Or you can bring me water now."

After some discussion and activity, one of the police officers approached, carrying a bottle of water.

"Arms up, pig!" shouted the hostage taker.

The policeman strode forward, one hand free, the other grasping the bottle.

The security guard mumbled something incoherently through the gag.

The kidnapper turned his head toward him for a second. "I will shoot you if you don't shut up!" He angrily turned his attention again on the approaching cop.

Both men immersed themselves in a stare down like two gunslingers of the Wild West. The stakes were unknown in this instance, but possibly critical to how the drama played out.

Ellen watched hopefully as her potential rescuer stepped tantalizingly closer. She was dead on her feet from being forced to stand for so long and having to endure the horrid man's touch. Her eyes pleaded for help. But the cop barely looked at her. She suddenly went limp.

The unexpected burden of Ellen's buckled body caught the terrorist off guard. He struggled to maintain his balance and hold her up. He overcompensated for the sudden weight load by excessively tightening the grip on her neck. There was an audible snap.

"Shit!" he cried out. He dropped the corpse on the hard floor and stared with sudden fear at the policeman holding the water bottle.

The policeman dropped the water bottle and surged ahead at full speed. The terrorist began to raise the gun when the cop tackled him.

Mary and Lauren, seemingly frozen in place, watched the nearby struggle as the two men crashed on the floor.

The athletic, well trained cop smashed the terrorist's gun hand on the floor. The impact propelled it from his hand. The cop then tasered the man, sending him into convulsions and his mouth frothing.

Two more heavily armed cops surged forward, assault rifles aimed at the unconscious man. The lethal weapons were armed with rubber bullets to prevent the heavy-duty bulletproof windows from cracking.

Lauren, still bound, managed to get on her knees. Chest heaving, she stared at her mother's body in shock. Her silent reaction quickly ceased when she began screaming through the cloth. A cop quickly strode over to her and removed the hand and mouth restraints. The girl's breath caught in her throat when she noticed the dead eyes gazing up at nothingness. The new orphan dropped to her knees, crying heavily.

Mary, just unfettered, peered at Lauren. She shuddered. *Poor girl. How awful! What a nightmare!* She resolutely stepped over knelt beside her. "Come here," she urged. Lauren, shuddering, allowed herself to be embraced by Mary.

"I'm so sorry."

Lauren looked at her, teardrops spilling down her pale face. "My mom is dead," she blurted.

Mary arms remained wrapped around her Lauren. Lauren's arms remained at her sides as she continued crying.

The terrorist was grabbed by two members of NYPD's elite ESU Unit known as the A-Team. He was shoved face down on the floor, tightly handcuffed with both hands behind him, and roughly lifted again to his feet. Then he was given the Miranda warning by the arresting police officer.

Mary wanted to record a video of the takedown and subsequent events, but she didn't want to abandon Lauren. She looked over Lauren's head as the rights were issued to the hostage taker.

"You have the right to remain silent. Anything you say can and will be used against you in a court of law. You have the right to an attorney. If you cannot afford an attorney, one will be provided for you. Do you understand the rights I have told you? With these rights in mind, do you wish to speak to me?"

The prisoner raised his head and glared at the cops. "Take those fucking handcuffs off me, you fascist pig!" Then, looking at Mary, he sneered, "You should write about me. I'll make you famous."

"She's not going to do a damn thing until you acknowledge the rights that I just read to you. Understand me?" the cop hotly said. He shook his head slightly at Mary.

"Okay," the man shouted. "I understand!"

"Calm down now buddy," he was told.

The handcuffed man, eyes flickering between his captor and Mary, relaxed a little bit.

A policeman in civilian clothes strode over to Mary and Lauren. He solemnly peered down at the Ellen's body. Anger crossed his face for an instant. He then scowled at Ellen's killer, looking like he wanted to beat the man to a pulp. But he managed to get control of himself and look questioningly at Mary.

"You both related to her?"

"I'm not. Lauren here is Ellen's daughter."

"I'm sorry for your loss," he said compassionately.

Lauren, sniffing, nodded at him.

"I saw my mother die," she blurted.

"I'm sorry, Lauren. I have to speak to your friend now."

Lauren nodded blankly at the cop.

"I'll be right back, Lauren," Mary soothingly said, a hand on Lauren's arm.

"Are you sure?" Lauren asked, desperation in her eyes.

"I promise." Mary glanced at the man. He nodded, projecting a small smile at Lauren. Then Mary followed him, as a policewoman, in body armor, went to Lauren and spoke to her.

They stopped about fifty feet away. "Is it true you're a writer?"

"Guilty as charged. I'm Mary Godwin with *Manhattan Magazine*."

"Ah." He paused, looking pensively at her. "You going to do as the perp said and write about him?"

Mary smiled in spite of herself. She looked quickly at the officer's name tag. "I came here as a sightseer, Sergeant Marston. But now I'm part of a tragic news story. Even so, I suppose that I shouldn't pass up on the opportunity. He," glancing at the handcuffed man, "has invited me to interview him. Is it okay to ask him a few questions here or do I have to wait until he's been booked?"

"He's been Mirandaed. If he's still willing to talk, go right ahead."

"Has he been ID'd?"

"He's not cooperating with us. Perhaps he'll open up with you. Are you game?"

Mary had never interviewed a convicted felon or an enemy of the United States. She briefly wondered if she was about to put herself on a terrorist hit list. She swallowed nervously. *I won't get anywhere by chickening out.* "Sure, let's do it."

She immediately thought about her phone, wondering if it was operable after being smashed. *Wait one minute! I have something else!* The journalist reached into her jeans pocket and snatched the small digital audio recorder that she'd concealed from the terrorist. It featured an in-built microphone and a backlit LCD display.

Marston nodded encouragingly. "You'll do fine, Miss Goodwin. We have your back."

"It's Godwin, not Goodwin."

"Godwin. I'll make a point to remember your name for the rest of my life," Marston gravely replied with sparkling eyes.

Mary smirked. *I hope he's not flirting with me after what has happened here. He seems nice though.* "Thanks, I guess."

Marston nodded, then turned around, and stepped toward the apprehended terrorist. Mary kept pace a few steps behind him.

Mary fed off Marston's confidence and quiet strength. The young journalist was surprised to discover that the tension and apprehension had mostly melted away, at least for the time being. Her mind feverishly worked out the questions she'd ask her former abductor. *Who are you? Why did you kidnap us? What's your objective? Who ordered you to do this or did you do it in your own misguided way? Easy now. I can't make him angry or he'll clam up.*

In what seemed like no time, Mary stood facing the man. She tried to shake off images and sounds of the violence he had committed. She again heard Ellen's neck break and her body drop on the floor and Lauren's mournful grieving. *Come on now. I'll be a disgrace to the magazine if I don't shape up. I must focus.*

Mary gathered herself. She observed the killer's eyes watching her.

"You finally ready or do I need to find a man to write about me?"

The insult increased her motivation and burned inside her. Sensing that he wanted to maintain the upper hand and provoke her, Mary did her best to act cool, calm, and collected, an almost unsurmountable task after the recent ordeal.

"Perhaps we should sit first. It will be better that way. Do you mind?" she asked him, glancing at Marston?

"That's not a good idea," Marston said, standing protectively near Mary, his full attention on the perpetrator.

Mary fidgeted with the recorder.

The man frowned at the device. "I did not agree to this."

"You consented to an interview. This is how it is done," Mary replied, almost hoping the man would call it off. She looked demurely at him, hoping her attitude would encourage him to proceed.

He shrugged. "Okay, go ahead."

She pressed PLAY and asked the first question. "What's your name?"

"Abu Musab Ali. What's yours?"

"You don't have to answer that," Marston advised her.

Mary didn't think revealing her identity would endanger her life. In any case, her name would appear in black ink as the writer of the magazine article. "That's okay, "she said, looking up at Marston for an instant before carefully regarding Abu Musab Ali. "My name is Mary Godwin. I work at *Manhattan Magazine*."

"Ah yes. That's right." Abu watched her bemusedly. "I will look for you on Twitter. You write very good."

Oh no! I wonder what other evil people are following me. Then again, perhaps it is best that I don't know.

"So tell me about yourself. Where were you born?"

"Brooklyn," he said smugly.

"Really. Why would someone from Brooklyn do what you did here today?"

"Number one, I am a Muslim. I am lost in Brooklyn, lost in America. God is not here."

"God being Allah?"

"Yes, very good. The real truth is that only true believers will be admitted to Heaven. All others, whether Christian, Jew, Buddhist or those who are Shiite or Sunni in name only won't be admitted. All Muslims who are unwilling to die for God will never make it past the holy gate into Heaven. Only those of us willing to live and die by the sword in the creation of a pure Islamic State will be spared. Nearly everybody living in this land of the infidels is my sworn enemy. I am sad to admit that you are one, too."

"We don't have to be enemies, do we?" *How do I rationalize with him?*

He laughed. His upper body began to rock forward and back, forward and back. His dark eyes drilled into hers like laser beams.

Mary steeled herself into showing she wouldn't back off. "Do you sympathize with those radicals who are slaughtering innocent people, including cutting heads off prisoners during public executions?"

"They do what is right and just, Allah be praised!"

"You're talking about ISIS."

He smiled proudly.

"The vast majority of Muslims do not believe in committing atrocities. You know that you are outnumbered by millions of reasonable, peace loving Muslim people."

"They will die. You will, too."

"Hey, that's enough. Mo more threats or the interview is over," Marston warned, glaring at the terrorist.

Mary appreciated the interruption. She pressed on. "You talk about death a lot. Abu, do you want to die?"

"Death will make me a martyr. So death is good. It's what I do now and later that will swell the number of young people that join us. Allah be praised!"

"And merciful?"

Abu smirked at Mary.

She continued. "It might surprise you that I've read the Koran. One passage really struck me. 'Whoever kills an innocent human being, it shall be as if he has killed all mankind, and whosoever saves the life of one, it shall be as if he had saved the life of all mankind,'" Mary finished. She felt like she was making progress.

Amu glared at her. He spat on the floor, and his upper torso rocked more aggressively.

Mary looked up at Marston. "I think I'm done." She was about to turn off the recorder when the interviewee spoke.

"I'm not finished with you yet," Abu Musab Ali said angrily. He attempted to move closer to her, but the police officers on either side of him held him fast.

"No you don't," one of the cops gruffly told him.

Mary backed off a few steps, warily regarding the ISIS sympathizer. She wanted to get out of there and never see him again. But a journalist had to do whatever was necessary to obtain every bit of information from multiple points of view. *It's my story. If I back off, my reputation will be irreparably damaged. Father will feel sorry for me. People in the office will avoid me. I'll have to resign.* Thinking about the consequences of shirking her responsibility strengthened Mary's determination to be the city's finest young newswomen.

Mary bravely stepped closer to Abu. "We'll talk again." She then spoke to Marston. "Please put it in the record that I am available to visit Abu Musab Ali in Rikers Island or wherever he will be held."

"Will do," Marston replied, writing in his pad. Then he nodded at the prisoner's escorts, signaling it was time to move. Marston whispered in Mary's ear. "Good job. See you around."

Mary felt the man's breath go through her. She stood, watching him walk away.

* * *

Mary's parents were home watching ongoing television coverage of the incident at One Trade Center when they were notified that Mary was identified as a witness. They immediately hailed a cab to take them downtown.

William Godwin was generally much calmer than his wife. Jane was more sensitive, more emotional. William was old school, controlling his reactions in public and slightly less so at home. He did not love Mary any less than Jane did, though the casual observer may have thought differently.

Their cab was half way to the Freedom Tower when William's phone rang. He didn't recognize the name on Caller ID, but took the call anyway. "Hello?" It was Mary. "Mary, are you okay?"

Jane looked over with teary eyes. "Tell her we are on our way."

William put the call on speaker mode. "We're on speaker, Mary. We'll be at One World Trade Center in a few minutes."

"Hello dear, are you okay?" Jane asked, edging closer to her husband to be closer to the phone.

Mary's voice came through clearly. "I'm safe and uninjured, Mom and Dad. Sorry I couldn't call you sooner. My phone is badly damaged. I'll tell you more when you're here." She instructed them where to meet her, then signed off.

"Why couldn't she talk longer?" Jane wondered.

"It doesn't matter. We'll be with her shortly," William replied, looking out the window at the busy city.

Jane dabbed her eyes with a tissue. "I can't let Mary see me like this. I must be strong."

William smiled encouragingly at her. "You will be," he replied hopefully.

* * *

A short time later, Mary was reunited with her parents in the bright, high-ceilinged lobby. Several dozen policemen and women either stood vigil or passed through the vast space. Some of them peered outside the windows where a press conference would soon begin.

After exchanging hugs with both parents, even her father, Mary spoke to them. She was very tired and happy to be alive. "I'm fine, Mom and Dad. Thank you for being here."

"What an awful nightmare you've gone through. Are you really all right?" Jane asked, looking with concern at her daughter's pale and strained face.

"Mom, I'm fine."

"You don't look it."

Thanks Mom. She turned to her father. "I interviewed him. His name is Abu Musab Ali."

"Good for you," he replied. "You're planning to put it in the magazine?"

"Yes, I am. And I think he'll want to talk to me some more."

"That's my girl."

Jane frowned at her husband. "Will, tell her that it's too dangerous. Don't let her see that monster again."

"Jane, it's perfectly safe. He'll be trussed like a chicken."

"Don't commit yourself just yet. Give it a day or two to decide," Godwin told Mary. "You won't be alone. You've got everybody at the magazine behind you. And NYPD will obviously keep you safe. Is Ali still upstairs?"

"No, he was taken away a few minutes before I called you."

"Thank God," Jane Godwin declared.

Mary noticed a woman stride into the lobby from outside and look over at her. She stopped a few feet away from the entrance and nodded at Mary.

"I've seen her before. Who is that?" Godwin asked Mary.

"Assistant US District Attorney Judy Green. She's already been assigned to prosecute Abu Musab Ali. I've got to go now," peering outside at the gathering multitude. "I'm supposed to say a few words to the media. Thanks for coming down. See you guys later. I love you both."

They said their farewells. Then Mary strode away. Her father pensively watched.

"I just realized that she may not be able to write that article after all," he said.

Before exiting the building, Green told Mary that Abu Musab Ali was being booked and charged with first-degree murder, first-degree kidnapping and other charges. Then they stepped outside and were immediately greeted by a phalanx of cameras and reporters. Dozens of questions were shouted simultaneously before the two women even arrived at the podium.

Green was a favorite federal prosecutor of the United States District Attorney for the borough of Manhattan. She was a sharp interrogator and strategist. The 28-year-old AUSA supplemented her questions in court with suggestive body language and a mesmerizing smile to bewitch judges, juries, and whomever else she needed to persuade. She had already turned down job offers with several of the city's legal powerhouses.

Green gave a 150-watt smile to Mary while stepping up to the podium. Seeing Mary hesitate, she waved Mary over to her side. A police helicopter roared overhead as Green peered confidently at the huge assemblage of local, national and international news people in attendance for the hastily arranged press conference. She glanced briefly at a staff member who shook his head reproachfully at her. Green shrugged subtly and plunged into her remarks.

Mary wondered what the disapproving look was about. She discovered the answer several minutes later when an official vehicle pulled up to the curb. Two grey-haired men climbed out, both dressed impeccably in tailored dark suits.

"Excuse us. Coming through."

The crowd parted obediently and reverently, opening a lane for the new arrivals. They were VIPS, namely the Police Commissioner and the United States District Attorney.

Green stopped speaking as soon as she noticed the slightly peeved, determined looking men rapidly approach the podium. She stepped back deferentially; her smile greatly diminished.

Mary immediately comprehended what was happening. *It's not Green's press conference. She started it prematurely. The conniver.* Mary gave the Assistant US Attorney (AUSA) an approving nod. *She's got guts. I hope some of that rubs off on me.* Mary curtsied slightly at the two men. They nodded politely with recognition, both having been guests at her father's parties and well acquainted with Mary's insightful articles about the city.

A reported shouted out a question at Mary about her ordeal just as the men positioned themselves at the dais. She looked deferentially at the powerful officials. The US District Attorney whispered in her ear. "Go ahead, Mary. Step over to the microphones and answer the question now. I will act as your counsel if you get into trouble. But I am supremely confident you'll do fine."

"Thank you, sir." Mary's heart pounded rapidly as she tightly grasped the hardwood podium and addressed her captive audience, knowing this was the defining moment of her relatively short life so far. Millions of television viewers, radio listeners, newspaper readers, and online media would know her name and form opinions about her, based entirely on her performance.

Mary cleared her throat and nodded at the expectant faces. She zeroed in on Tamara Rogers, a well-respected television reporter "Tamara, thank you for your question," she began, noting the smile on Tamara's face at being recognized and named.

She continued, her eyes slowly scanning the group. *I might as well plug Dad's magazine.* "My name is Mary Godwin. I work at *Manhattan Magazine*. Today, I was an eyewitness and victim in yet another act of terrorism by an American born citizen. I will not and cannot go into the particulars because doing so could adversely affect the prosecution." She looked down a moment to collect her thoughts before continuing.

"I am thankful to be able to stand before you now. But I am heartbroken that the life of a lovely woman was taken for no good reason." Mary's eyes moistened. She tried to control her emotions. "Terrorism must stop. I appeal to radicals to turn to constructive measures instead." She nodded again at her audience. "Thank you." She backed away from the dais.

"What about the FBI?" a reporter asked.

The Police Commissioner stepped up to the microphone, adjusted its angle, and spoke. "The FBI has already begun its investigation and will obviously pursue issues such as the radicalization of the perpetrator, Abu Musab Ali. The FBI will issue statements when appropriate. That's all I will say now on the matter." He covered the microphone while whispering with the US District Attorney (USDA).

Another reporter asked a question. "Commissioner, is ISIS connected to what happened in the Observatory?"

The Commissioner reacted with annoyance as he had declared that he had no more to say. But he fielded the question with evident reluctance. "I am not aware at this time that ISIS has acknowledged that the perpetrator is one of their own." He promptly moved aside.

The USDA then edged to the podium.

"Only a short statement. We will prosecute Abu Musab Ali to the full extent of the law. Terrorists will get no safe haven in our great city. The United States v Abu Musab Ali will see to it. That is all."

The podium was abandoned as a fury of questions ensued. The impromptu press conference was over. Mary watched Judy Green being reprimanded by her boss for beginning the press conference without him. The Assistant US Attorney nodded respectfully, yet Mary couldn't help but notice the fire in her eyes.

Several news people made an effort to speak to Mary privately. She was normally very receptive to interacting with her peers. She sensed that this was not an appropriate time, especially after noticing Judy frown at her.

"Sorry but I have to go back inside," Mary told her small audience. She quickly entered the lobby, half expecting to see her parents again. They weren't there. Their absence both disappointed and relieved her. She briefly thought about Percy, thinking he must be worried sick about her.

Mary assumed she would be spending considerable time with the prosecuting attorney, beginning with the examination before trial in which Mary would go over every detail of her experience. Then there was the matter of her eventual court appearance, and the testimony she would be required to provide. Mary looked forward to seeing Green in action in court, but having to relive the terrible experience was too much for her to contemplate. Grimacing, she felt her blood pressure rise accompanied by discomfort in her stomach.

Mary was shaken out of her nightmare by repeated taps on her right shoulder and somebody repeating her name. She snapped to, noticing Judy Green watched her with concern.

"Do I dare ask what terrible place you were at?" Green asked.

"Actually I was thinking of you?"

"Really? How so?"

"I was dreading having to testify."

"I know you'll do fine. Listen Mary, I hope you know that you don't expect to be releasing a magazine article right away about it."

"No way!"

"Yeah, you'll have to wait until a jury comes back with a verdict. Or perhaps longer, depending if it's appealed by Abu Musab Ali's defense team."

"Oh no!"

"Sorry. You must know deep inside that writing about it wouldn't be permitted. It would be a conflict of interest and impair my case. The judge could potentially disallow your testimony."

Mary's disappointment was tempered by the faint hope that she could be excused from appearing in front of the judge and jury.

"Wipe that smile off your face, honey. Don't even think for a second that you can weasel out of the legal proceedings. You were a principal player upstairs. If I don't call you as a witness, the defense surely will. Do you understand?"

Mary sighed deeply. She nodded reprovingly, realizing she had lost out on a major career opportunity. Somebody else would write it. "So if Abu Musab Ali wants me to interview him?"

"Sorry, Mary. You can't."

"That really sucks."

"You'll only have to pour your heart and soul into something else that will get your mind off it."

Mary sighed deeply. "Right."

She wondered what that would be.

Chapter 5

Howard Peters sat down on the living room couch and turned on the television. He surfed different channels with the remote before selecting a news channel. He spiked a couple of asparagus spears and raised the fork to his mouth while listlessly watching a recap of the lone wolf incident down at One World Trade Center. His dark, cruel eyes watched Mary at the news conference. He stopped chewing, absorbed by what he saw on the flat screen.

"Did I or did I not see that bitch in the park today? I did, didn't I? It's gotta be her. I'll check the camera later, but I'm frigging sure it was her. Look at her standing there like she thinks she knows anything about suffering. She hasn't a clue. Wait until I give her the special treatment."

Peters licked his lips and shut up. He replayed her one minute at the podium over and over, memorized her voice, her poise, her face and yes indeed, the shape of her slender, vibrant looking body. He turned off the television and continued staring at the screen, not really seeing it.

"She'll do just fine. I'll teach her all about pain and suffering. She'll be able to write a dissertation on the subject by the time we're done. But she'll never get it published."

He speared more asparagus, shoved it in his mouth, and chewed thoughtfully.

Chapter 6

Mary waited for the elevator that would take her up to Percy's apartment. She was numb and tired. She hadn't spoken to her fiancé since leaving the apartment that morning. Two calls to him on the phone she had borrowed at One World Trade Center went unanswered. The only reason she could come up with was that he had gone out and left the phone home.

She desperately needed love and comfort from the man who on the day of their wedding would promise to have and to hold her, for better, for worse, in sickness and in health. That was not too much to ask for even as an engaged couple.

I'm sure he has a good explanation. There's no reason to be concerned about Percy. He's probably waiting inside with a bouquet of red roses to bestow on me like he's prone to do! The thought cheered her a little, but not as much as it should. She stepped into the empty elevator, pressed the floor button and stood thinking.

He must know about what happened to me. I'm sure every tv network has aired the story, even the news conference. He would have seen me there. He must have called me on my phone. Of course he did. He's probably beside himself with worry and frustration that I didn't take his calls. But, how could I? The phone is bagged and tagged.

Her mind reverted again to her ordeal. She saw Ellen fall on the floor and the lone wolf's leer. She continued to stand in the elevator cab until she discovered the door had opened.

Mary mechanically stepped off the elevator and stepped to the apartment door. She heaved a deep sigh and tried the door knob. It was locked. The apartment was probably empty. She fumbled for her keys and managed with some effort to unlock the door. Mary entered the apartment and gently closed the door.

She took a step, then immediately stopped when her ears heard a woman's laughter from somewhere in the residence. *Is Percy watching a movie?* Then she heard Percy's unmistakable voice. Mary couldn't make it out, but the tone was clear. He used it with her when in a romantic mood.

Her chest tightened and stomach tensed.

Mary quietly stepped forward, straining her ears to hear any human sounds, no matter how low. The effort was almost too much for her. She had trouble concentrating. She felt lethargic, too, another effect of acute shock sustained downtown.

Stealthily approaching the living room, Mary thought she heard murmuring and moans. Dreading what she'd see, she forced her feet forward, step by step. Her heart beat loudly in her ears. She repeated the same two words to herself over and over again. *Please no, please no, please no.*

Mary stopped once more, this time directly on the door saddle of the large room, and watched the pair. Percy sat at the piano. His hair was tousled and his clothing disheveled. He gazed lustily at a familiar looking beautiful woman seated beside him on the bench. Her face was partially hidden by her trademark long, black hair. Mary observed their bodies brushing each other as Percy played a song.

Emily Taylor began singing, her classically trained Tony Award winning voice disarming anybody within earshot of her. Even Mary's rancor directed at her fiancé's obvious indiscretion faded, charmed by the magical sweetness of Emily's voice.

Mary, still apparently unseen, entered the living room and sat in a leather chair facing the piano. Emily and Percy were too absorbed by the music and each other to notice her right away. Mary captured the lovey-dovey moment by taking a snapshot of them with the brand new phone she had purchased on the way home. The romantic pair remained oblivious to her presence.

The growing of anger relentlessly surging within Mary temporarily overcame the depression and fog she'd been in. *How long do I have to sit here and take this shit!!!*

Percy tore his eyes away from Emily that very moment and watched Mary toying with the engagement ring that adorned the third finger of her left hand. A semblance of guilt was quickly followed by feigned exuberance.

"You know Emily, don't you, my love? We're working on that new song that I wrote for her, you know; the one I told you about this morning."

Emily's face transformed from bliss to disappointment to serenity. She stood up gracefully and approached Mary, smiling beatifically. "Hello, Mary. It's so nice to see you again."

Mary saw no need to be polite. She glumly remained seated, accepting Emily's kisses on both cheeks. *This is the first and hopefully last time I have to deal with a situation like this. How am I supposed to behave?*

Percy observed Mary carefully. "How was your day?" he asked.

Mary's jaw dropped. "How was my day? You don't know? Seriously?" she asked incredulously, turning from Percy to Emily and Percy again.

"Percy stood and walked over. "What's wrong? Tell me."

"You don't know what happened at the Freedom Tower today?"

"Mary, I've had the phone off all day and the ringer off on the landline phone. You know I hate interruptions when I'm working. Why? Were you trying to reach me or something?"

"I was held prisoner with other people up in the observatory. I saw a woman die." Mary started crying hard.

Emily looked shocked and embarrassed.

Percy got on his knees in front of Mary and held her hands. "I'm so sorry."

Mary wasn't sure if he alluded to her devastating experience or her interrupting his interlude with Emily.

"Poor Mary," Emily said. "Here, come sit with me, darling." Percy released Mary. Emily escorted Mary to a couch. They sat together. "You probably need a good stiff drink." She looked at Percy. "Go get one, love."

Love? Is that just for Percy or does she call very man that? A dull ache began to take root in her head.

Emily looked at Mary with a calculating look on her pretty, tanned face. "You must be feeling horrible, darling."

Mary, looking down, could only nod.

Percy returned with an uncorked bottle of chilled white wine and three glasses. He set the crystal wine glassware down on a nearby table and poured out the yellow-gold liquid. He gave Mary the fullest one. He winked at Emily when Mary wasn't looking.

Mary held the glass in both hands and stared at it. Then, without thinking, she drained the narrow wine glass. She held it out to Percy in a daze.

"You want more?" he asked her, glancing furtively at Emily.

"Uh huh," Mary replied.

Her glass was refilled. Percy and Emily sipped at their 2018 Elenora's Selection Chardonnay from Buena Vista Winery, both entertained by Mary's out of character and entirely excusable binge drinking.

The vintage was meant to be enjoyed with sips, not gulps. But Mary didn't care. She needed to forget that day and she did her best to find oblivion whether her companions approved or not. *I can get drunk if I want. It's what I need to do now, Abu what's his name and Percy and Emily be damned!*

Percy carefully watched Mary's transformation from sober to intoxication. He hoped that his fiancé would somehow forget about Emily. He understood that discovering him alone with Emily produced an untenable situation that could have long lasting consequences. *I must get the sultry siren out of the apartment and put Mary to bed.* Unfortunately, despite being a sophisticated lady's man, he did not know what to do first.

He looked once more at Mary. Her fourth glass was empty and hung precariously in her hand. Her head sagged. She appeared to be asleep.

"Do you think she's awake?" he whispered into Emily's ear. Her perfume and closeness were almost too much for him. He imagined making love to Emily right there. Having a comatose Mary added another element to the turn on. *Maybe a drunken Mary will enjoy a threesome.*

Emily turned her head to him, and lowered a hand. "Does that excite you, love?"

Percy, keeping an eyes on Mary, kissed Emily. It was a long, deep kiss, full of desire and hope.

When Mary mumbled something, Percy and Emily broke apart, out of breath and ready for more.

"You poor darling," Emily whispered, finally raising her hand.

"You know I want you," he managed, "but you must leave now before we go any further again."

Emily pouted but agreed.

Mary's eyes barely opened as Percy quietly escorted Emily from the room. In the elevator vestibule, he pressed the down button. They embraced and kissed again. Then Emily thanked Percy for the love song and impassioned demonstration of what the lyrics meant. She left Percy aching for more when the elevator door opened.

Percy watched her step in and lean against the back wall of the cab with a suggestive grin. He sorrowfully nodded as the door slid shut and went inside the apartment to attend to Mary.

Chapter 7

Percy looked disapprovingly at Mary and decided that he did not want to carry her to the bedroom. He preferred to awaken her and help steer her there. The reason had little to do with his own strength. Mary was light enough to manage. He just wasn't in the mood to hoist and cradle her in his arms. He would have carried Emily in a heat beat.

He blamed Mary for Emily's leaving. *If I wasn't engaged, I would do whatever I want with Emily in any room of the apartment. I almost did anyway,* he ruefully contemplated. He wondered, not for the first time, if getting married was such a good idea.

Mary stirred.

I guess it's that time.

"Wake up, Mary!"

Mary heard a voice call her name. She didn't want to open her eyes. *Leave me alone! Let me sleep!*

She risked a peek at Percy and was sorry for it. He wore a huge scowl on his face which detracted from his looks. Seeing that woke her up even more than caffeine. *I don't want to look at him again.*

"Rise and shine, Mary!"

She opened her eyes again, this time until she was ready to sleep in her own bed.

"All right, I'm awake. Are you happy now?" she said, glaring at Percy.

He didn't look at all happy. He grunted, "Up now, I'll help you to the bed."

Leaning on Percy's shoulder, she staggered to their bedroom. The combination of the wine and unwanted exertion made her head spin.

"Here you go," Percy announced, easing Mary onto the bed.

"Where's your girlfriend?" Mary asked, sitting on the side of the bed.

"What?" he asked.

"Emily!!!!"

"She left."

"You sound so sad, Percy," Mary exclaimed, looking up at him.

"You're drunk. Lay down and get some sleep."

She looked up at his exasperated face. "Not drunk enough!"

He shook his head. "Listen Mary, I need to go out."

Mary tried to stand so she could slap him, but was unable to move. "Go then."

Percy turned to leave. He almost made it to the bedroom door.

"Go and do your worst with her for all I care!" Mary cried out angrily. Her bitter words came at a price as the headache intensified.

Percy stopped dead in his tracks and turned around. "What a thing to say."

Mary struggled to focus on his face, fearing she would collapse on the bed if she didn't concentrate.

"You're too drunk to know what's you're saying," Percy said in an accusatory tone.

"Thank God for booze."

"What do you want from me, Mary?"

"I want a head to lean on when I need it. How would you feel after being held hostage and seeing someone die? And instead of being consoled by you when I got home, I basically saw you in the arms of another woman."

"I don't know what to say."

"No, I guess not." Mary looked at Percy through bloodshot eyes, not seeing the caring, loving man she had hoped for. She saw an entirely different person, one whom she did not want as a husband or lover. She looked down at the floor, unable to watch him anymore.

Percy stood near the door, staring at her. What he thought was anybody's guess. If Mary looked up, she would have seen conflicting emotions on his face.

Does he know that we have arrived, possibly against our will, at this important crossroad? Will we survive this? Or will Percy stay on course and do as he pleases?

Mary heard him move a little closer to her. She was conflicted with opposing emotions. She still hoped for the overdue hug and she wanted to give him hell. "I need to sleep. We need to talk in the morning."

Percy nodded. "Goodnight," he said. "I'll be in the other room."

Mary lay down and closed her eyes, hoping that her brain would allow sleep to take hold.

Mary slept fitfully that long night. She stirred at 3:04 AM, needing to use the bathroom. Returning to the bedroom she looked at Percy's side of the bed. It was empty! *He's probably sleeping in the living room or guest room.* Still feeling regret and anger, she decided to try to get more sleep instead of looking for him.

His absence weighted on her when she rose from the bed a few hours later. He hadn't returned to their bed for some reason. Mary stood and stretched briefly. *Where is he?* She used the bathroom and then stepped into the hall.

A door closed softly. Mary thought it was the front door. *Is he going out? He's rarely even awake at this hour.* She ran toward the front entrance, almost running into Percy as he strode away from the door.

Mary stood silently, arms crossed, waiting for Percy to explain himself. *I'm such an idiot. Why did I rush into a relationship with the man, knowing full well what he is? Do I allow him a chance to redeem himself or should I walk away now?*

She saw her wide-eyed future husband struggle to recover from being caught in a compromising situation. *Does he love me? Does he love Emily? Does he only love himself?*

Percy, smiling weakly, greeted her. "Mary, you startled me."

He stepped up to Mary and hugged her. Her arms hung limply. She used all of her willpower to keep them at her sides and not to cry. *I must be strong.* Smelling a feminine scent not her own, she raised her arms part way, and backed away from Percy.

He looked at her, clearly stunned. "Can we discuss this?"

"Do that, Percy," she said stonily. "How long have you been unfaithful?"

"Mary, what do you want me to say?"

"What about the truth? Isn't that what you owe me?"

Percy nodded. "Of course, darling."

"Don't call me that! It's an Emily word."

Mary stormed off, leaving her nonplused fiancé behind. She held off the angry and heartbroken tears until she stepped into the bedroom. *This is it! What did I do to make him abandon me?*

She wiped her sodden eyes with tissue and noticed Percy regarding her sadly. She fetched a suitcase from a walk-in closet and began throwing clothes in.

"What are you doing?"

"What does it look like?" barely sparing a glance at him while packing. *He looks terrible. Is he really sorry?* She turned her head to be certain and was shocked to see him on his knees crying.

Mary rushed over to Percy. She squatted, facing him, and pressed his head against her breasts. The sobs continued for a short time while she wondered what to do next. She was full of disappointment, anger and compassion.

The sobs ended.

Percy raised his head and kissed her lightly on the lips. He moved his head back and peered at her cautiously as she hadn't kissed him back.

"Soul meets soul on lovers' lips."

"That's beautiful, Percy. Is it one of yours?"

"Look it up," Percy Shelley replied with a knowing smile. His face turned serious. "I'm sorry I hurt you."

"Do you love her?"

Percy gazed at Mary, but looked away quickly from her penetrating stare.

"You're supposed to love and make love to me and nobody else. If that's too much to ask, then you need to let me know right now so we can end immediately the engagement. I will not tolerate any exceptions. Do you understand me, Percy?"

"Yes, damn it!"

Mary was saddened by Percy's tone. She needed clarification. "Am I asking too much of you?"

She realized this was the crucial moment of their relationship. Mary carefully watched Percy's reaction. His lips pressed together as he assumed a thoughtful countenance. An immediate response from the man would have been ideal. Any delay created serious doubt in her mind that they would have a happy future together. Severely disappointed, she rose to her feet.

Percy looking up at her unhappily. "I'm sorry," he said. "I'd be deceiving both of us if I told you what you want to hear."

"That's what I thought," Mary declared grimly. "Thanks for your honesty."

"You're ending the engagement?" Percy asked.

"Don't blame me, Percy! I'm not the guilty person here."

"You're awfully conventional," he replied with a pointed finger. "I guess you don't believe in unconditional love."

Mary was too astonished to reply. Sighing, she retrieved another suitcase and continued packing.

Percy watched her. "Where will you go?" he said softly.

"Back to my parents' house. Where else?" she exclaimed bitterly.

Percy nodded. Mary closed the full suitcases, lifted them off the bed and walked toward the bedroom door. Percy reached out when Mary was about to pass him. "Here, let me carry them for you."

Mary used all of her strength and willpower not to look at Percy. "No thanks." She stared straight ahead, trying not to think about the growing feeling of desolation within her. She wanted to hear Percy say something that would stop her from leaving. But it seemed like a lost cause. At the apartment entrance, she set the suitcases down and turned to Percy. She pulled off the engagement ring and held it out to him.

Percy looked down at the ring. "I don't want it," he muttered. His eyes glared, wet and angry at it.

Mary set it down on the key table. She fumbled in a pocket and deposited her two apartment keys next to the ring. She looked up at Percy in despair, still silently urging him to say something that would make her stay.

"I'm sorry," he said. "You're doing the right thing."

Mary swallowed hard. "Bye, Percy."

He fidgeted.

Mary opened the door, retrieved the luggage, and walked to the elevator. She pressed the button and waited, feeling eyes on her back. It seemed like forever before she heard the cab move up the elevator shaft. She felt a sense of relief, carrying the heavy suitcases inside the cab, and even more so when the door closed a few seconds later.

She was gone.

Chapter 8

Peters leaned back in the chair, hands interlocked behind his head, looking smugly at the image on the computer monitor of Mary Godwin. *All bases covered in so little time. I am the best!*

He had completed a google search of her, accumulating enough useful information on his intended target to mark step one as done. He knew where Mary worked, her relationship with Shelley, and where he lived. He also had the address of William and Jane Godwin. Peters knew that Mary had moved from their home into Shelley's place. He considered it logical that she would visit her dear mommy and daddy periodically.

She's a spoiled, rich bitch who deserves a dose of humility from yours truly. I sure know how it feels to be put in one's place. It frigging sucks, especially if done for no real good reason. I'll do to you what that Rosefield bastard should receive. It's time for another muscle memory. He punched his abdomen hard. With all of the sit-ups and crunches he did every day, the self-inflicted battering barely hurt.

He reviewed his mental checklist, pushed the chair back on its wheels, and nimbly jumped to his feet. He absently rubbed his short hair. It was the same length as when he served in Afghanistan and Iraq.

Peters opened the refrigerator and grabbed the large carton containing two dozen brown eggs. He set it down on the counter, took a tall mug out of a cabinet, and began cracking eggshells. He tossed four in the trash receptacle and then gulped down the raw eggs. After rinsing the gooey mug in the sink he walked purposefully to the bedroom.

He dropped onto the thick carpet and did one hundred pushups, nice and slow, to exercise his core. His face reddened from the effort and strain on his muscles. Half way through the routine, his brain told him he couldn't do anymore. But he kept soldiering on, motivated by a primal urge to punish those who deserved it.

Finished, he jumped to his feet, breathing hard, and burped. It smelled eggy.

He stripped down, neatly placing his garments on the bed and stepped into the bathroom. Peters stood in front of the mirror, admiring his body. He enjoyed being ripped. It felt good to be better than other people. Grunting with satisfaction, he turned on the shower and began planning the second phase of the operation. Surveillance.

Chapter 9

The taxi stopped in front of the Godwins' four-story townhouse. Mary's eyes were closed, but she wasn't asleep. She wanted very much to sleep for days without interruption. She seemed to be wandering some grey area in between sleep and wakefulness.

The cab driver looked at her through the rear-view mirror. "Miss, we're there." He paused a beat. His passenger didn't respond, forcing him to raise his voice. "Lady!"

Mary opened her glazed eyes. "Where am I?" she asked herself.

"See for yourself."

Mary gazed out the window to her left, immediately recognizing the townhouse. "Here we are." She took forever to pay the fare with her ATM card. She forgot all about the suitcases.

Thankfully, the driver was honest. He fetched them from the trunk and handed them to her. "Good luck to you," he said before climbing back in the car and driving away.

Mary needed good luck and then some. She stood at the front entrance, searching blindly for the house keys. She was exhausted and empty inside. Too much trauma, too little sleep. Even standing was an effort. She leaned against the door, a solid masterpiece only installed the previous year after the original had been destroyed.

While she continued her search for the keys to the building, the lock snapped loudly and the door opened. William Godwin opened his mouth to greet Mary as she fell to the ground. Reacting quickly, he managed to grab her just before she hit the marble floor. Godwin staggered backwards, gripping her, before regaining his balance. He still had fast reflexes and a strong body kept in shape by playing squash and working out at a chic club on Park Avenue.

Mary felt like a ragdoll. She couldn't believe what was happening to her. *Did I black out? What's wrong with me?*

She stood, shaking a little. He father propped her up to make sure she did not fall again.

"My God!" he exclaimed, looking intently at Mary. "Has something else happened to you?"

Jane hurried down the stairs, staring anxiously at her husband and daughter. She rushed over. "What's wrong?" she asked.

"I'm sorry. I was stupidly leaning against the door when Dad opened it."

"Why were you leaning against the door? Are you ill?" William asked.

"Look at her! She's pale and has a fever!" Jane exclaimed, a hand on Mary's forehead.

"I had to leave. I had to come here," Mary muttered.

"Percy let you leave in your condition?" William inquired doubtfully.

"I left him," Mary replied.

"What do you mean, dear?" asked Jane.

"We're over. I returned the ring," Mary uttered in a voice barely above a whisper. *How many more questions?*

"You ended the engagement. Why?" William asked.

"Listen, I'm done answering questions, at least until I get some sleep. Do you mind?" Mary forced herself to appear in more control of herself than she really was. "Dad, you can let go. I'm okay now," she said testily. "Thanks for saving me from a hard fall."

William reluctantly released her. "You're entirely welcome," he replied with a weak smile.

"Oh, my suitcases."

"Where are they?" Jane asked.

"Outside, by the door." Mary turned to fetch them. The door was still open.

"Will, can you carry them for her? She's not up to it."

"Of course. Mary, go to bed. I've got them."

Mary allowed her father to be the gallant knight and dictating father.

He carried the suitcases inside, set them down, and closed the door. "All set," he said with a frown, lifting them again. He walked to the staircase and began climbing the steps.

Mary and her stepmother embraced. "Mom, we'll talk later."

"I know we will, dear. Sleep well."

Jane Godwin anxiously watched Mary trudge up the stairs after her father.

Mary lay in bed, eyes tightly shut, but not asleep. She worried that sleep would bring bad dreams and take her to places she did not want to go to. She was told dreams are cathartic, that they purged bad memories. Or perhaps they hinted at what she really wanted to do in life. Either way, she fought off sleep as long as possible. Just before drifting away, the weary young woman asked herself why she needed to punish herself in her dreams and nightmares. *What's the point?*

Her subconscious mind had her messing up in school and at work. She envisioned herself missing class, not turning in homework, failing exams, not listening to what her editor told her, and missing deadlines.

None of those misdeeds actually occurred. They were all figments of her hyperactive imagination.

The nightmare was a bad one. Mary relived the traumatic experience at One World Trade Center. It was even worse than the actual event because she knew what was going to happen and couldn't prevent it. The sleeping Mary desperately attempted to steer her mind in another direction, clinging to the idea that she could somehow save Ellen's life and alter history.

Wishful thinking never seemed to occur in her sleep. Instead, she again saw Abu Musab Ali strangle Ellen. There was a significant difference from reality. In the dream, she was unbound and free to move. She saw herself sprinting in slow motion toward Ellen when the woman collapsed. Mary was too slow to save Ellen.

She called out, "No!"

As dawn approached, Mary fell into a deep, dreamless sleep.

Chapter 10

Peters was in no rush to kill his intended target. *No siree, Bob*. He wanted to get to know her habits so well that her movements could be easily anticipated. In his warped mind, the killer thought that watching her from a safe distance for a protracted period of time was a courtship. Lyrics from The King & I, a classic musical, struck a certain chord while he researched Mary Godwin. *Getting to know you, getting to know all about you.*

Mary Godwin would evolve from being a stranger to a vibrant woman he intimately knew. Only then would he plan how to lure her to her death.

He had two preliminary tasks to perform. First, he must acquire her telephone numbers to enable him to call and text her at any hour of the day or night. Next, he needed to surveille the buildings, blocks, and neighborhoods where Mary Godwin lived and worked.

Feeling a tingle of anticipation, Peters went online to search for the basic information he needed. He clicked the google.com bookmark and keyed in M-A-R-Y G-O-O-D-W-I-N with two fingers. The results disoriented him. None of the images came close to what his Mary looked like.

He slapped his head. "What the! Where is she? I mean I plugged in her name correctly, didn't I?"

He slowly and deliberately re-entered her first name followed by a space and G-O-D-W-I-N. Then he clicked on the search icon.

"There she is!!!" He wondered what had gone wrong the first attempt. Then it hit him. "I misspelled her frigging name! He punished himself with a well-deserved gut punch. The unforgiving blow to his heavily muscled, bruised abdomen hurt. It was the price for screwing up again.

He glared at an image of Mary Godwin and songwriter Percy Shelley together at a gala fundraiser on Broadway. The accompanying description indicated that they were engaged, but no date had yet been set for the wedding.

"I'll save you the trouble of having to organize the wedding. You can thank me soon in person," he said, leering at the picture.

"Are you two getting some? I bet my bottom dollar that you are. Shelley looks like a real letch. Perhaps I should pay you a visit, maybe catch you both going at it. I can get Shelley to write a song about me." He laughed.

The search produced more interesting results. He read up on *Manhattan Magazine* and the Godwins. He was disgusted that she worked for her father. *She was born with a silver spoon.*

"You can't get away from the old man. You're daddy's little girl. I bet you want to marry someone just like him. Is pretty boy Shelley like him? I don't think so, but I'll find out soon enough."

Peters wrote down the telephone numbers and address for Percy Shelley, the magazine, and Mary's parents. Then he sat back, closed his eyes, and waited for his brain to formulate a plan.

Chapter 11

Knock, Knock, Knock.

Mary, on the periphery of awareness, was irritated by the sound. *I need more sleep.* She put the pillow over her head.

"Mary, are you awake?" a distant woman's voice called out.

Mary pressed down on the pillow, hanging on desperately to sleep.

"You have to take this phone call. Mary!" Then softly, "I think she's awake, John."

Mary moaned. She forced herself into a sitting position on the edge of the bed. Her eyes still refused to open.

"It's late. Are you ill, dear?" Jane Godwin inquired from beyond the locked door. "Please open the door. I have John, that young detective from Maine on the phone for you. He says it's important."

"Coming,' Mary murmured. She stood, opened her eyes and tried to shake the cobwebs. She stepped over to the bedroom door, unlocked it, and opened the door part way. Mary looked at her stepmother with glassy eyes. Mary reached for the phone.

"Good morning, dear."

"The phone, Mom." She was in no mood for pleasantries.

Jane handed the phone to Mary. "Come down for breakfast when you're ready." Then she turned and walked away.

Mary closed the door and locked it again. Privacy was a necessary part of living with her parents.

She sat cross-legged on the bed. "Hi, John. Sorry about that. What is it?"

"Hi, Mary," the unfamiliar voice said in a perverted tone.

This isn't John. Why did Mom think it was him?

Mary looked sharply at the call ID. It read UNKNOWN. "Who is this?"

"I'm an admirer. We haven't met yet."

"How did you get this number?"

The connection was lost.

The voice creeped her out. The caller was obviously not John Pounds, a detective at the Maine State Police that she knew from last summer on Islesboro. Pounds had been on the island investigating a murder. She had spent some time with the Statie getting acclimated with police procedures, thinking that knowledge could prove useful as a print journalist.

Mary shivered from the unsettling call. *I can't just sit here on my butt and ignore it.*

She set down the portable house phone on the night table and grabbed her own. She absentmindedly noticed a slew of messages. Ignoring them, she autodialed a long-distance number. "Hi John, its Mary." They exchanged small talk before she got down to business.

"John, did you call me a few minutes ago?"

"No, why?" Pounds's voice asked.

"My mother took a call from someone she thought was you."

"Did the caller identify himself as me?"

"Good question. I'll ask her."

"Wait Mary. Did you look at Caller ID?"

"Yes. It read UNKNOWN. He sounded perverted. It was disgusting."

"What did he say?"

"'Hi Mary. We haven't met yet but we're going to. Something like that. Then he hung up.'"

"Huh. It's probably nothing. You should have dialed *59 right after hanging up. Listen, I saw you on the news. Are you okay?'"

Mary's mood sunk to a new low. She fought back the tears.

"Mary?"

"I'm all right, thanks," she said in a trembling voice.

"You went through a terrible ordeal. Perhaps it's not my place," he said, pausing.

"What?" she asked sniffling.

"Mary, there are counselors who can help you handle and get though the trauma."

"You think I need a psychiatrist?" *Perhaps I do.*

"Don't take it the wrong way. I'm just saying as a friend that they're a good resource to help you cope. Even cops see them. It's just something to consider, Mary."

"Okay thanks, I guess. I should get going, John."

"Call me anytime, Mary. Use me as a soundboard or whatever."

"Right. Thanks."

After ending the call, Mary sighed heavily and lowered her head. She tried not to think, just be, but dark thoughts kept nagging at her. She curled up in bed and got under the covers.

"Mary?"

Moving back here was not such a good idea. But where else could I go? Mary covered her ears and began humming with the hope those actions would miraculously block out her stepmother and everything else.

* * *

Gwen Peabody was her best friend and old college roommate. Gwen was an appraiser at Cabot Auctions & Appraisals in Boston. She had gone to bed on Saturday night worrying about Mary, particularly because her texts and voice messages to Mary had been ignored. *She must be a wreck. I'll surprise her with a quick trip on the Acela in the morning.*

On Sunday morning, Gwen again struck out getting a reply from Mary. That gave her two options. She could call Percy or the Godwins. She decided to try Percy first because Mary lived with him.

The man is incorrigible. He better not flirt with me again. But that's just the way he is, isn't it? He can't help himself.

She walked into the kitchen in her panties. She ground Godiva Hazelnut Crème coffee beans, poured water into the coffeemaker and set it on brew. Then she sat down and called Shelley. After three rings, she was about to give up when his strained voice came through the speaker.

"Gwen, is she having you run interference?"

"Would do you mean? Mary's not there?"

"You don't know?"

"What's going on, Percy?"

"Well, Gwen, you should really hear it from her."

"Tell me," Gwen demanded, not really wanting to hear bad news, yet insistent that he tell her whatever it was. She breathed in the aromatic percolating coffee.

"She left me."

Gwen heard sorrow, disbelief, and anger in his voice. She was too stunned to speak.

"Gwen?"

"What happened? Where is Mary?"

"At her parents. I refuse to explain. She's your friend."

Mary needs me. "Okay, let me go."

"Will you pass along a message to Mary?"

"No way!"

She ended the call, not caring about being rude. She didn't want to be used by the man. *I wonder what happened. Why did Mary leave him? What did he do?*

She poured herself a cup of steaming coffee and called the Godwins.

Chapter 12

Howard Peters thought that the gods smiled down on him. He believed that a lot of Greek and Roman mythology was based on real events and people. He admired Theseus and Odysseus. His favorite Roman was Brutus. *Here was a man who wasn't afraid to do what he had to do, even kill a friend who happened to be the most powerful man in Rome. Here was a man of principle who did what had to be done. What a hero!*

Peters raised a glass of fresh squeezed orange juice to the bust of the Roman senator and gulped down the thick sweet liquid. Then he paced the living room, replaying in his mind the morning's phone calls.

At the outset he hadn't known where Mary was. But he did have the newly acquired phone numbers. He called the boyfriend first, thinking perhaps she'd needed some good loving to get her mind off the nerve-racking incident at One World Trade Center. *I sure wish I'd been at the Freedom Tower. If it was me, I would have taken out a lot more than just one middle-aged woman. I would have taught that Ali bastard a thing or two. What a loser! Must Moslems are. I saw and killed my share of them. And what thanks did I get? That bastard Rosefield will get his medicine someday.*

Thinking about what the military had done to him during his last enlistment infuriated Peters. He burned the anger with long reps of pushups and squats. Soreness evolved into pain. He stopped, unable to push the muscles any further. He appreciated pain. He couldn't understand why others did not.

He jumped to his feet and paced the apartment. His thoughts reverted to the morning's phone calls. Then he stopped, angry again at himself. *Why did I allow my mind to deviate from the phone calls to that Islamic terrorist? I must be more focused. I'm better than that!*

He brutally punched his abdomen nine times. Nine was his favorite number and his favorite song, *Revolution 9*, was recorded by The Beatles.

Finally at peace with himself, Peters stood in the military 'at ease' position, feet spread and interlocking his hands behind him. He gazed straight ahead and concentrated. The memory of making the first call came clearly.

He listened carefully when the connection was made between his blocked phone number and the recipient's phone. The first ring went unanswered, the second ring, too. Then, he heard an annoyed clipped voice.

"I'd appreciate it if you don't hang up on me," Shelley said.

What's the asshole talking about?

"Sadly, it wasn't me, though by the sound of your voice you probably deserved it," Peters said in his best gruff Froggy imitation.

"Who is this?"

"Did you give Mary some good lovin' last night?"

"Do I know you?"

"Let me speak to the foxy lady."

"She's not here."

Peters heard a click, swore loudly and pressed redial.

After seven rings, Percy answered. "Hello!"

"Never hang up on me, asshole." Peters ended the call, somewhat mollified that Shelley was the worse for wear. He replayed Shelley's words and tone in his mind. "Sweet Mary must have done something to get that effete sounding wimp sounding so pussy-whipped."

He then dialed the Godwin's home phone. Using the same voice, he was very cordial with Mary's mother. He told her he had laryngitis. Haha! The woman for some reason asked if his name was John. He almost laughed, but managed to control himself, replying that yes, that was him. Then, after a very long, trying wait, Mary finally got on the line. *She'll pay for keeping me waiting!*

Peters thought that the brief conversation had the desired disturbing effect. She did not sound cool, calm, and in control at all. Even her greeting sounded forced. She definitely seemed undone by his voice.

She's sampled my appetizer and did not like the taste at all. Wait until she has the entrée! He began to laugh, stopping himself suddenly. *This is serious shit! Shape up, private!*

Chapter 13

Hearing her dear friend's voice released a new stream of tears. "Oh, Gwen."

"Mary, I'm coming down to see you today."

"You are?" Mary replied. A faint trace of hope stirred in her chest.

"You know it, sister. We can hang out and talk, go for a walk, do whatever."

"Gwen, you're the best!"

"Ha! I'll see in four hours. Gotta run if I'm going to make that train. Bye!"

"Bye."

Mary now had motivation to get up. She stripped and showered. Emerging sometime later, one of her grandmother's sayings crossed her mind. *I'm feeling human.* It seemed very appropriate.

Thinking of Beatrice saddened Mary. She wished the grand old lady was still alive. Back in the day, they spent many wonderful hours going through thick scrapbooks and albums containing memorable images and newspaper articles from her early years as a stage actress, singer, and dancer. The career was cut short when she married her wealthy husband. At the time, it was considered scandalous to marry an actor. As a socialite, Beatrice turned to philanthropy, writing, and sculpting.

"I miss you, nana. You'd be a great comfort right now. Well, I guess you still are, even though I can't cuddle up with you anymore." Mary turned to gaze at a favorite photograph of Beatrice and her taken on the shoreline of Penobscot Bay in Mid Coast Maine. "I love you."

Beatrice gave her granddaughter strength and new resolve to push on. *I'll have a lot of fun with Gwen. And going to work tomorrow will do me a world of good.*

Mary got dressed and put on makeup to diminish the evidence she'd been crying heavily. Occasionally her eyes glanced at the phone. *Will he call? Does he even care a little about me?*

She refused to say his name out loud or in her thoughts. Perhaps, if he called, she'd think differently. Either way, if there should be a call, Mary strongly believed that Percy should be the one to make it. He was the one who needed to apologize.

She went downstairs with a certain spring in her step to await Gwen's arrival.

Chapter 14

Peters watchfully walked down the Godwin's street, as alert as he would have been on a reconnaissance mission on Afghanistan. The veteran stopped across the street and up the block from his destination. He observed an attractive redheaded woman ring the doorbell of the Godwin townhouse.

He fought a powerful urge to grab and drag her away and then ravage her. *I need a piece of that! I gotta put her ahead of little Miss Mary.* He watched the door open. He almost drooled when Mary hugged the hot number. *A twofer?*

His right hand reached under his long shirt for the scabbard. *Don't be stupid! You know better than that! Come back later.*

The young women went inside but left the front door partially open. *Are they inviting me inside? No, they must be heading out shortly. Better back into the alley over here.*

He did so and then waited.

* * *

Gwen's arrival saved Mary from further cross examination by her parents, especially Jane, about her personal life. Saved by the doorbell, she ran to the door, flung it open, and urgently hugged Gwen.

"Thank God you're here!" she whispered, eyes misty, trying not to think about her parents. They meant well but could be annoying nevertheless.

"You've come through for me more times than I can remember," Gwen whispered back. "Shall we go inside? I better say hi to your parents."

"Of course," Mary answered, lowering her arms, and moving aside. She allowed Gwen, an oversized leather bag slung on a shoulder, past her. Mary neglected to shut the door.

Gwen warmly greeted the Godwins. She had spent several enjoyable nights in the townhouse and at their island home in Maine. Her own parents got along well with them. They were fellow members of a few heritage organizations. Gwen and Mary considered the functions too stodgy for their taste, but knew that they would eventually change their minds when they got to a certain age.

"So, what do you two have planned," Jane asked Gwen and Mary.

The two friends eyed each other thoughtfully. Usually Mary took the lead, but she wasn't her usual self. "We're going out for walk and grab a bite," Gwen replied.

A pigeon poked its head inside the open doorway, perhaps looking for crumbs. It cooed. Jane shrieked. Will Godwin shooed it out and shut the door.

"Isn't that bad luck?" Jane asked, as her husband comforted her was a pat on the shoulder.

"Don't be silly," he commented.

Gwen chimed in. "I heard that birds flying inside a house can bring bad luck. But that's only an old wives' tale. Right?"

"You think I'm superstitious?" Jane asked.

"Let's go," Mary urged, clearly not liking the subject matter and the way the conversation was going.

"I'll leave my bag here if you don't mind," Gwen declared.

Godwin looked expectantly at his wife. After noticing the glum expression on her face, he replied. "That's fine, Gwen. Put it down on the chair behind you."

Gwen turned around and placed the bag on an antique chair. Everyone watched as she removed a credit card from the bag and stuffed it in a pocket. She faced them with a smile. "Okay."

Godwin opened the door and bowed as the Mary and Gwen glided past him. He closed the door behind their retreating forms and turned to Jane.

"That was weird," Mary commented. Being outside was already helping the stress headache.

She and Gwen walked briskly on the sidewalk, unaware of a man across the street stepping out of the shadows of a building.

"What do you mean?" Gwen replied.

"I was ready to burst. I really was."

"Tell me about it."

Mary waited until they passed a couple of teenagers. "I'm really ready for a change of scenery. Perhaps unwinding on the island."

"Well, it's still off season, so you'll have plenty of peace and quiet up there. Or you can come back to Boston with me. We can do that now if you'd like."

Gwen stopped in case Mary agreed. Mary reacted in slow motion.

The man trailing them abruptly halted, his eyes trained on them.

Gwen moved a couple of steps until they stood facing each other, only inches apart. They peered into the others' eyes with complete openness and trust.

"Tell me what you want to do, Mary."

Mary's eyes moistened. "I want to undo the past 24 hours. I know that is impossible. I have to learn to cope with what's happened to me, don't I?"

"Yes, you do, but not alone. That's why I'm right here, right now." She drew Mary into a long, strong embrace. Neither cared about the people walking past them. Two friends hugging was as much part of the New York experience as anything else.

Chapter 15

"What the fuck are they doing?" Peters asked, as a woman walked up the cement sidewalk toward him. She looked at him nervously and crossed the street before passing by. She peered back at him a few times.

"Get lost, you paranoid bitch!" he shouted as she hurried away.

The woman's skittish behavior annoyed him royally. He was sorely tempted to give her a real dose of fear by chasing her. Instead, he turned his attention back to Mary and her friend and leered at them hugging.

"Are they making out? Those little minxes! Right on the street, for God's Sake! I bet they won't notice if I got a little closer and take some juicy pics. I better make sure they don't mark me. That would complicate matters a whole lot."

Pulling his phone out, Peters looked from left to right to make sure the coast was clear. He crossed to the same side of the street as the two women and calculated whether or not he'd be seen. They stood in the sun, he in a shaded area. Chances were good that the brightness would partially screen him. That was good enough for him to record a video of them.

Moving forward very slowly, he inched ever closer to Mary and her attractive friend. He was close enough to hear their voices, but still too far to understand what they were saying.

Damn frustrating!

Peters raised the volume on the audio setting to maximum and listened. That helped slightly, although the voices came through sounding tinny. He cursed when the women began walking. He followed at what he thought was a safe distance.

* * *

Mary and Gwen walked down the street. "Gwen, that sounds really tempting. Getting out of the city for a while is just what I need. When's the next train?"

Gwen laughed. "There's one almost every hour."

Mary's phone rang. Her heart skipped a beat when she saw that it was Percy. She was conflicted about taking the call.

Gwen watched her reaction. "Who is it?" she asked as she peered down at the screen. "Oh."

Mary grimaced at Gwen, took a deep breath, and answered on the third ring. "Hi," she said in a pained voice, her heart in her throat.

"Mary, when are you coming back?"

"Percy, I gave you the ring. Do you know what that means?"

"I miss you."

"You do?" Mary glanced at Gwen, who was watching her closely was an unreadable expression.

"Mary, I'm here waiting for you."

"What about what's her name, Percy?"

"That's not fair."

"Neither was fooling around with her when you're about to get married. You hurt me a lot."

"Mary, I know and I'm truly sorry. Please believe me. When can I see you?"

"Percy, I can't see you and don't know what good it will do. I'm going out of town anyway."

"Please don't. I must see you now."

"I do not need any more pressure from you or anybody else, Percy. I need some time to know what I want to do. If you care at all about me, then you'll just have to respect where I'm coming from.

Can you do that, Percy, or must you have your way, everybody else be damned?"

The building anger and resentment inside her purged the depression. It felt good. Mary waited for a reply, wondering if she had been too harsh.

"Percy?"

"I will let you take more time. I owe you that," Percy said resignedly.

"That's right, you do. I'm glad to hear it."

"Go girl!" Gwen said.

"Who's that?" Percy asked, an edge in his voice.

"Does it matter, Percy?" Mary asked irritably.

"No, I guess not."

"Listen, I'm going to go now, before anything more is said that will be regretted later. Bye, Percy."

She ended the call before he could reply.

* * *

Peters stood about thirty feet away, facing a mannequin in a store window. He had been listening attentively to Mary, and viewing her reflection. He remained there when the conversation ended and the two women walked away.

What a toughie that one is! Let's see how tough she really is when she's my POW. Gotta hand it to her though. She put that prissy boyfriend in his place. Payback's a bitch, isn't it!

Peters thought about the orphanages and temporary homes he had lived in for only days at a time before being sent back to the orphanages. He vividly remembered the fights he had instigated at school. Beating up other kids was well worth being punished by the principal. His memories leaped ahead to his enlistment. The Army was by far the best time because it satisfied his urge to kill.

He blinked at the glass, confused that Mary and his friend were not there anymore. Panicking, he spun around and scanned the area. They had vanished.

Three teenage boys approached, all looking hard at him. He angrily punched his abdomen with as much force as possible, flinching from the impact.

The teenagers grinned at each other. One of them called out. "Hey Mister, do that again."

Peters faced the trio. He dropped the phone in a pocket, clenched both fists, spread his feet apart, and coldly stared at the boys.

"Little boy, step over here and say that again. You know, all three of you punks are more than welcome to take me on. Hell, call your friends! The more the merrier! What do you say?"

The adolescents were not yet full grown. Only one of them measured up to Peters' 5'10" height. They stopped at a safe distance from Peters. There was no trace of humor on their faces anymore.

Then as Peters took a menacing step forward, and then another, uncertainty quickly turned to fear. "Let's get out of here," their spokesman strongly suggested. They turned tail and ran away.

Peters considered pursuit, but thought better of it. He stood, laughing loudly, wanting to belittle them. *Those kids don't know how lucky they are! They don't know that I've got better things to do right now, like track down Mary Godwin and her hot girlfriend.*

* * *

Gwen and Mary had ducked inside a coffee shop down the block on Third Avenue to order a couple of lattes. When they reemerged on the street, Gwen paused upon seeing the beginning of the alteration. "Let's get out of here," she told Mary after pointing across the street.

"Gwen, we're safe. This is a low crime neighborhood," Mary said, staring at the juveniles. "I want to see what happens."

"Always the journalist, aren't you? You'll probably find a way to write one of your magazine articles about the incident. Will you hold it against me if we leave now? I hate violence."

"No, not at all."

They returned to the house for a few minutes. Mary packed a small suitcase while Gwen chatted with Mary's parents. When the friends stepped outside again with a suitcase and shoulder bag respectively, the altercation was over and none of the participants were visible. One lurked nearby, unseen.

Chapter 16

Peters observed the women step outside and looked up the street. He was upset when an Uber stopped in front of the residence and they got into the car. The move caught him off guard. He had fully expected to be following them on foot.

His easily inflamed temper got the better of him. *Friggin bitches! Now what?*

He bitterly watched the car motor away. Then he turned his attention to the townhouse. He studied the exterior from left to tight and back again, as an idea formed his devious mind.

Then, feeling better, he marched off.

* * *

The Acela Express sped northeast at more than 110 miles an hour for a good part of the trip from Penn Station on Manhattan's West Side to South Station in Boston. As the distance separating Mary and her beloved hometown widened, she felt more relaxed and at peace. The train ride was not much more than a blur.

Allowing exhaustion to overtake her, she fell into a very shallow sleep. Drifting in and out, her head resting against the upright leather cushion beside Gwen, she distinctly heard the subtle, steady click-clack sound of the locomotive on the steel tracks. Connecticut and Rhode Island hurtled past the sleeping women. Then the dim sights and sounds of the train transformed into the pleasing notes of a piano. She dreamed about watching Percy leering at her while making love to a beautiful woman.

She somehow managed to awaken before more bad thoughts eroded her self-esteem. *Has sleep become my dark enemy? Will every night be like this?* Staring blankly ahead, she shivered with dread.

"You were tossing and turning. I was contemplating awakening you."

Mary turned to look at Gwen, thankful she wasn't alone. "I can't get a peaceful nap or good night's sleep anymore."

"Do you want to tell me what you dreamed about?"

Mary shook her head. "No, I just want to forget. Temporary amnesia would be just what the doctor ordered. I'm sorry to be like this."

"Not at all, Mary. You don't deserve what you've been going through. Maybe you need a prescription for sleeping pills."

"I would if I knew for sure that pills would keep the dreams away." She yawned.

"It might be worth going to the doctor, Mary, and see what he or she recommends."

"Good idea, Gwen."

The PA announced the train's imminent arrival at Back Bay. The next stop and end of the Amtrak line was South Station.

A Lyft driver dropped them in off front of Gwen's residence on Chestnut Street in the historic neighborhood of Beacon Hill. The historic city village was known for its iconic narrow, hilly cobblestone streets. Gaslight lamps adorned brick sidewalks and stately old buildings.

The concierge greeted them as they entered the lobby. He loaded their bags and recently delivered groceries on a luggage cart.

"I thought we'd eat in tonight," Gwen explained in response to Mary's questioning look.

"Sounds good to me."

They kept quiet, each suspecting the concierge would like nothing more than to hear something indiscreet. Mary examined the décor as they approached the elevator. This was her first time here. Gwen had moved out of her parents' Brookline home four months earlier, wanting independence and a walking commute to her office.

Mary and Gwen sat at the kitchen table, liberally sipping from their wineglasses in between bites of grilled steak salad.

"You know I have work tomorrow," Gwen said.

"Can you take the day off?"

"I wish I could, Mary, but no. Tomorrow is actually the deadline to complete the catalogue for an upcoming major auction. I have a pressure cooker of a day ahead of me." Gwen grabbed Mary's hand and held it. "Sorry."

Mary smiled sadly at Gwen, wondering if the Boston trip was a bad idea.

"What are you thinking?" Gwen asked, giving Mary's hand a gentle squeeze.

"I'm thinking that perhaps I should have remained in New York."

"Nonsense! You can enjoy the current exhibits at the Fine Arts or Gardner. Or check out Beacon Hill. There are a lot of nice shops in the area, as you know. You can check out the history landmarks you didn't see in college."

"True."

"So you'll be Boston Strong tomorrow?"

Mary laughed. "I will." Turning misty-eyed, she added, "I'll stop for a moment near the marathon finishing line on Boylston and pay my respects to the bomb victims."

They sat there solemnly a moment. Then they clicked their wineglasses and drained the delicious contents.

"Let's hang out in the living room," Gwen suggested, standing.

"Okay but let me do the dishes first."

"They can wait," Gwen declared with a grin, carrying a bottle and her glass into the other room.

Shrugging, Mary followed her friend. She was a little drunk and ready for anything.

They plunked down, side by side, on a couch. Gwen refilled the glasses and took a big swig of the Merlot. Mary decided to do one better with two full swallows.

"Can I sleep with you tonight?" she asked.

Gwen stared at her uncertainly, lips slightly parted. "What do you mean?"

"I don't want to be alone. Those dreams," she explained.

"Of course. I'm here for you."

Chapter 17

Mary awakened feeling much refreshed. Her last memory before falling asleep was laying on her side pressed against Gwen's backside, an arm around her waist. *I can't feel any snugger than this.* She smiled to herself, remembering what they had done.

The tantalizing aroma of fresh brewed coffee permeated the bedroom, followed closely by the dawning realization that Gwen could have gone to work.

She jumped out of bed naked and quickly put on a t-shirt and panties. Then she went to look for Gwen. "Gwen?"

"In the kitchen," she heard Gwen call out.

"Oh good," Mary replied with relief.

Entering the kitchen, she saw that Gwen was dressed for work and hurriedly chewing the last bite of a cantaloupe. They quickly stepped over to one another and hugged. Mary wanted more but understood her friend was probably about to rush off to her office. She was pleasantly surprised when Gwen kissed her deeply. The short but intense interlude ended too quickly.

"I shouldn't have done that," Gwen exclaimed in a raspy voice. "But it should keep you going until I see you later," she commented with a wicked smile.

"I'm really glad you did. And thanks for last night," Mary replied huskily.

Gwen, with some difficulty, diverted her eyes from Mary's intense gaze. "I loved it. You look like you slept better. No nightmares?"

"None. I slept like a baby."

Gwen looked at her shyly. "You know, I usually don't do that stuff."

"I don't either. Do you think I'm turning, Gwen?"

"I think you need love wherever you can right now. It has more healing powers than anything. But no, you're not gay. Perhaps a little bit?"

Mary could accept that. "I don't want to make you late," she said, glancing at her wristwatch. It was 8:16 AM.

"I'm good." She looked guiltily at the full sink. "I have left a sink full of dirty dishes though."

"I'll be happy to take care of them, Gwen."

"Great. I should run."

Mary followed her to the apartment entrance where Gwen retrieved and flung her long-strapped, leather bag over a shoulder. "I'll see you at 6. We can meet somewhere if you'd like."

"I'll text you this afternoon," Mary replied. She'd explore the area and make the decision where to meet her. Being assertive was one of her attributes.

They hugged quickly. Gwen opened the door and hurried off.

Mary held the door open, watched the elevator close, and then determinately closed the apartment door. *Now what? I might as well get the dishes done.* She returned to the kitchen, trying not to think, hoping to stretch her good mood. It was a challenge.

Feeling appreciative for what Gwen did for her, Mary busied herself with the dishes and tidying up the kitchen. It was the least she could do.

Contented, Mary went into the living room. She gazed out a window at the private deck. *Do I want to veg out sitting out there, maybe grab some rays and check the phone for messages? Or should I go exploring like Gwen recommended?*

Mary decided catch up on her emails and was unpleasantly surprised to discover one from Judy Green. *Wow! She doesn't waste time.* The Assistant United States District Attorney reminded Mary about her commitment to give testimony to the Grand Jury. *Ugh!!!!* In preparation, she was asked to describe her grim experience in a Word attachment. Green instructed her to leave nothing out, no matter how mundane it might seem, beginning with the trip downtown and her frame of mind at the time.

The email ruined Mary's good mood. Her chest and stomach tightened when she thought about having to relive the horrible memories she so desperately wanted to forget. *There goes my R&R. I want to forget what happened, not rehash it! Can I can pretend that I got amnesia and went into shock? That must happen to people who experience a traumatic event. And I've had two of them - The Freedom Tower and Percy's infidelity!*

Deep down, Mary knew she had to do her part to make sure the terrorist got the justice he deserved. It wasn't her way to shirk her responsibilities, especially as her magazine articles sort of made her a public figure.

Will Mary believe me if I lie to her? So where does that leave me? Up a creek without a paddle. That's where! I have no choice. I have to get down with it, prove I have what it takes to get the job down in spite of everything. Damn it!

Mary devoted more than three hours writing five painstaking pages. She forced herself to reread it, constantly editing the document until it looked like one of her fine magazine pieces. The journalist attached it to her reply to Green and notified her that she was in Boston getting some badly needed time off, and didn't know when she would return to New York City.

After the email was sent, Mary went into the kitchen with one purpose in mind. She wanted to drink every bit of alcohol Gwen kept there. Unfortunately there was only one bottle of wine. At least, it was full. *I can drink it all. It would be so easy.* Reaching for the bottle, she paused. *Perhaps too easy.*

I'm stronger than this. Mary lowered her arm. *I can deal with this. I don't want Gwen to come home and see me passed out in a pool of vomit. What would she think of me then? That I'm pathetic? A loser?*

Anger surged through her. She turned around and stormed out of the kitchen and a minute later from the apartment.

Chapter 18

Peters slammed the apartment door and angrily secured the locks and chain. He was frustrated and infuriated about losing his prey. It was highly unusual for a target to disappear on him. She was not at the *Manhattan Magazine* office, the Godwin's townhouse or Percy Shelley's apartment.

"Where is she? How dare the vixen escape me! I hate that!"

He badly wanted to punch the nearest wall. He had repaired more than his share of fist holes over the years. Instead, he punched himself some more, pretending it was Mary's face. The image of her broken nose felt so good. His mood lifted.

"Is she on some secret assignment?" he wondered aloud, pacing up and down the hallway. "The damned receptionist at her office was more than useless. What a lowlife!"

Peters paced back and forth, counting each step until he got to ten thousand. The exercise gradually calmed him.

"Okay, which location should I stake out again? The boyfriend? Mommy and daddy's place? Her office? Little Miss Mary, we'll see how your garden grows!" He laughed. The mirth could not quite extinguish the anger that filled his dark, hate-filled eyes.

* * *

Mary put on her sunglasses and trod up cobblestoned Acorn Street, avoiding eye contact with other pedestrians. Normally inclined to return the smiles of friendly looking strangers, she was not up to it now. Instead, she averted looking at faces and hid behind the dark lens.

She stopped to take a few photographs of the three-hundred-year-old narrow block-long thoroughfare.

Standing as still as a post, Mary pretended that the 21st Century did not exist. Time travel seemed to be just beyond her reach. She envisioned 19th Century artisans transporting their wares on horse drawn wagons past her position.

The bustling city became quieter, shorter, and smaller. The winding Charles River was wider in past centuries, especially in Back Bay. She no longer heard any motor vehicles nor did she see any skyscrapers. Church steeples now dominated the low urban skyline.

Three of her favorite authors lived in the region. She would give anything to take a carriage to visit Nathaniel Hawthorne and Louisa May Alcott, who were neighbors in Concord. Or she could interview Herman Melville in Pittsfield. Wishful thinking.

A driver looked down from high atop a wagon seat, smiled, and topped his hat at her. He looked familiar. *Impossible! He looks like that police intelligence operative, Gary Marston.*

The repeated blasts of a car horn ended the reverie. Startled, Mary turned to see the impatient driver of a BMW glaring at her. He signaled with the abrupt wave of a hand for her to move aside.

What? Where am I?

Unnerved, Mary backed onto the narrow sidewalk.

The car surged ahead until it was next to her. The driver slammed hard on the brake and turned to her. "You should watch yourself," the driver said. "I could have run you over. Be thankful that I didn't."

Am I imagining this, too? "Excuse me?"

"Are you deaf and dumb or just one of them? What is wrong with you, standing in the middle of the street like you were in another dimension?"

What a bastard! What do I do? Turn around and walk in the opposite direction or film him and the license plate? Will that tick him off more? What will he do then?

The man shook his head. "You're pathetic." Then he turned his arrogant-looking face away and stepped on the accelerator. Mary watched helplessly as the horn sounded, forcing other pedestrians to move quickly close to the old buildings.

Her heart pounded in her ears as she stood staring at the vehicle making a turn at the end of the street. *I can't seem to catch a break no matter where I am. There are bad people everywhere! Even in Boston.*

She looked up the block to make sure the BMW driver wasn't returning to harass her again. Acorn Street was thankfully once again free of cars as it customarily was. Inhaling a shaky breath, Mary began walking quickly, determined to enjoy the rest of the day.

She asked herself if her life had taken a permanent downturn.

Don't be silly! Once I go back to work, all will be good. I'll bounce back and will be as good as new again! A string of 70-hour work weeks will get me back where I need to be. Strong as ever!

She did some self-analysis and arrived at a remarkable conclusion. She had been faced down by three men in as many days. The first man was Abu Musab Ali, next came Percy Shelly swiftly on

Ali's heels and lastly the rude, Type A driver on Acorn Street. *I won't let the deplorable actions of any of them defeat me.*

A little while later, Mary was enjoying the Public Garden. She watched people photographing a pair of swans that swam single file in the lagoon there. Apparently, they were named Romeo and Juliet and both were females. That made her smile.

Two men, not much older than Mary, and dressed in business casual attire, approached. They were deep in a conversation, but stopped speaking as they sat down on a nearby bench. They nodded at Mary and she smiled politely back at them. They quietly continued their discussion as Mary listened in, her eyes on the water.

"The guards deny they beat him up," said the bearded man."

"That means squat. Some of them are more sadistic than those behind bars," the clean shaved man said.

"Well maybe."

"Either they beat him up or he did it to himself. "

"That's crazy. You're saying the terrorist is a masochist. Why would he beat himself up like that?"

Mary glanced over at the men when she heard the "terrorist" word. *Must be someone else.* Feeling dread build up inside her, she pulled out her media badge and interrupted the men.

"Excuse me, I'm a journalist," she said, displaying the photo ID. "I overheard you both. What's going on?"

The men gazed at the badge and each other. "You of all people don't know?" asked the bearded man.

"What do you mean?" Mary asked, afraid that she know the answer to her question.

"Your face has been all over the net. I saw you at that news conference at the Freedom Tower the other day. That was you, right??"

Mary slowly nodded her response. "What prisoner were you discussing a minute ago?" She asked, looking from one to the other.

"The Observatory Terrorist, who else!!!"

She stood. "You were talking about Abu Musab Ali?"

"Yeah, you really haven't heard?"

"I wouldn't be asking you if I know the answer!" Mary exclaimed more heatedly than she wanted. She forced herself to calm down. "Tell me everything now, please." She intended to go online after extracting more information from them.

"Sure, sorry. So it's been reported that Ali has complained about being abused by the guards. He supposedly won't name names, mind you. His lawyer has pictures of the cuts and bruises and is threatening to have the trial moved out of New York City."

"Oh no!" *This is too much.*

"What are you going to do?"

"I can't tell you that, but thanks for telling me." Mary turned and walked away quickly. Both men watched her intently.

"Go Red Sox!" one of them taunted. Mary was not a huge baseball fan and did not particularly care about the intense Yankees-Red Sox rivalry that persisted decade after decade irregardless of what team was doing better. So the Red Sox fan's affront went ignored.

Mary pulled out her phone and immediately discovered why she hadn't known about the unsettling development in New York City. The device had somehow shutdown on its own accord. *When did I use it last? On Acorn Street. Where I pretended to be in 19th Century. But that was make believe, right?*

She involuntarily shivered in reaction to the implausible possibility that the phone could have stopped working at that precise time. *That's ridiculous! It's only a coincidence. I must have accidently shut it down. That's the only logical explanation. I've got to hang on to logic to keep myself together. Falling apart is not an option.*

Mary leaned against an elm tree on the Boston Common, hoping to absorb some of the old tree's strength. She went online and immediately found corroborating news bulletins. Her search was interrupted by an incoming text from Judy Green.

Have you heard the news? Why have you been

ignoring my texts and phone messages?

I have an important update that hasn't yet been

made public. CALL ME!!!

Mary, concerned that the Assistant US District Attorney thought she was negligent and a liability, immediately replied.

Sorry. Phone issues. Will call now.

She phoned Green. *That should settle her down, assuming she believes me. I'll know soon enough.* Green answered on the second ring.

"Mary, have you heard about Ali?"

"My phone shutdown without my knowing it. I just heard about him. I'm really shocked that he's injured. Was it another inmate or a guard who did it?"

"Neither, Mary. And don't mention his name on the phone with anyone. Listen carefully. What I'm about to reveal is privileged information. You can only discuss it with me, got it?"

"Yes, what is it?"

"He injured himself. We have evidence."

"Judy, what evidence?"

"He forgot to clean under his nails after scraping and punching himself. We have skin and blood fragments proving he's the guilty party. He intentionally inflicted it to himself, Mary."

"Why?"

"Great question. He refuses to admit his guilt and his attorney isn't being much more cooperative. I believe he may have injured himself to get the guards blamed in order to get the trial moved out of the city. In any case, they won't get the change of venue as the judge is now aware of the defendant's culpability."

"That's good."

"Mary, thank you for the excellent deposition you sent me this morning. It really demonstrates your journalistic skills."

"Thanks. I put a lot into it."

"I can tell. I know this ordeal has taken a toll out of you. It'll be over soon enough."

"How soon is that? Every day is nearly as rough as the day before."

"Really? It's that bad?"

"Yes, it is. I'm trying to battle through it, man up, but it's not easy."

"I know. By the way, he's still demanding to see you. He said he'll only cooperate if you interview him. But we both know that can't happen, don't we?"

Mary fought against the anxiety. Her skin turned clammy.

"Mary?"

"Is he at the federal facility on Park Row?"

"Mary, you can't go there! I forbid you!"

"I know. I'm just curious. Are you saying he hasn't granted any media interviews?"

"That's correct, he's refused, including one with your friend at *Manhattan Magazine*."

"Judy, who is that?"

"Mary, I don't want to be put in the middle of an intrigue. Your father has to tell you that."

"Okay, I guess. I won't put you on the spot, unlike you are with me." Mary heard a sigh on the other end of the line.

"Listen Mary, I want you and I to be rock solid. I'm counting on you to give great testimony to the grand jury."

"When does that happen?" Mary asked in a strangled voice.

"It's not that bad. You'll see."

"When?"

"Next Tuesday, eight days from now. We'll meet before then down here in my office. We'll do it nice and easy. You'll see."

"So you say, Judy. What about Lauren? Will she will be giving testimony?"

"Yes, she will. She's a hero, like you are."

"Is it humane to put her through the ordeal?"

"Mary, Lauren wants justice more than anyone. She wants her mother's killer put away for life. No, that's not quite true. Lauren wants him executed by a firing squad but we both know that won't ever happen."

"Will I see her?"

"Mary, that's not a good idea."

"Oh, why?"

"Listen to me. I can probably get an indictment without her, but having Lauren testify will convince the grand jury beyond a reasonable doubt that a federal crime has been committed."

"What federal crime was committed?"

"Mary, are you interviewing me?" Green asked sharply.

Mary almost laughed, but wasn't quite there. "No, Judy, I'm just curious. It's just that if I get myself involved in something, I need to know as much as possible about it from different angles."

"Fair enough. You have one minute to ask away."

"Okay. What federal crime was committed?"

"Domestic terrorism. It is a violation of the Patriot Act."

"That's what happened in the Freedom Tower."

There was a slight pause before Mary heard the reply. "Mary, are you asking or telling me?"

"Just asking, Judy. I'm done for now."

"Mary, maybe you should become a prosecutor. You seem to have the knack for it."

"No way! Not interested, but thanks."

"Our professions have something in common, you know."

"What's that, Judy?"

"The pursuit of truth. Don't you agree?"

"I guess so," Mary concurred after a few seconds of thinking it over. "We have to persistently dig for the truth, often uncovering lies and deceit in the process."

"Sounds about right. By the way, Gary Marston says 'hi.'"

Mary felt an electric current run through her. "He does? He's with NYPD, right?"

Yeah, he's an intelligence operative at the Anti-Terrorist Deployment Group of the NYPD Counterterrorism Command. Gary's a sharp guy. He likes you."

"He does?"

"Yes."

"I'm not dating anyone now. I can't."

"You don't have to tell me anymore unless it will make you feel better."

"Is that how you speak to those on the stand?"

"I'm just being nosy. Sorry."

I liked him. He seemed to possess the right combination of strength and compassion. And good looking!

"Anyway, Gary's on my short witness list and I'm glad about that."

"Okay, say 'hi' back." Mary smiled to herself.

"I will. Now listen, Mary. I should run. I'll send you the specifics for when you come down here. Let me know if you have any questions after receiving my email."

"Okay, I will."

"Mary, see you soon."

"Okay, bye." Mary ended the call. She held the phone and stared in space, thinking about the conversation. The good news was that she and the Assistant US Attorney got along. They were not far from forming a friendship. Having a friend in the New York offices of the U.S. Justice Department could provide useful in her writing career.

An incoming call startled her. It was Percy. A pang of lost love and desolation immobilized her for a moment. She thought about severing the connection or letting him leave a message. Instead, she bravely took the call, answering on the third ring.

"What is it, Percy?" she asked, trying to sound calm, but not quite succeeding.

"Mary, when are you coming home?"

Oh God! Is he serious? "You need to give me time and space."

"Are you back in the city?"

"Percy, I'm not ready to see you. Don't you know how much you hurt me? Or have you already forgotten?"

"I'm suffering, too. Don't you care about me anymore?"

The realization that Percy always turned the conversation around to make himself seem the martyr flooded back to her. Nothing was his fault. Woe is me.

"You can come over when you get back."

Mary heard the trace of pleading in his voice. *Does that mean he loves me or is he trying to manipulate my emotions?* She tried to resist. "I'm not ready for that, Percy."

"I'll have to be content in knowing that my eyes will gaze wondrously upon you soon."

"Percy, please save your poetry for what's her name. Bye."

She was well aware that the ploy generally weakened her ability to fend off his advances. It was proof that he was trying to seduce her one more time and win her back. *Not this time, Percy. I refuse to be betrayed again.*

Chapter 19

The marine layer formed over the Atlantic Ocean. A heavy fog bank surged westward. New York City lay directly in its path.

Peters welcomed the thick blanket more than any other city resident. The air mass would provide the perfect cover for the illegal work that needed to be done right away. He actually believed that the weather was a signal from the powers on high or below that he was doing the right thing.

Peters strode resolutely down the block, dressed in grey, to blend in with the thick vapor. He could barely see ten feet in any direction. The traffic was understandably lighter than normal and when he saw vehicles, they seemed to be emerging from another world.

He stopped at the service gate of the Godwin's townhouse and scanned his surroundings. He couldn't see across the street which meant nobody over there could see him. The street itself was barely visible.

He easily scaled the wet black wrought iron fence, vigilantly listening for movement on the sidewalk, street and from within the building. All was quiet. So far, so good. Perched near the top of the fence, he inserted his hand in a pocket of his waterproof jacket. Two senses kicked in around the same time. He felt the hard object in there and he heard an approaching vehicle.

Goddammit!

He stood on a metal bar, one hand gripping the fence, the other in a pocket, silently cursing and urging the vehicle to pass by without stopping. Screeching brakes would signify that he was seen. He remained as still as a corpse, knowing movement would attract attention.

Keep moving, idiot!

The vehicle motored slowly past his position. Peters exhaled.

A few minutes later, he stood on the sidewalk, staring up at the small device. It was a combination mini camera and motion detector. The compact security unit was attached to the western corner of the limestone façade, held there by a special epoxy. The front door was only ten feet to his right.

Mission accomplished! Now I'll see everyone who enters and exits the front door. Mary better be one of them, and soon, if she knows what's good for her!

He walked away, his mind rehashing slights he had received, and plotting revenge.

* * *

Mary still had three hours to kill before meeting Gwen. She filled the time sightseeing on board an amphibious craft, the ever-popular Duck tour. The guide had a purple beard. Mary wasn't sure if it was real or not. His name was Paul Reverse.

Near the Boston Public Library, the guide's informative, colorful and sometimes humorous description of the historical events that occurred in the buildings they passed was interrupted by a pedestrian who apparently recognized Paul.

The middle-aged man called out, "Hey, Paul!!!"

Paul waved vaguely back at his recent passenger, foreseeing a comic tragedy in the making. The pedestrian, focused entirely on Paul, didn't see where he was walking.

Mary grimaced when the man tripped over a refuse container, almost falling yet heroically managing to stay upright on both feet. Mary heard Paul Reverse and some of the passengers laugh. She wondered if the pratfall was a rehearsed segment of the tour.

Two hours later, after a short voyage up the Charles River and completion of the fun and informative excursion around the old city,

Mary entered The Sky Restaurant, a restaurant perched atop the Adams Tower. The dining establishment offered panoramic 360-degree views of Boston from the 75th floor of the iconic skyscraper. Mary was fortunate to have succeeded in reserving a table to the ever-popular hotspot. The establishment was in demand as much as a former restaurant on the top floor of The Prudential Center.

The first to arrive, Mary was escorted to the table for two. She promptly ordered a drink and admired the vista below. She took some photos and uploaded them on her social media sites, unaware who may view them for better or for worse.

* * *

Peters viciously shattered the computer mouse with his fist. The resulting pain was well deserved after being unable to locate the contrary Mary Godwin. He angrily installed a replacement device; several were on hand for such an accident. Then he went back online to continue the search for the elusive woman. This time he searched her Twitter account and sure enough, there were a bunch of recently posted images.

"Got you!!!" he exclaimed, leering triumphantly at the screen. "Why the hell would you be in that cesspool of a city? Did that minx you were with take you there? Is that it? Are you a traitor to New York? Do you like the Boston Red Sucks, Mary Godwin?"

Peters glared at the contemptible pictures of the Boston skyline for a long time, allowing his mood to darken. Being a champion of negative energy, the bitterness and contempt made him feel stronger.

"This proves that she totally deserves to be exterminated! I will be doing New York City a public service. It will earn me the respect I've deserved and been denied for so long."

He continued scrolling through Mary's tweets. "When are you returning to Gotham? I can't wait forever. Don't make me go up there? That would cost you even more pain. Is that what you want? Is that why you're playing hard to get?"

* * *

Mary stared out the window of the southbound train as the southern suburbs of Boston flew by. She felt the Acela accelerate on the tracks. Although she loved getting to a destination quickly, speeding home to New York City did not thrill her. For a fleeting moment, she had considered taking the Downeaster train to Portland Maine and then hopping on the bus to Lincolnville Beach. There, she would board the ferry to Islesboro, her summer sanctuary.

Being on that island paradise is so tempting right now. I would have the house to myself for a couple of months. I would have no worries. Just bliss, watching the waves and reading some good books by a roaring fire. But I can't wriggle out of my legal responsibility. Crap!

She sipped from the large clear plastic container of iced coffee, thinking about the dinner with Gwen. Her good friend had been in a very bad mood that evening from a grueling day at work. Gwen constantly complained about her boss.

"He despises me because of my last name," Gwen told her.

"What makes you say that?" Mary replied, wondering if Gwen's claim could be true.

"Someone at the office I trust overheard Selby talking about me."

"What did Selby specifically say, Gwen?"

Gwen finished chewing and swallowed. "He said that I was born with a silver spoon in my mouth."

Mary laughed. "That's pathetic. It's not your fault your family has money. He's probably jealous and insecure."

Gwen almost coughed up a mouthful of sautéed lobster tails. When she finally swallowed, her face flushed, she replied. "Insecure? He's a pompous ass. He treats me like an idiot, going out of his way whenever possible to criticize my work. He enjoys marking up my reports in red ink with short critical comments that have very little to do with reality. It's gotten to the point that whenever I see an email from him in my inbox, I feel so much despair and anger that I'm afraid to open it. I think he's trying to make me quit my job."

Mary watched a tear meander down Gwen's face. She reached across the table and held her hand. Gwen used her free hand to dab the wet cheek with a napkin.

"Mary, I need your help. My confidence is really shaken badly. What should I do?"

Mary's reverie was interrupted when the conductor stopped and spoke to her. "Ticket please."

Mary handed it to him, watched it being scanned, then accepted the checked ticket back with a smile of acknowledgement.

Her mind returned to the restaurant.

Mary was concerned about what the job was doing to Gwen. Having a prejudicial and resentful boss was a stressful and unfair situation. There could be no happy ending, unless one of them left the company.

Gwen looked across the dining table at Mary with troubled eyes. "What are you thinking?"

"I wish I could give you advice about how to handle your boss, Gwen."

"That's sweet of you. It'll work out somehow."

"Well, there may be one possibility. You know that the criticisms are unjustified. So if you get along with his boss then go to him or her and file a complaint. It wouldn't hurt to have someone back you up like your associate who could attest to Selby's bias against you."

Gwen squeezed Mary's hands. "Thanks, Mary. I think that's what I'll do. I really appreciate our time together. I'm sorry that you have to see me like this."

"Come on, Gwen. I was deep down in the dumps until coming up to Boston with you. You really saved me."

"Then you should consider spending more time here, perhaps even a move. I'm sure you could put your investigative journalist skills to work in Boston."

Mary nodded unenthusiastically.

Mary continued ruminating as the train journeyed southwestward through Fairfield County, Connecticut. Her mind continued drifted on its own accord from what Gwen told her to something that had been nagging her for the better part of a year. She had a story to tell, potentially more powerful than the ordeal in the Observatory, and infinitely more frightening. *No, I mustn't go there. What's the point in tormenting myself? I can barely face him without cringing.*

Her body shook for a few seconds. She let it go its course. Nobody seemed to notice.

Instead, I've got to focus on getting through the next few weeks, giving testimony and putting Percy firmly behind me. It's time to get my mind solidly into producing quality articles.

Mary felt somewhat better at postponing the inevitable one more time. She buried it as deep as possible within the deep recesses of her mind as the train hurtled on the tracks toward New York City.

Chapter 20

Howard Peters lived on the ground floor in a rent stabilized apartment. The late 19th century building was originally a mansion. During the middle of last century, it was converted to one bedroom and two-bedroom apartments. His apartment was in the rear section of the building. Unbeknownst to anybody else currently alive, including the building superintendent, the Peters residence contained a secret room accessible through a removable panel in the back wall of the bedroom closet.

He had been thrilled the first time the opening was accidently discovered. That occurred five years before Peters first laid eyes on Mary Godwin.

Someone, possibly the developer who converted the building into multifamily units, or possibly even the original building owner, had plastered and painted over the opening in an effort to conceal it.

But why?

Peters had been squatting on the closet floor, spit polishing his old army boots. The combat veteran occasionally wore them, but only inside the apartment, and on certain special occasions such as the anniversary of his involuntary discharge from The United States Armed Forces.

He stopped shining for a moment, raised a boot to his eyes, and looked dispassionately at the reflection of his unhandsome mean-looking face. His arms ached from the two hours passed in painstakingly making the boots look like they would pass muster by the drill sergeant. If they did not measure up, he would be assigned latrine duty.

Remembering that punishment like it was yesterday, a wave of anger surged within him. He hurled the leather boot at the rear wall with all of his might. There was something odd about the sound the boot made when it struck the wall.

Peters duck walked over to the point of impact and stared closely at the resulting crack. Frowning, he rapped his knuckles on and around the damaged area. He felt and heard differences in the vertical surface. He withdrew and unclenched his fist, curious about the significance of what it meant.

"There's an area that's not solid. Is it possible there's a void? I gotta check it out, investigate as it were." Curious, he was tempted to kick it in, but held back because brute force, this time, did not seem appropriate. He would be creating unnecessary repair work for himself to do and making noise that his snoopy neighbors would wonder and complain about. The less they knew about his actions, the better.

During the next 23 minutes, he slowly, deliberately, and, as quietly as possible, mapped out the outline of the void on the wall using a pencil. Then, sweating heavily from the concerted effort, he backed up to survey his work with excitement and approval.

"Well, what do you know! That could be the portal to my future. I'm the frigging discoverer of some dark secret! Is there pirate's treasure on the other side? Dead bodies? Jimmy Hoffa?"

He laughed loudly. Remembering the neighbors, he clamped a hand over his mouth hard, His smashed lips deservedly smarted. He barely felt any discomfort, as his mind was busy calculating the best way to excavate.

"Why not use my trusty combat knife? Yeah, a four inch, serrated, stainless steel blade will cut through anything. This should be so easy," he growled, thinking about a night's work several years earlier.

When Peters completed cutting through the rectangular plaster and paint perimeter, he cleaned up his beloved knife and put it back in the scabbard. He tried to ignore the pounding headache that seemingly had a life of its own. It impaired his ability to think clearly. *It's some kind of a short doorway. But where's the damn knob? How am I supposed to get it open without one of them?*

The two-foot-wide by three-foot-tall cutout exposed a glossy hardwood surface. Peters discovered it was a sliding door. The portal required a combination of a lubricant, crowbar and muscle power to completely open the entrance to whatever lay beyond.

Cool stale air assaulted his nostrils as he stood staring into the darkness. Eager to explore, he quickly retrieved a flashlight from the kitchen and aimed the stream of light at the space past the closet. He stepped into the adjoining space, saying, "That's one small step for man, one giant leap for mankind."

He stood on a small stoop at the top of a narrow landing that led in one direction – downward. He searched the walls around him for a light switch. Sure enough, a vintage push-button light switch was within his grasp. He pressed one of the buttons, fully expecting that nothing would happen. The relic from the early 20th century proved him wrong when a series of ancient incandescent light bulbs flickered on.

"I'll be a son of a bitch!"

Impatient to enjoy the moment more than a few seconds, he started down the stairs, still holding the unneeded flashlight in his left hand. The temperature cooled slightly where the stairs made a 90-degree turn.

The intrepid explorer's eyes took note of the cracked plaster walls and the identifiable tracks his shoes made in the heavy layer of dust. Ten steps below the sharp bend, he set foot on the basement floor, stopped, and looked around.

The windowless chamber occupied half of the building's footprint. The owner of the old house had constructed a wall, sealing off the space from the rest of the basement level. Peters remembered that was where the modernized furnace, hot water heater, and electrical panel were located.

Peters felt like the place was reserved for him. *I will do great things here, away from prying eyes and for my own gratification. I will hone my craft to perfection.* He laughed. The thick walls and ceiling absorbed the unpleasant sound.

A canvas tarp covered an unknown object in the center of the room. Curious about what he may being taking possession of, Peters strode over to the draped shape and flung back the heavy cloth. A bronze sculpture of a man's head was exposed to his view. The base stood on an antique work table.

Peters was exhilarated by the man's facial expression - pure terror.

Time seemed to stop as the sadist wondrously stared and admired the head. "What beauty! A genius created this masterpiece!" He wanted to know if the sculptor or sculptress had used a live or dead model. *Such inspiration! I wish I had been a fly on the wall to watch this art being created!*

A terrible yearning built up deep within him. He needed to emulate the work of art in his own way. *I must get some sculpting tools and create my own studio down here. Then I'll bring a muse down here. I'll use my fine tools on that special person. It shouldn't be too difficult to manipulate all kinds of expressions on that face. No, not at all.*

The horrible visions he imagined filled him with sexual tension that could only be relieved one way.

Chapter 21

The Acela train's PA system announced that Penn Station was the next stop. Mary reached for the coffee cup from the drop tray and swallowed the few remaining drops of liquid caffeine.

Nobody in the city knows I'm back. She checked her voicemail, grimly noticing too many calls from her parents. *I don't want to talk to mom and dad. Mom's worried about me way too much. Why does she still treat me like a little girl? Will I treat my daughter the same way? Will I ever want to get married? After what Percy did, the idea of being a spinster doesn't really seem so bad.* She sighed, turned her head to the window, and stared dolefully at her reflection.

As the train sped through the tunnel under the big city, Mary tried to persuade herself that she was right in returning home with days to spare before the grand jury was convened.

I've wallowed in self-pity long enough and sat on my ass long enough. Too much free time allows too many negative thoughts to turn me in the wrong direction. That's not me!

To hell with Percy! Let him see what happens when that prima donna tires of him. To hell with terrorists! I'll personally make sure that one of them will serve time for his monstrous actions! It's the least I can do for Lauren.

Her phone vibrated. Mary jumped in her seat, startled, a clear indicator she had a long way to go in getting her nerves back to normal. Noticing that the caller was Judy Green did nothing to calm her down. *What does she want now?* She braced herself and took the call.

"Judy, tell me that you are excusing me from giving testimony."

"Mary, your testimony is more important than ever. There's been another development."

Mary tensed even more. "What happened?"

"Lauren's had a tricyclic antidepressant overdose."

"That's terrible. Is it okay to visit her?"

"Mary, forget about it. Her father doesn't want Lauren to have any visitors other than family at the hospital. Mary, where are you?"

"On the Acela. I'm almost at Penn Station."

"Good. You know where my office is, right?"

"One Hogan Place. Don't worry, I know how to get there.

"Of course. Come by tomorrow morning, say 10. Okay?"

"Okay," Mary replied petulantly.

"I'll provide lunch Mary."

"I'll be there that long?" Mary updated her calendar as she spoke.

"Hey, it won't be torture."

"No?" Mary replied doubtingly.

The signal was lost under the hundreds of tons of rebar and concrete. She reverted to staring out the window, her mind drifting to stories about homeless people living in abandoned tunnels beneath the city that never sleeps. Some of them lived contentedly underground despite the absence of hygiene, electricity, electronics, running water and indoor plumbing. Thinking about their plight saddened Mary but also made her appreciative about her life.

All in all, I'm really fortunate in spite of the recent adversity. It's up to me to make it better.

And poor Lauren. It's totally unfair. Would seeing me really harm her? Is her father being paranoid? Should I find out which hospital she's at? She could use a friend at a time like this. Or would seeing me remind her of the nightmare we shared and worsen her condition?

Chapter 22

Peters never tired of watching the *Saw* movies. He owned copies of all eight films in the franchise. Whenever he needed to bolster his mood, all he had to do was play one. Sometimes he played a double feature. They made him hungry. He always stuffed his mouth with heavily buttered and salted popcorn during the especially gory scenes. Every bloody death and violent torture orchestrated by the admirable character, Jigsaw, was well deserved and worth watching over and over again, sometimes in slow motion. Peters wished that his little den of horrors in his private basement was as large and intricate as what he saw in those movies.

* * *

Mary strode briskly on the busy sidewalk flanking 7th Avenue. She was unsure about her destination. Her choices were the townhouse and office.

It doesn't really matter where I go. I mean, Dad said not to return to work until after the grand jury, but I can't just stay home twiddling my thumbs. Being there is stifling, yet comforting in a way. I never expected to live there again but what choice did I have? It's not my fault what happened.

Being back in New York exacerbated the heartache inside her and the trauma of what happened in the Freedom Tower.

I should have seen it coming. I knew all about his reputation from my friends here and on the island. And there were warning signs in the New York pictorials and online gossip columns. Did he play me for a fool? Did he ever really want to marry me?

Mary fought down the turmoil of conflicting emotions, knowing full well that anything others than being cool, calm and alert on the city streets was unquestionably not a good thing.

She would learn the hard way that it could mean the difference between life and death.

* * *

He was thoroughly enjoying the eighteenth viewing of *Saw VI* when a loud beep from the computer diverted his attention. The high-pitched sound could only mean one thing.

Peters enthusiastically paused the movie and stepped quickly to the desktop PC. *Who's at the Godwin's front door? It had better be Miss Mary! I'm sick and tired of seeing her stupid parents and the other idiots who go in and out of the place every frigging day.* He was also peeved that perhaps he had missed her when he had been out of the apartment.

A wave of euphoria consumed him when he peered at the screen. He pumped his fists. "The bitch is back! The bitch is frigging back!"

He stared at the monitor, watching Mary inserted a key in the keyhole, turned it, opened the door, and entered the building. Her appearance only served to whet his appetite.

"Don't worry, it won't be very long now. You will soon never be seen again, at least alive and in one piece."

Chapter 23

Sometime before his life intersected with Mary Godwin, he was Detective First Grade Gary Marston. He possessed exceptional problem solving and analytical skills and was respected and liked by his fellow officers. His testimony and strength on the witness stand was generally considered a win-win for prosecutors.

The detective led everyone to believe that he wanted to remain in the huge metropolitan police force until retirement. That was not the case.

He was due for a promotion according to hints dropped by his precinct commander, Captain O'Malley. The likelihood of becoming a sergeant meant that his higher rank would expose him more to the top brass. O'Malley considered Marston a natural, with his easy smile and intelligence, attributes that could enable him to climb the hierarchy as far as he wanted.

Marston was riding high at the moment due to the successful end of an investigation resulting in multiple arrests and the seizure of more than one hundred stolen illegal assault rifles and other firearms. Marston had orchestrated the whole operation, including his own undercover infiltration in the gun trafficking ring.

Marston wanted to use his new stature to make a lateral move. He had not yet shared his thoughts with anybody. To be fair to himself and the captain, he needed to make a decision before his upcoming performance review.

That happened a year ago.

Less than a month later, Marston got his wish, a much-wanted transfer to the Anti-Terrorist Deployment Group of the NYPD Counterterrorism Command. Homeland Security would have been happy to have him, but being a loyal New Yorker, the Brooklyn resident preferred to stay with NYPD.

Serving on the front lines of safeguarding New York City and the United States put his patriotism to good use. Although several terrorist incidents had occurred since 9/11, a significantly higher number of threats had been prevented, resulting in saving thousands of lives.

His wide-ranging responsibilities included intelligence analysis, surveillance, and first responder liaison. During a terrorism event, he customarily followed the heavily armed members of the Critical Response Command, known as the CRC, to the scene. Once the perpetrator was apprehended, he coordinating the sharing of extracting information with other segments of the intelligence and legal communities including the U.S. District Courts.

In the instance of Abu Musab Ali, he would only close the book on the terrorist after the judge's sentencing. That was a long ways off, probably close to a year or so.

Marston was ready to leave Judy Green's small office. He was confident about their combined efforts to put Abu Musab Ali in prison for a long time. Judy was his favorite Assistant US Attorney. They had some good times at a neighborhood bar but were just friends.

Standing and stretching, he noticed a mischievous look on her face.

"By the way, Gary, I think Mary Godwin may be interested in you."

He was surprised by the exhilaration that he felt at hearing the unexpected news. *Easy does it. I liked her right off the bat, but that's true with a lot of women.*

He looked keenly at Judy. She grinned back at him.

"What makes you say that?" he asked as nonchalantly as possible.

Judy grinned wryly. "I know these things."

The operative could not think of a smart reply. "Oh?" was all that he could muster. He had suspicions that Judy was pulling his leg. It wouldn't be the first time.

"I'm serious, Gary."

"You're matchmaking me with her."

"Excellent deduction," she said with a wink. "What are friends for?"

"Well, I'll say hi to her when I'm in court for the grand jury proceeding. See how that goes."

Judy nodded at him, her manner suddenly serious. "It'll go well. I'm ready."

"I know you are. I guess I'm still pissed about that stunt he pulled in the MCC (Metropolitan Correction Center). It'll be interesting to see how Abu Musab Ali's attorney uses that."

"Yeah, but it has nothing to do with why the grand jury is meeting, as you know. The grand jury will deliver an arraignment indicating there is probable cause that Abu Musab Ali is guilty."

"Judy, I know that. I'm jumping ahead to the actual trial."

"Don't let it bother you."

Marston nodded. "Well, I better get back to operations to keep us safe."

"See you," Judy said.

Marston gave her a thumbs up and left.

He stepped outside 1 Saint Andrews Plaza. The building was ideally located a long block from the federal courthouse at 500 Pearl Street. The Metropolitan Correction Center was situated between both those structures on Park Row. And Marston's office? NYPD was situated just across Park Row at 1 Police Plaza. In other words, he rarely had more than a five-minute walk during his work day.

His mind was more on Mary Godwin than work as he crossed the two-way thoroughfare.

Is she available? Am I even her type? I'm middle class but she's a step or two up the social ladder from me. Does that really matter anymore? After all, New York's the great melting pot.

So, yeah, I'll try to figure how she reacts to seeing me in the court building. If I can. I probably have an easier time knowing what a terrorist is thinking than what a woman is thinking. My intelligence work is no help for that!

Marston was cutting himself short. He usually did okay. Most women were mesmerized by his deep blue eyes, handsome face, and easy manner.

The man was oblivious to those attributes as he took long, quick steps past a huge red steel plop art sculpture adjacent to the police fortress. But by the time Marston entered the building, his thoughts were entirely focused on the job-related tasks that required his complete attention.

Chapter 24

Mary leaned against the exterior kitchen wall, exhaling nicotine vapor from an e-cigarette. She needed it after a stressful prolonged three-way conversation with her parents. That had sent her fleeing out the service entrance into the alleyway. Hearing the distinguishable sound of her stepmother's approaching footsteps, she quickly pushed off the wall and shuffled down the alley in the direction of the tall metal gate.

Give me a break, Mother, or I'm leaving again.

Mary grabbed hold of the iron with both hands and imagined herself caged in a jail cell. The comparison was not difficult for her to comprehend, although that was perhaps somewhat unfair to the jailers, her parents.

Suddenly feeling watched, she gazed through the gate at the street. She noticed a car passing by and a woman on the far sidewalk, but nobody looking back at her.

Spinning around, she saw her mother frowning at her. "I'll be inside soon. Don't worry, I'm fine out here."

Jane Godwin smiled encouragingly. "I can keep you company, dear. I promise not to talk."

Yeah, right.

"Mother, please!"

"Mary, I don't like you calling me that!"

"What?"

"You only call me 'mother' when you're upset about something or angry at me. So which is it?"

Mary realized that her stepmother was right on both counts. *I'm using the formal term as an exclamation and probably not in a very complimentary manner.* The dynamics of their relationships changed in that moment as her respect increased for the woman.

She walked toward her stepmother. "Mom, you're right. I'm sorry."

Mary rested the e-cigarette on a ledge and embraced Jane. They separated after a short time.

"Thank you, Mary. That meant the world to me."

"Me too, Mom."

Jane looked past her daughter toward the street and frowned. "Let's go inside, shall we?"

Mary resisted looking in the same direction for an instant. Shrugging inwardly, she avoided looking past the service gate and fetched the e-cigarette. Then she followed Jane inside.

Mary was not a poet. But she had heard enough of her ex-fiancé's recitations to perhaps incorporate them in her psyche. Just before drifting off to sleep the night before her testimony, she inadvertently composed a short poem.

When tomorrow becomes today,

I will be on my way.

I will not at all mind

To be back at the grind.

She was thankfully too sleepy to wonder why she would emulate Percy.

She was jittery the next morning. To calm herself, she listened to Hammock on her music app. The duo's ambient music usually relaxed her.

Instead of the usual caffeinated coffee which would only irritate her nerves, Mary made herself a cup of herb tea. She ignored her stepmother's prying eyes and questions, pretending she couldn't hear them over the earbuds. When Jane tapped her should, Mary reluctantly removed them, sighed internally, and looked questioningly at her.

"Dear, I know you're not looking forward to court this morning."

Why bring it up then, Mother! She could only manage to say, "Right." She inserted the earbuds again, hoping that was the end of the unwanted discussion. Deep inside, she was aware that her stepmother deemed that a discussion was more beneficial than keeping it to herself. Sometimes it worked, but not this morning. She only wanted to get the ordeal over with. Then she could get on with her life.

Before departing with time to spare, Mary yielded to her stepmother. She assured Jane that she would survive the court proceeding and come out wiser and stronger.

Then, bracing herself, she opened the door and exited the townhouse, entirely unaware of the remote-control device perched several yards away.

Chapter 25

The morning sun slowly climbed up the steep Manhattan skyline. Pedestrians seeking warmth and brightness strode purposefully on the sunny side of the street. Those seeking cooler temperatures and regular daylight sought the shady sidewalks. Most of the foot travelers at that hour were on their way to work.

Howard Peters covertly stood in the shade at the end of the block, nursing a cup of black coffee. He watched Mary step outside and stop. *It's about time, woman! Now what!* He cursed to himself when William Godwin followed her outside. When they walked together in his direction, Peters lowered the tip of his cap.

Father and daughter seemed deep in conversation, but every now and then she scanned her surroundings for no apparent reason that Peters could understand.

Peters tried to look inconspicuous. He stared at his phone, oblivious to Mary's brief but intense gaze at him when she stepped past his position. A few quick heartbeats later, he dared look up to take a fleeting look at her, only to find the brazen young woman peering over her shoulders at him. Her hand was raised, her phone aimed at him.

He looked away grimacing. *Damn her! Does she have a sixth sense or what? She's made me! Now what?*

He stood stock still waiting for his brain to focus on a tangible thought. Meanwhile, his target rounded a corner and moved out of sight.

* * *

"Dad, did you see that man?"

Godwin looked all around. A number of men were visible. "Which one?"

"We passed him just before rounding the corner. I don't think he wanted me to notice him. I took his picture." She felt good about that. The next step was to somehow learn his identity and determining his interest in her.

"Listen, Mary. People do the oddest things. There are a lot of strange people in our great city." He looked down at her and frowned at her glum expression. "We can go back if you want and speak to the man. I will do the talking."

Mary sighed. "That's all right. I guess I'm paranoid."

Her father briefly touched her shoulder briefly. "No you're not, young lady. You have been through the ringer. There is no harm in being observant. None at all."

Mary nodded unenthusiastically. *Okay, get a grip.* "Thanks, Dad. You're right."

She fought an urge to look back to see if the man was there. *Don't be ridiculous!*

They walked quickly down Park Avenue to 59th Street. There, they would go their separate ways, he to the magazine offices on Third Avenue, she to the IRT subway station on Lexington Avenue.

Just before reaching the corner where they'd diverge, Godwin took Mary's hand and walked her over to the side of a building. The congested pedestrian traffic swerved around them.

Godwin faced his daughter. He raised her face up to him with a finger under her chin. "Now listen to me."

Mary looked up at him with unfocused eyes.

Godwin regarded Mary closely. "Mary, do you hear me?"

Mary forced herself to the surface. She peered at her father with a weak smile. "I hear you."

"Good. You'll do fine. I've checked out Judy Green. She's a good attorney. Perhaps a little hard-nosed, but she has an excellent conviction rate."

"Dad, you didn't have to do that. Investigating people is something I do, too, you know. It's part of my job description. I know what I'm doing."

"I know you do. I'm just being an overprotective father."

Mary responded with a smile that reached her eyes. She reached up on her tiptoes and kissed him on a cheek, not caring how a public platonic kiss may look to the throng passing by. "Dad, have a good dad"

"Swing by the office after you get out of court," he replied.

"I will."

They parted company. A minute later, Mary descended the stairs down to the Lexington Avenue Line of the massive subway system.

* * *

"Damn her eyes!" Peters exclaimed. An elderly woman, waiting for her dog to do his business at a hydrant, nervously watched him. Peters gave her a dirty look. Unnerved, she turned away, pulling at her dog who was still doing his business.

Peters grinned at the sight of the dog peeing all over the place, including on some dressy polished shoes. Then his mind thought back to Mary Godwin. *How could that bitch have the audacity of casing me with those penetrating witchy eyes of hers? Doesn't she know that's against the rules? And why on Earth am I standing here like an idiot while she and her old man get away?*

Failing to get an answer, Peters double marched to the street corner. There, he tried to appear casual while peering around the bend. *There!* They were almost a block ahead of him. *I better get a move on.*

He fell into the pedestrian traffic flow moving in the same direction as the Godwins, barely keeping them in view.

His deviant mind wondered about Mary and her father. *Does he slip into her bed at night and keep her warm? Little Miss Mary looks like she'd enjoy that. They're both perverts. Terminating her will make the world a better place. I'm a frigging hero!* He leered at women passing him. Those who peered back at him quickly looked away.

Peters gradually narrowed the distance behind the Godwins. He made sure that there a small crowd separating him from father and daughter in case Mary looked behind her again. Realizing how observant she was enhanced the manhunt.

A hunter should never get distracted by thoughts having nothing to do with the task at hand. Be that as it may, he did not pay enough attention to the Godwins to react smoothly when they suddenly huddled next to a building. He was only a few seconds from colliding into them.

Peters caused a minor commotion when he abruptly swerved into a tiny empty spot in the moving multitude. People who found themselves behind him had to slow down and sidestep in order to avoid stepping on his heels.

He turned his head away from Mary, hoping that the astute young woman had not noticed him. That could compromise the mission more, even possibly forcing him to end it. There would be no end to the pain and suffering he would do to himself if that came to pass.

Peters needed to know if he had escaped unnoticed. He stepped over the curb onto the street and backtracked until she was barely visible, in glimpses, beyond the evermoving throng of commuters. She appeared to be pensively focused on her old man. That was good. He breathed easier, particularly so when Mary and her father parted company. He almost laughed when she kissed the man on the cheek.

Who is she kidding? I bet there's a lot of tongue action when they're alone. Sick!

The killer shook his head like a dog to clear the perverse yet tantalizing image from his internal monitor.

Shape up! It's time to follow her sweet scent.

After allowed her to pass him, he recontinued the pursuit, following her into the heavily congested subway station.

Peters had a few anxious moments in the subway. He had neglected to carry the necessary MetroCard to get through the turnstile. Without the polyester smart card, he would be unable to pursue Mary onto the platform and board a train. When he saw Mary swipe her card, he cut to the front of a long line of subterranean travelers waiting to purchase a MetroCard

"Give me a two fare. I've got an emergency," he declared loudly and gruffly in response to a slew of agitated four-letter complaints. An MTA cop glanced in his direction but took no action.

Frigging lowlifes!

He paid and waited, baring his upper teeth. The long seconds seemed like minutes. At last, the card was handed to him. Then, passing through the turnstile, Peters heard the rumble of an arriving train. He didn't know if that was hers or not. A crackly voice on a loudspeaker announced the arrival of a downtown train. *Downtown is more likely than uptown. Let's go!*

He sprinted for the stairway down to the downtown platform as screaming brakes penetrated his eardrums. Following customary etiquette, the people waiting to board the train allowed passengers to exit first. Then the throng herded into the subway cars

Peters leaped from the second to last stair onto the platform shouting, "Move it! Move it!"

He shoved his way through the crowd moving in the opposite direction, determined to board the train before the doors closed. A stooped elderly man stood in his way. Peters knocked him aside as the doors began to slide shut. He ignored the cry of pain of the old man hitting the unforgiving concrete floor. He listened instead to a recorded announcement. "Stand clear of the closing doors please." He made it through the closing gap just in time.

He stood, a hand grasping a metal pole, eyes darting around in search of her. *Where are you?* He did not see her in the densely crowded car. Every seat was occupied and straphangers were lined up from end to end. Everybody avoided his unfriendly probing stare. It was a reaction he expected from them. *That's right. Look away from me if you know what's good for you!*

He didn't know which car Mary was in nor was he certain she was even on that train. He caught somebody frowning at him. "What're you looking at?" Peters growled. The person lowered his gaze immediately.

Peters got in motion, forcefully moving toward the front of the train.

* * *

Mary's body swayed as the train sped around a curve. She held onto the grubby metal handhold as her body leaned to the right. There was no chance of banging into the straphanger next to her because his torso angled in the same direction.

She used the thumb of her free hand to navigate the internet for news, read emails, and browse her friends' social media. These relaxing activities kept her mind busy and pleasantly diverted from that morning's rehearsal with Green. She was too preoccupied to notice the other passengers.

Chapter 26

Peters observed Mary Godwin working her phone from his vantage point at the opposite end of the subway car. He dared not get any closer due to the proximity of an alert-looking cop standing alertly near her.

When the train burst out of the dark tunnel into the Brooklyn Bridge station, Peters noticed the cop looking at him with suspicion. *Fuck you, copper.* He turned his head back to his mark, almost missing her edging toward a door. He did the same.

* * *

Mary, a purposeful fast walker, wove her way on the platform through the crowd as much as she could. Her mind was on a text from Gwen, who had been gushing about some obscure historical papers discovered in an old house in Boston.

That's the big difference between us. She loves the old stuff. I'm into what's happening right now and what will happen in the future, especially how the city will manage to survive being, perpetually flooded in several feet of salt water. The subways, the basements, ugh.

She pushed through the turnstile and climbed up the crowded stairwell. At the top, she stepped out of the bottleneck, happy to inhale the relatively fresh air of downtown Manhattan. It was far better than the heavy, stale underground air.

If Mary had looked upward in the southwest direction, the upper floors of One World Trade Center would have been clearly visible. She intentionally avoided doing that. Instead, she stepped aside, deciding to reply to Gwen. Expressing an interest in her friend's find would make Gwen happy, and raise her own flagging spirits, too.

She was too busy writing to notice Peters walk past, stealing an evil glance at her.

* * *

Peters sat on a bench, his head down, eyes up. To pass the time, he counted the number of legs that moved by him. Counting was a habit, an occupation to keep himself busy. OCD personified. Millions have the condition, but his symptoms were perhaps unique.

Every eight seconds, he turned his head toward Mary to make sure she had not somehow vanished. Frankly, that would not have surprised him very much. He almost expected the unexpected from her.

No, she's still there, moving those delectable looking fingers on her frigging phone. What's she doing? Writing a damned dissertation or something? I mean I don't have all day! Actually I do, don't I?

Occasionally, he was caught looking at people's pelvic regions and received dirty looks from them. He was oblivious, as his vision rose no higher than that. Then a pair of shapely legs turned in his direction.

Ah oh!

He raised his head and eyes, strangely excited that he had been caught. That quickly evolved to shock and anger when he looked into the fiery eyes of Mary Godwin.

The gall of this bitch! She really needs to be put down and quick!

Peters struggled to regain his composure, hoping he was looking at her calmly. He decided to play the part of the victim by going on the offensive. "Why are you staring at me, lady? That is just rude, don't you think?"

Mary glowered at him. "Don't play the innocent one with me! Why have you been following me?"

A number of pedestrians passing by, glanced warily at them, eager to put the quarreling man and woman safely behind. Peters certainly did not want them involved.

"You're mistaken. I'm following nobody. Can't you see I'm sitting here minding my own damn business?"

Peters was stunned when she took another picture of him. He was sorely tempted to leap up and kill her then and there with his trusty knife. Looking daggers at her, he begrudgingly perceived that he would never get away with committing murder in front of dozens of witnesses. He swallowed hard.

"By the way, you need my permission to take my picture and you don't have it. Delete it now!" He stood, itching to grab the phone from her measly hand. He took a step forward.

"Erase the frigging picture now or I call over those cops down the block!"

* * *

Mary cautiously backed up a step, intimidated by the malevolence in his eyes and sudden aggressive behavior. The ill will oozing from him at her was even more frightening than Abu Musab Ali. She had a bad feeling that this man was capable of committing far worse atrocities then the Arab-American.

She took another step back, afraid to take her eyes off the man. She almost collided with people crowding around to witness the altercation.

"Stay away from me," she uttered through clenched teeth.

The man then sneered. "You won't see me again unless I want you to. Better put, you won't see me until, well, never mind that."

Hearing the threat was more than Mary could take. She quickly turned on her heels and urged herself quickly away, eager to disappear from the man's sight as fast as possible. The crowd of rubberneckers moved aside so she could pass through. Despite being thoroughly unnerved, her mind was clear.

Oh God, please keep me safe from that scary man. I bet he has a police record or he's been locked up in a psycho ward.

I'll ask Judy to check him out. The FBI apparently has a state-of-the-art facial recognition system. Hopefully she can pull some strings to get someone to check.

Or should I contact Gary Marston? He made me feel safe once before after he, er, oh damn it! Get a hold of yourself, Mary!

This is going to be a long morning. Facing a grand jury is the last thing I need after this latest in a seemingly never-ending series of nightmare events.

She glanced over a shoulder to see if the man was following her. He hadn't moved other than animatingly pointing a finger up at a very tall man.

Walking quickly, her nostrils detected a foul odor. A moment later, Mary saw a shrouded form laying on a nearby bench. An empty liquor bottle lay on the ground nearby.

Poor homeless person. A drink now is a terrible idea but it is really tempting.

Sighing, she kept forcing her way forward and soon found herself pushing through the brass and glass revolving door of One St. Andrew's Plaza where federal criminals were prosecuted to the full extent of the law.

* * *

Peters was very fortunate not to have attracted the unwanted attention of NYPD during his run-in with Mary Godwin. But now, a pair of police officers approached him while he was quarreling loudly with an argumentative straggler. The situation would have been dicey if he hadn't at the last moment told the idiot what he could do to himself.

He hightailed it in the direction his intended victim had taken a few minutes earlier. *Those cops better not try to stop me!* He badly wanted to sprint ahead to catch up with her. But that would raise the cops' suspicions.

Where did she go? Have I lost her?

He stopped and scanned ahead, knowing from experience that his eagle-like eyes would have better success recognizing her from a stationary position.

"Yeah, there she is!" he told the homeless person reclining on a bench. The vagrant slowly sat up and grunted something unintelligible.

Peters ignored the wretch and walked on toward the federal courthouse Mary had just entered. He knew better than to ever to set foot in that place under his own recognizance.

I ain't that crazy. Right?

Approaching the court building that also housed the offices of the United States District Attorney more than made him uncomfortable. The edifice reminded him of bad times to come if he was not careful.

What is she doing in there? Does it have something to do with me? He felt his stomach muscles tighten at the thought. *No, it can't be. Must be something else.*

A cop exited, stopped, and looked up and down the street. The man squinted at him. Peters smiled and bent down to retie his shoe laces.

This should deceive the bastard. It's worked before anyway.

He double knotted, then slowly raised himself. He glanced up to see if he was being watched. The cop wasn't there.

Where'd he go? Probably to get some donuts.

Peters wanted to wait around for Mary Godwin's reappearance. But the place gave him the creeps. He could be easily arrested and escorted to the US District Attorney's office to be summarily charged with a litany of crimes.

I'm being frigging paranoid.

He stepped around the corner, eyes darting in all directions. A patrol car stopped a few yards away. The front passenger side window rolled down.

Shit on a stick! Stay cool as a cucumber now. He walked away slowly, trying to look like he did not have a care in the world.

But the policewoman in the passenger seat had discerned something abnormal in Peters' face and eyes. She had learned all about suspicious behavior at the police academy and on subsequent duty on the city streets.

Stepping out of the squad car, she called out to him as he strode down the street. "Sir, stop now!"

Being on NYPD's radar sucked big time. Cooperation was essential. He stopped and turned around, with a puzzled look on his face. "You talking to me, Officer?"

"Sir, please step over here."

God damn it!

"Yes, ma'am!" With maximum effort, Peters attempted to look at her with a friendly smile, but a leered manifested on his face instead. He reluctantly stepped over to the police woman.

She watched him narrowly.

What's her problem? She ain't getting any?

"That's close enough," she ordered when Peters was no more than a few feet away.

He obeyed the command, barely overcoming the urge to give her a mock salute.

"I need to see some photo ID."

"ID?" Peters asked, feigning confusion. He just had to give her a tough time. Being overtly compliant even with NYPD was more than they deserved.

"Identification such as a Driver's License," she said wearily.

"How are you doing anyway?" Peters inquired insincerely. He reached in a rear pocket, and removed the requested item.

"Don't worry about me," she replied testily, reaching for the New York State driver's license. She examined it carefully, looked up at Peter's face, and down again at the rectangular plastic card. She nodded slightly before returning it to Peters.

"So, Mr. Reynolds, what business do you have being downtown?"

Peters slipped the fake card in a pocket. "I walk around different parts of our fine city every day. Today, I'm exploring downtown."

The police officer frowned, then utilized a hard stare. "Really?"

You can't scare me as long as you can with that idiotic look, bitch! I can scare you far worse if I wanted to. Consider today your lucky day.

He looked smugly at the cop. His overconfidence did not last very long.

"Let me see that ID again, Mr. Reynolds."

"Is there a problem?"

She extended her hand impatiently. Peters tendered the ID again, no longer grinning.

"Wait here," she ordered gruffly.

Peters helplessly watched her take the card to the patrol car and scan it. *It's okay. She won't learn anything. Mr. Tom Reynolds has no criminal record. He's a boring, honest citizen.* While NYPD ran a search on Reynolds, Peters looked around in case Mary Godwin showed herself. No such luck.

The driver's license was returned a short time later with a curt nod. He was amused that the policewoman seemed disappointed not to have found anything incriminating. They parted company quietly, she to the cruiser and Peters reverting to strolling down the block. He felt her penetrating eyes on him until rounding a corner.

Chapter 27

Mary's court rehearsal in Green's office in The Daniel Patrick Moynihan United States Courthouse at 500 Pearl Street generally went smoothly. The Assistant United States Attorney smiled often and offered encouraging words as they reviewed what had happened on the top floor of the city's tallest skyscraper and what to expect with the Grand Jury.

Green prepped Mary, using the exact questions she would direct at her during the actual grand jury session. The AUSA interrupted the witness a few times when Mary expanded her answered too much or acted flustered.

Then, just as Mary was feeling somewhat relaxed, Green informed her that the jurists had assembled and were waiting.

The star witness stared at Green. "It's now?" she asked nervously.

"Now it is. Let's do it. Remember, Mary, we're on the same side. It'll be over before you know it."

"I sure hope so."

They descended the stairs side-by-side. Judy Green attempted to relax Mary with questions about her music tastes and sharing her own. The diversion helped.

Mary sat in the witness's chair. A microphone was positioned on a table in front of her. After being sworn in by the grand jury foreman, she smiled shyly at the seventeen citizens facing her. They were a microcosm of the city's population. There were men and women, whites, blacks, Hispanics and an Asian.

Green asked her a series of easy questions about Mary's experience in the Observatory before the abduction. She answered calmly but instead of speaking to the

"Are you all right, Mary?" Green asked, approaching her.

"Yes, thank you. I'm just a little nervous," she said, her green eyes focused on the assistant federal prosecutor, now standing only a foot away. She winked at Mary. Mary smiled in return, feeling reassured by the gesture.

"Now, Mary, I know this is difficult. But you must tell the court what you saw Abu Musab Ali do next."

"Abu Musab Ali grabbed Ellen, held her in front of him as a human shield so that the police couldn't shoot him."

"Did you see where his hands were?"

"Well, I saw one was wrapped around her neck." Mary looked down, not wanting to continue."

"Go on please," Judy requested gently yet firmly. "What happened next?"

Judy had instructed her during the prepping to look directly at the jurors when answering questions and to modulate her words. Mary had to keep reminding herself to do that. She looked from Judy to the jurists and back at Judy again, shaking her head slightly.

"Take your time, Mary. We're nearly done here."

Mary, shaking slightly, reluctantly faced the jurors. The men and women grand jurists returned her gaze attentively with a mixture of somberness, frowns, anxiety, encouraging smiles, and even a nod.

She finally spoke, making sure every word was pronounced clearly. "I remember clearly that one hand propped her up, the other hand held a gun. Ellen then sagged and the pressure on her neck intensified until I heard her neck break. It is a sound I will remember to my death." Mary blinked back tears.

"Abu Musab Ali broke Ellen's neck?" Judy asked, glancing at each jurist.

"Yes, after the snapping sound, she collapsed on the floor and never moved again."

Mary's mind replayed the image over and over again.

"Mary?"

Mary looked blankly at Judy, then the jury. *Isn't it enough? Is there more? What have I forgotten?* "I'm sorry."

Judy looked at her "That's all, Mary." The prosecutor then faced the jurists and asked if they had any questions for Mary.

Mary closed her eyes, praying that they had heard enough from her to indict the bastard of murder. *Please no more.*

She failed to see the foreman hand a piece of paper to Green, who then read it and whispered something to the man, before stepping over to Mary.

"Mary, you are excused," she said kindly.

Mary looked at her keenly, wondering if she had heard Judy correctly. Then she rose stiffly to her feet, feeling used and abused. She mechanically followed Judy out of the courtroom to the adjoining hallway. Not quite believing the ordeal was over and feeling drained and shattered, she was not paying attention to her surroundings. She almost knocked a man over.

A pair of strong hands grabbed her shoulders. Mary looked up blankly at Gary Marston's concerned face.

"Are you all right, Miss Godwin?" he inquired, his hands still holding her.

"What?" she asked, spellbound by his intense eyes.

He looked concerned about her. "You look like you've been through a war."

They gazed at one another, his arms still holding her just in case.

"Do you want to let go? Of my arms, I mean?"

He released his grip, winking at Judy who stood nearby, eyebrows raised and smiling knowingly.

"I've been thinking about you," Marston said. "How are you doing?"

"Well, as you observed, I'm a bit shell shocked."

"That's par for the course, Mary."

"You're a golfer?"

"Whenever I can. It gets my mind off work. You play?"

"Golf's not my favorite but I can play. Are you asking me out, sir?"

"Call me Gary."

"Well Gary, I'm sure we'd have fun. Where do you play?"

Judy glanced at her watch and frowned.

"Here and there," Marston replied, ending the smile as Judy nodded at him.

"The jury's waiting on you, Gary," Judy sternly informed him.

"Right," Marston replied. He handed Mary his card. Their hands brushed, sending a cascade of warmth through Mary. "Call me anytime, okay."

"I will," she whispered.

Chapter 28

Mary walked three miles uptown to the landmark building housing the offices of *Manhattan Magazine*. The invigorating hike succeeded in calming her nerves.

Mary did not see her stalker keeping pace a safe distance behind her nor was she aware that he slipped a tracking device in her open shoulder bag.

Her mind wavered between two intense happenings – her testimony and the brief interlude with Marston. *Will I ever see him again? Should I? He's really sexy. I guess that answers my question.*

Approaching the magazine's entrance, she wondered which staff writer at the magazine had been assigned the news story. She did not look forward to being questioned by whomever that person was.

Immediately after entering the periodical's large suite, she retreated to the bathroom, carefully avoiding eye contact with her coworkers. Despite the long walk, she was not in the mood to be speaking to anybody, small talk or otherwise. She entered a stall, bolted the door, and sat down on the toilet fully clothed.

Why am I here? I guess I'm not ready to face the music. Maybe I should go out of town again until the story's old news. I'll hide for six months. Her mind went out on a tangent. After several minutes has passed, she returned to the present situation.

She shook her head. *Here I am rambling, delaying the inevitable. Toughen up! Some people here think I'm daddy's little girl. Just because my father runs the magazine doesn't mean that I can be a slouch. No way! Just the opposite. I have to set the standard by working harder than everyone else here.*

I'll write the best damn piece and prove I can be an asset to any publisher on the planet!

Mary unbolted the stall door, stepped to the sink, and turned on the faucet. She lowered her head and cupped cool water on her face as the bathroom door flew open. She sensed the unknown woman who had just entered was staring at her. *That's just rude. I bet I know who it is. I'll ignore her, pretend she's not there.* She scooped some more soothing water.

The other woman stood a few feet away, looking at her own reflection, applying makeup and admiring herself. Her eyes flickered toward Mary as she brushed her long black hair, before reverting her gaze back at her own face in the mirror. She cleared her throat.

Mary turned off the water, reached for a soft cloth from the top of a pile conveniently stacked on the vanity, and dried her face. Then she stood and faced other woman standing there regarding her with an unfriendly gaze.

Julia Newman was the best young writer at the magazine. 30, good looking, and charming when she wanted to be, she was also a tiger, and a well-dressed one at that. Julia and Mary were not friends and likely never would be. Mary was always annoyed whenever she caught Julia flirting with her father.

"Julia, what do you want?"

"Hello to you, too, Mary. You may as well know that I'm writing the article, or a series of them," she added, gloating. "I need to interview you as soon as possible."

"I hope you don't plan to do it in here. That's a bit unorthodox, even for you. I'll let you know when I'm ready. Don't press me," she said in a strained voice, walking past her colleague and out of the lavatory.

Julia stared disdainfully at her back.

Without thinking, Mary marched directly to the publisher's plush office, barely acknowledging wary nods and greetings on the way.

William Godwin raised his eyes from the galley proof of an article slated to be included in the next issue. His ready smile turned to worry as he examined his daughter's haggard face.

"Mary, I'm glad you're here. How was the grand jury testimony? Please close the door and take a seat."

The moment she sat, Mary burst out, "You gave Julia the damn story."

"Well, it wasn't exactly my decision. As a matter of fact, I abstained, leaving the decision to Jerry. After all, the editor decides and approves writing assignments around here." He paused. "You don't look well. Was the grand jury that bad?"

Mary glared at her father. "Well what did you expect?"

"Of course," he replied gently. "It's no wonder you look the way you do."

"Thanks a lot," Mary said, hurt by her father's blunt honesty.

"Now, now." Godwin moved around the large desk and stepped over to her and took her in his arms. When they separated, she felt more in control of her emotions and her self-esteem was largely restored.

Godwin further helped her mindset by acclimating his daughter about the contents of the current and ensuing weekly issue of the magazine. Mary understood that her father fostered hopes that she would succeed him some day as the publisher. She did not completely rule out seeing her name at the top of the masthead. But that accomplishment lay years ahead of her.

Before departing the publisher's office, Mary promised to cooperate with Julia. She wanted to get the interview over with and committed to stop by the correspondent's desk shortly.

Godwin smiled at her. "That's my girl."

"Will I always be that?"

"You're damn right!" He turned serious then. "Are you ready as yet to write?"

"Sure, I think so."

"Listen, you can't write until you're fully committed to doing so. Otherwise the results will be like milquetoast. That's not you, Mary. As long as you have worked here, you've put your heart and soul into every word. You write with passion. If you can, put your troubles aside. Or allow them to motivate you." He looked at her intensely, his deep blue eyes boring into Mary.

He's right as usual. I usually can't get enough here. Now I'm feeling like a shell. Maybe I should sit down and do what he said. Will the thrill return? It better. If not, well, we'll see.

Mary sensed an improvement in her attitude. She committed herself to resuscitate her desire to be the best she could be.

Farewell Percy Shelley. We were never meant to be together for long. Abu Musab Ali, you will be punished to the full extent of the law and I will continue to do the right thing, starting off by making sure that Julia doesn't twist and turn the story away from what actually occurred.

Mary smiled at her father. "I'm ready now. I have a lot to prove to myself."

"Mary, I am certain your contributions here will be praised far and near."

"Thanks, dad. Now I better get going. See you later." Feeling her inner drive kick in, she left her father's office.

Chapter 29

Peters watching Mary enter the building that he knew housed the magazine offices. Licking a cherry flavored lollipop, he leered at her backside until it disappeared from view. He was satisfied with himself at tailing her for such a long distance without losing her in a crowd or being observed by her.

Savoring the succulent candy, he wondered if she was somehow off her game or had he sharpened his. *She normally has cat eyes and a sixth sense about me. But not today. Why is that? Did she have a bad time in the courthouse? If she did, then that's good for me. Yeah!*

Peters eagerly anticipated the chocolate center of the lollipop. He resisted nibbling at the delicious treat. Every time that happened, he bit his gums as punishment. *No gain, no pain.*

She's gone back to daddy. He'll make her feel better. What sickos! Will I have to put both of them out of their misery or just his little girl? And is today the big day? I've got the room all ready for the lucky lady. Hmm.

He enthusiastically made loud smacking sounds. He enjoyed the shocked and disgusted stares of pedestrians walking past him. A few glares managed to annoy him; an open invitation for him to retaliate.

"Keep your damn eyes on where you're going if you know what's good for you," he warned.

Gradually, realization dawned in his brain that he could be remembered later on by people saying he was seen loitering near the Godwin's place of employment not long before her mysterious disappearance. That meant she would have a stay of execution for at least another day.

He moved to a safer vantage point and continued his vigil, wondering what Mary Godwin was doing and when she'd leave the building.

Chapter 30

Mary sat across the conference room table from Julia Newman. The interview was finally done and she almost was, too. She watched Julia eject the freshly recorded DVD and insert it in a plastic case labeled in blank ink with Mary's name and today's date.

She better not try to release any footage without my consent or more importantly, by the editor or publisher.

Julia looked over at Mary with an unreadable expression on her face. "Mary, you can leave or do you have something to add that you may have forgotten?"

"One thing. Nobody other than *Manhattan Magazine* management and us will ever see the interview unless permission is granted, right?"

Julia responded with a half-smile.

Mary stood and looked fiercely down at the senior correspondent. "Do we need to go to Jerry with this?"

"Not really."

Mary stared at Julia, wishing she could trust her, but unable to do so. Frustrated, worn out, and stressed by having to relive the events at the top of the Freedom Tower three times in one day, Mary then opened the door and exited the room.

* * *

Julia's insincere smile vanished immediately after Mary's departure. The scowl on her face that replaced it came at a cost. Any semblance of being pretty was gone. She simply looked mean and arrogant.

She considered the vague silent reply to Mary an easily breakable half measure. She had recently made plans to leave the magazine. *Hell, I didn't really promise her a damned thing. If Mary was her usual sharp self, she would have pressed me for a written promise. But the princess was off kilter. She made it uncommonly easy for me and will pay dearly because of being off her A-game.*

Julia rose, strode out the room, and smugly strutted to her desk. It was situated in an open bullpen area. Her so-called office contained a desk and two chairs surrounded by a short cubicle.

Julia sneaked a quick look around to see if anyone was watching her. Apparently not. She needed to get the task done without being caught in the act. The journalist thought she might be able to explain the reason for making a backup of the digital disc, but she was not positive her excuse would be accepted.

Having saved the DVD to her computer, she inserted a blank disc. Her eyes scanned the work stations again. Again, everybody seemed to be focused on their own work. So far so good.

She uploaded the saved file onto the blank disc. Her head began to pulse while waiting for the transfer to be completed. She glanced up and caught a pair of green eyes observing her. *Damn her! What does she see? I'll offer the princess a smile. She'll never know.*

Julia smiled insincerely at Mary before checking the status of the upload. She saw that there was 1:29 until completion. No good.

I feel her probing eyes still watching me. She faintly heard Mary's voice. *Who is she talking to? Who cares!*

1:10.

Don't look away from the damn screen. I can count backwards a lot faster than this.

: 55.

Come on! Hurry up!

"Hi, Julia. What are you doing?"

She breathed out, then inhaled slowly and deeply while considering what to do and say. She spun around, smiling sweetly. She hoped that would disarm her visitor as it had so many other times.

"Hello, Jerry," she greeted the magazine's senior editor. "It's an honor to have you stop by."

Jerry smiled back without any real warmth. "I asked you a question. Tell me what you're up to. Does it have something to do with Mary's interview?"

"Yes, it does. That's really perceptive of you," she replied.

"Don't patronize me, Julia. You should know better."

Her smile wavered, then vanished altogether as her confidence faltered. "Very well. I have nothing to hide."

"Ah," the editor remarked.

"What?' Julia hissed.

"You were about to say."

"Yes, um, I'm making a backup of the interview in case I accidently misplace it."

"That is not necessary, Julia, is it? I am well aware that you access your office files from off-site and your plans to have it published by another publication."

"You do?" trying unsuccessfully to flash a disarming smile. She glanced at the computer screen. The copying of the file was 100% completed.

"Give me the DVD, Julia, and the office keys," he said disappointedly

"How did you find out?" she asked.

"Julia, I won't share that with you. Do I need to call security? Do you want everybody to watch you being escorted out of the building?"

Julia's eyes scanned the other cubicles. More than twenty people gawked back at her, including Mary. Julia's face reddened with anger. Her mind searched for a way to leave the office in possession of the DVD. She could still write the story about the Freedom Tower incident for the media company she was going to but it wouldn't be nearly deep enough without having the contents of plastic and metal disc in her possession.

She reluctantly moved the newly completed file to the desktop Recycle Bin. Then she looked up at Jerry to see if he'd make her remove the disc from the external drive.

Her devious mind conceived a desperate plan. Could she use guile to persuade the security guard that night to get her back in the office and retrieve the disc?

Julia shutdown the computer with a smirk. She then filled her shoulder bag with candy, aspirin and other innocuous personal articles from the top drawer of the desk. Then she stood, heaved the heavy-laden bag over her shoulder and stepped through the open gap.

Without warning, Mary blocked her path.

Julia wanted to slap her face hard. She instead stopped and glared at her.

* * *

Mary's brain fog had begun to clear immediately after sitting at her desk, following the intercession with her father. The familiarity of the space and memories of the hundreds of hours following leads and wearing out the keyboard both calmed her and sharpened her senses. That was when she reflected on Julia's interview and remarks that followed.

She determinately gazed at her nemesis.

What is she doing over there? She thought her father should be alerted. Swiveling around, she saw him engaged in an intense conversation with the editor. More than once they looked at Julia.

What's going on? It looks serious. And what does Julia have to do with it? She noticed her father nod at Jerry just before their tete-a-tete ended.

Mary astutely surmised what Julia was up to. She knew from experience that there was no end to the opportunist's guile. While Julia stuffed her bag, Mary decided that she had to make sure her instincts were correct. She strode resolutely over to her father and briefed him what Julia was doing. Then she waited at her work station until Julia loaded her bag. At that point, she moved to a position that would block Julia's path.

Mary understood that she was about to make a permanent enemy of Julia by humiliating her in front of everybody. *Is it worth it? Do I want to have to deal with her trying to get even with me in the years to come? Yes, I do for the sake of setting a standard of integrity. My fellow associates here will shortly learn what I stand for.*

The magazine personnel parted as Julia headed from her former desk to the office entrance. Mary was the only person who did not move aside. Braving the confrontation, she braced herself.

Julia stopped abruptly, inches from tripping over Mary.

Mary wrapped her arms around the unpleasantly surprised journalist and whispered softly in her ear. "Don't worry, the disc you left will be secured after you leave here."

"I hate you," Julia replied, spittle flying from her mouth.

Mary took a side step to unblock her adversary's path to the office main entrance. She received one final up close and personal view of the anger and hatred flickering in Julia's eyes before the woman broke away and stormed out of the office, never to set foot in *Manhattan Magazine* again.

The entire magazine staff witnessed the close encounter of the two investigative journalists and Julia's dramatic exit. Stunned silence was followed by incessant chatter and a strained return to normalcy.

Mary returned to the vacation desk to retrieve the disc from the computer. She discovered that Jerry had already ejected the disc and held it in a hand. William Godwin stood beside him.

"That went well, didn't it?" William Godwin muttered. "In retrospect, I should have given Julia her marching orders behind the closed door of my office."

Jerry found an empty jewel case in the desk and inserted the disc in it. "Well, what's done is done."

"I wonder if there are any files on the hard drive with questionable content."

Mary chimed in. "I can do that. It'll keep me occupied a while."

"Thanks but Carl will examine the files."

Godwin commented, "I appreciate your spirit and understand your eagerness to look at Julia's work. Frankly, it is not appropriate. I do not want people here thinking that you have a vendetta against Julia."

"What about the big article Julia was working on? Do I have to go through another interview with whomever you will reassign the article to?"

"No, there's no need. The one interview will suffice. It should all be on the DVD. You may, of course, be asked a few questions, right Jerry?"

"Yes. See me in my office when you're ready to discuss your next assignment."

"Will do."

Mary returned to her desk. She stared at the vacated work station with mixed emotions, wondering what Julia may have accidently left in a drawer. She reprimanded herself and got to work opening and replying to her work-related emails. Then she went to see Jerry.

* * *

Howard Peters thought that he had better things to do than hang out indefinitely near the magazine's office. *What am I doing hanging around here like a bum? I just have to access the tracker I so cleverly dropped in her bag to know her whereabouts.*

He decided to go home to plot Mary's death. He challenged himself not to have a morsel of food or drop of liquid until the plan was ready to go.

Just as he turned to leave his vantage point to leave, a familiar figure strode energetically past him.

"Frigging Rosefield!"

The object of his derision stopped almost immediately and turned around to see who had addressed him so disrespectfully. Two centuries earlier, the words would have been grounds for a duel, but not today. The strained expression on his face acknowledged the offense and the subsequent recognition on the congressman's crimson face acknowledged the insult.

The two men faced each other silently, each taking the measure of the other. Animosity was the prominent emotion, especially from Peters.

"Private Peters," Rosefield said without emotion.

"Lieutenant," Peters replied gruffly. "It's been too long. You know, I've been thinking of looking you up, paying you a visit."

"Why?" Rosefield asked guardedly.

"To catch up on old times together. "We're brothers, you know," he added derisively.

"Brothers indeed. Ha!"

"You think that's funny, Rosefield?"

The former unit commander frowned at him. "What on Earth are you talking about?"

"Brothers in arms should never lose one another. Right, Lieutenant?"

"Peters, do not call me that. You can call me congressman or major or, well, I would actually prefer not being addressed by you at all."

"Once a bastard, always a bastard. I know you're hoping to be a frigging senator or president like you're privileged or something. Take my word, congressman is as high as you'll ever be."

"You better not be threatening me, Peters," Rosefield growled.

Peters grinned maliciously at Rosefield, turned around, and walked away.

Rosefield shook his head, thinking he should have recorded his former subordinate and wondering if he should take the man's words seriously. He had seen the man's work firsthand and did he know Peters enjoyed killing. *Yes, I better remain vigilant, perhaps even investigate the man's activity since he was discharged from the Army.*

Looking to his left and right, he crossed the street to see William Godwin.

Chapter 31

Mary considered it fortuitous when she was assigned to do a piece neglected by Julia Newman about the use of facial recognition software to nab criminals. She quickly discovered that it was being used by the FBI, NYPD, and police departments across the nation. It was very similar to the system used by the military and intelligence communities to track terrorists in the Mideast and other locations around the planet.

Her fascination with the subject was subliminally connected to her experience with terrorism and the stalker. Feeling invigorated, she immersed herself in the investigatory phase of the assignment.

Mary's online search produced a great deal of results. She read about the FBI Next Identification system or NGI for short. In use since September 2014, the biometrical authentication system matched up a prodigious quantity of fingerprints, retina scans, videos and still photographs. Many of the available photos were taken by police after making arrests. Others were harvested from the hundreds of millions of photographs posted on popular social media sites such as Facebook and Instagram.

Mary discovered that the hundreds of surveillance cameras operating on street corners around the city were used to identify and arrest criminals. There was something about the citywide cameras that triggered a vague thought in her mind, but she could not quite determine what it was. She shrugged and continued her research.

She was too engrossed in her work to notice Theodore Rosefield and her father watching her from Godwin's office.

By early evening, Mary had made excellent progress. The next step, she decided, was gaining access to NYPD's operations center. Observing technicians review video feeds and photography was essential to write a comprehensive essay.

She had several contacts at One Police Plaza, the address for the NYPD headquarters. For the fun of it, she decided to call Marston. She shut her eyes and daydreamed about him.

"Mary?"

Did I drift off at my desk? She opened her eyes and peered up at the man himself. *No, it can't be. I'm dreaming.*

Blushing from embarrassment and guilt, Mary blinked at Marston.

His initial bemused gaze was replaced with a grin and then concern "I'm sorry if I startled you, Mary. I was told you are still here. I hope you don't mind my stopping by."

Mary shook her head in response, still stunned by coincidence of thinking of the man one moment and seeing him the next.

Mary regained the power of speech. "Please do."

He sat down, grinning at her. "If you've forgotten, my name is Gary."

"Gary," she repeated, not noticing his temporary awkwardness around her.

Marston nodded, seemingly pleased at hearing her recite his name. Then his expression turned more serious. "Have you recovered from your grand jury testimony?"

"Oh yes, I'm much better now that I'm working again. Why are you here, Gary?" *Why did I ask him that?*

Marston observed her carefully for a moment.

Mary felt unaccustomedly shy under such close scrutiny. "I feel like I'm back in the court room."

"Mary, I'm sorry. Do you want me to leave?"

"I'm glad you're here. Is it about Abu Musab Ali?"

"You'd prefer if it wasn't," he declared.

"That's right. I'm sick of his name and everything else about him."

Marston leaned forward, resting a tanned hand close to her pale one.

She gazed down at it. *He must have gone to somewhere warm and sunny. Did he take someone?*

Marston smiled kindly at her. "I see that one of your strengths is observing. That must be why your articles are so well thought out."

"Thanks. I try to make them specific, diverse, and sweeping."

"Mary, you cover the bases well."

"Thanks, I guess." She looked back at his hand, noting the absence of a wedding band. She met his gaze, feeling brave. "I feel like getting a drink. What about you?"

His smile deepened. "I'd like that."

"So you're off duty?"

Marston put his hands together as if they were bound by handcuffs. "Guilty as charged."

Mary laughed.

"Is now good?" he asked, glancing at the monitor.

"Yes, I'm almost ready." She moved a file to her active assignment folder, closed the active programs and logged off the computer. "I want to discuss something with you on our way to the bar."

"Anything to do with One World Trade Center?" Marston inquired guardedly.

"No, it is something else."

She stood, retrieved her handbag, hoisted it over a shoulder and faced him.

Mary regarded the slight smile on his face. "What's funny?"

"Nothing, nothing at all. I'll follow you."

At the end of the workday, Mary usually looked toward the publisher's office to see if her father was still in. Now, her mind was too distracted by Marston to think about doing that. She did not know that he had been observing her interplay with the intelligence operative.

Marston, always aware of his surroundings, noticed Godwin watching them. He saw the perplexed look on his face. He acknowledged Mary's father with a respectful nod.

Mary noticed Marston's alertness on the street. His eyes swept up and down the sidewalk, occasionally making eye contact with pedestrians as the couple walked to their designated destination, P.J. Clarke's, on Third Avenue.

I doubt if he misses much. I should emulate him more that way. It sure doesn't hurt to be more observant and careful.

They were fortunate to get a table for two near the back of the ever-popular Irish bar and restaurant. The establishment had survived nearly two centuries in the ever-changing city. Its clientele once included Marilyn Monroe and Frank Sinatra, among others.

Gary and Mary ordered drinks, he a screwdriver and she a pinot noir.

Marston looked intently at Mary's pensive face. "What are you thinking about?"

"How I should be more alert to what's happening. Be more like you." Mary glanced at him to gauge his reaction.

"I get the impression that you know what's going on around you, too. Anyway, it's a necessity for me. It is an essential part of NYPD training. Vigilance counters terrorism."

Mary tensed up when she heard the "t" word.

Marston frowned at her. "What's wrong?"

Mary swallowed hard. "I'm still trying to come to grips with what I witnessed. Hearing the terrorism and terrorist words still unnerves me."

"You saw a sampling of the worst in people. That can change you. The city may not seem as safe for the time being. But you should know that my associates and I are working hard to counter the threats and make New York as safe as possible from foreign and domestic threats."

Mary nodded. She assumed that Gary was talking about the joint efforts of the law enforcement and intelligence communities to thwart the attacks before they happened.

"In any event, Mary, as I've already expressed, being on the alert for suspicious behavior and activity is second nature. It's sort of like another layer of skin."

"I, um, never mind." Mary looked away suddenly, overcome with doubt. *Should I even tell Gary about that man who's been following me? He would probably think that I'm paranoid.*

"What? Tell me, Mary." Marston gently placed a hand on Mary's chin and turned her face toward his.

He certainly likes to touch me. First my hand, now my chin. What's next? Mary, slow down. Focus on the here and now. "Some guy's been following me. It's probably nothing but paranoia."

"Tell me about him."

A waiter delivered their drink order. He placed the glasses on the red and white checkered tablecloth and distributed menus to the pair.

Mary patiently waited until the waiter left. Then she told her date everything she could remember about the persistent scary man. Marston coaxed more details out of her than she thought possible.

Finished, Mary picked up her wine glass, surprised that it was empty. Gary got the waiter's attention and signaled for another round.

"Perhaps we can ID the man together," he suggested.

"You and I?" she asked doubtfully.

"Sure, why not. It would be fun working together. You gave me some useful locations where you saw him. There are plenty of cameras downtown. They are all around the perimeter of the courthouses and government buildings. Like London, you know. I'm sure the perp's on camera, no matter how careful he thought he was."

Their waiter brought two full glasses and left with the empties after Marston told him they weren't yet ready to order dinner.

"Do you believe in coincidences?" she asked.

"Well, they do happen. Why are you asking?"

"This is what I was researching today. Facial recognition software." She took a deep sip of the delicious dark wine. *Easy does it or he'll be carrying me out of here. He looks strong enough to do that easily.*

"Cool. Tell me more." Marston took a long swig, his eyes panning the crowd just in case Mary's stalker was there. He didn't see anyone matching the description nor a man looking at their table other than the waitstaff. Disappointed, he turned his hungry gaze back on Mary.

Mary was still sober enough to see his roving eyes. "You don't know what he looks other than what I told you and you still had to look?"

"Mary, you never know. Perps can be unpredictable sometimes. Always expect the unexpected and you'll never be surprised."

"I can understand that."

He chuckled. "I seriously doubt he'd risk being seen again by you. And if he dared come here, the man could possibly be wearing a disguise."

Marston watched her scan the crowd.

"No, he's not here," she decided, much relieved and very glad to have Gary as a soundboard and possibly much more.

Marston stared thoughtfully at his drink, then looked across the table. "I know it's none of my business but are you seeing anybody?"

"Gary, you don't beat around the bush."

He laughed. "No, I don't. I don't like wasting time."

"No, I'm not. I would have replied differently a week ago. I was engaged to marry someone but it didn't work out." She sighed.

Marston placed a hand gently on hers. "I'm sorry that he hurt you."

They gazed silently at each other. After a time, Marston retracted his hand to pick up the menu. He studied it as Mary made a similar effort. Sighing again, she closed it, still undecided what to order.

Just thinking about Percy for an instant has set me back. What if he changes? Would I take him back? Can an amoral romantic change his ways? Thinking it out made her feel better.

When the waiter returned, Mary asked Marston to order for both of them. She was not up for making any more decisions that evening.

Time seemed to skip ahead. Before long, their Maryland crab cake appetizer was set down on the center of the table with two plates. The couple eagerly dug in.

Delicious! The rich red wine accentuated her taste buds very nicely.

Marston grinned, watching her savor every bite. He sat back, allowing her to grab the last large morsel.

Mary swallowed the last tidbit, put the fork down, and gently dabbed her soft lips with a napkin. The comfort food made her feel infinitely better. She looked across the table, feeling more and more comfortable with him. Being out on a date felt really good and long overdue.

He seemed to welcome the attention, too. His eyes remained locked on hers, but she had noticed his eyes roam to her breasts when she ate. That didn't bother Mary at all.

"While we're waiting for the entrée, Mary, do you mind if we discuss our strategy on identifying the man who's been stalking you?"

"No, not at all."

"We should find him in the system."

Mary's stomach flexed slightly. "You think he's a criminal?"

"It's a valid possibility. We can look at the video feeds near the front entrance of the USDA's building and the courthouse. There are other mounted cameras located between the subway exits and those buildings. If we can't match him up, you should sit with one of the departmental artists. A good sketch is almost as good as a photograph in ID'ing perps."

Mary nodded. She was not thrilled about the prospect of seeing images of the creep but if it would help get him off her back it would be worthwhile.

She also wanted to learn why man had picked her. Did she remind him of someone he knew in the past? Was he a harmless freak whose goal in life was following young women or was he something more dangerous? Mary would use whatever she learned her magazine assignment. If that meant spending more time with Gary, then that was icing on the cake.

I'll do it! Then she repeated her affirmation out loud. "I'll do it! We'll do it together, right?"

"As much as possible, Mary. I have a lot on my plate, but I'll make the time, whenever possible, to be there for and with you."

"Thanks, Gary." She dazzled him with a warm seductive smile.

The waiter delivered their entrée and set the heaping plates down in front of them, advising the diners not to touch the hot plates with their fingers. Mary and Gary promptly dug in and ate without much conversation, dividing time between enjoying the food, sipping their drinks, and contemplating the rest of the evening.

Mary asked herself if Gary was a rebound, a substitute for Percy Shelley. *Could be but I don't care. I need to move on just as I'm sure Percy surely has.* She grabbed the wine glass and took a few sips, watching Gary put a forkful in his mouth.

When she was stuffed and finished eating, Mary sighed contently. Gary nodded at her and signaled the waiter for the check.

Chapter 32

Peters had a good handle on Mary Godwin's movements. Between the monitoring devices in her bag and the service gate to the townhouse, he kept tabs where she was around the clock.

He noticed that she had not moved a single inch during the past hour. *I verified earlier that she left the office. Where the hell has she gone to?* He checked her precise position. *P.J. Clarke's? Is she drinking down her sorrows? Alone? I don't know. Should I hurry over there and see for myself?*

He was in denial about an escalating need to see her because his emotional and mental states were in flux. While believing that he would ultimately control his victims in the way they died, until that happened, they possessed him in varying degrees. Of course, they were ignorant about his craving until it was too late.

What does it matter if I go to the restaurant? Not a frigging thing! So long as she keeps that bag nearby, it won't matter where I am or she is. When she's my prisoner, I'll save the tracker for her successor.

You'll be in the ground, girlie, just like my mom!

Thinking about his dead mother was unbearable. *Why did I do that? Why punish myself? It's not my fault what happened to her. She wanted to die so she could be with dear dead Dad. She wanted to be rotting in the ground with him more than she wanted to be alive with me, damn her! What a miserable mother she was to abandon me like that! What makes a parent want to do that? I'm glad that I'll never have to go through that. Nobody's going to make me be a good-for-nothing father!*

Peters punched himself fiercely in the stomach as many times as he could tolerate. After the beating, he lay on his back shedding dry tears.

A little while later, he angrily and moodily sat in front of the computer monitor, looking at images of Mary Godwin he had screensaved. He blamed her for making him remember his mother.

His forefinger rubbed the image on the screen and let his imagination run rampant. As he fantasized, an almost desperate need to be with her built up in his chest. He saw her lying on the long table, pleading for him to end her life. There would be no mercy.

I am thankfully not afflicted with empathy and compassion. They are weaknesses that I am not cursed with.

"Do you know how special you are to have the opportunity to die in my company and care?" Peters asked. He sensed that Mary would appreciate his depravity. *In death we trust!*

Thinking of death triggered old memories, a defining moment of his life. The image changed to rural Afghanistan.

No, not there!

* * *

Peters dredged up the night he had snuck out of camp, unseen by the two soldiers manning the perimeter. He wore a black shirt, Army fatigues and boots. An Enhanced Night Vision Goggle was secured to his helmet. His face was darkened with a liberal application of greasy eye black as he needed to be invisible, seen only if he wished it.

Peters checked the time. 1:32 AM. He moved stealthily, descending a hill from the camp's strategic high ground down to a relatively flat plateau. He peered intently through the lens, careful to avoid pitfalls. Everything he saw was green except animals and people. Their body heat signature radiated red and yellow colors.

He trudged through an enormous opium poppy field. The Taliban made a ton of money cultivating the native plant, converting it to heroin, and selling the opiate at an enormous profit. Peters was told the Taliban was his enemy, but destroying poppy plants wasn't permitted. There was a lot of aspects about the war that made no sense to him. *What a frigging stupid war! It's a complete waste of time being here. The Brits discovered that, then the damned Russians, and now the U.S. of A. I might as well stomp the shit out of the poppies a while and then get back to camp. That'll teach the infidels a lesson.*

Trampling up and down the rows was hard work, but a lot of fun, too. Destroying enemy crops reminded him of his military hero, General William Tecumseh Sherman. After his victory in Atlanta, his Union army lay waste to Georgia all the way to Savannah, probably shortening the Civil War by months.

The new moon made for an optimally dark night to ravage the plants without being spotted by the farmers. Taking a break, he recalled seeing a shed on the far side of the field when on patrol the previous day. *Perhaps I should burn the damned place. I could shorten the war just like Sherman.* He raised the night vision goggles to his eyes and searched for the building. *Where the fuck is it? Did the Afghanis move it?*

He glanced at his watch. 2:33 AM. *That's crazy. Have I been out that long? Maybe I should call it a night and get back.*

Peters heard a low noise somewhere in the field. He stopped and spun toward the sound. He saw nothing out of the ordinary. No movement. Had he imagined it?

There was another rustle behind him. He did a 180, swiveling his M16A2 semiautomatic rifle in front of him. *Who or what kind of animal could be out here in the middle of the night?* He lowered into a squatting position. The poppies towered above him, some close to four feet tall. The plants he had not yet trampled were nearly ready to be harvested.

Peters pulled his trusty combat knife from its sheaf. He preferred being up close and personal. A good gutting was exactly what he needed. Gunshots would awaken his fellow Army Rangers. He'd never make it back to his tent unseen once his unit was awake, alert and prepared to fire on anybody approaching their position.

The elite combat soldier could not afford being caught outside camp. He was AWOL, having left his post without permission. His record would be blemished. The prospect of being locked up in the brig for up to one month with loss of pay was nothing to look forward to.

No, siree! I better butcher these bastards and get back to my cozy beddy-bye before anybody's the wiser.

Slowing his breathing so that it was inaudible, Peters glared at the undergrowth he crouched in, listening intently. He began to regret the probability he was alone. *Do the Afgoons even have a clue that I'm here?*

As it turned out, several Afghanis were awake. With the U.S. encampment on the nearby ridge, they made sure that at least one of their number stayed away and be watchful. The American invaders were tolerated if they did not tamper with the locals' livelihood.

The adolescent Afghani boy on duty was finishing up urinating by a tree when he heard a swishing sound coming from the far end of the poppy field. He went to awaken his cousin, a Taliban soldier.

Shaking him awake, he whispered that a goat or two probably got loose and was scampering about in the cultivated ground. The Taliban grabbed two rifles, handing one to his surprised cousin. Fearing damage to their cash crop, the pair went together to investigate. They split up and maneuvered around the plants, careful not to harm any.

Neither expected to find an American soldier ravaging the plants.

Peters heard movement from two directions. Unafraid, he considered his options. He could sprint all the way to camp or stand his ground. Only one choice was acceptable. Standing down was not it.

The Taliban soldier was nearby. However, his young cousin was the one who stumbled on the intruder's position.

Peters barely saw the shape in the darkness before it tripped over him. The impact caused the Afghani's rifle to fly out of his hand.

Peters reacted very quickly, using his training and instincts to gain the upper hand. He could not allow the enemy to cry out, thus warning his compatriots. Peters drove a fist into the man's sternum as the Afghani's hands urgently searched for his rifle. Peters pulled his knife from the scabbard and slashed the sharp steel blade across the winded Afghani's throat. He gurgled a little too loudly for Pete's liking.

"Shut up," Peters whispered, now slicing open the man's stomach. The blood thirsty Army Ranger became frenzied by the carnage. He only managed to stop when his ears detected movement nearby. He rose up to face the other the figure hurtling toward him. Peters roared fiercely. The crazed shriek must have terrorized the attacker as he suddenly stopped, turned, and ran away.

Where did he go? In case he goes running to get his Afgoon buddies, I better head back to camp. There'll be plenty more opportunities to kill soon enough, I hope. Isn't war glorious?

Listening for pursuit, Peters sprinted away, knocking down dozens of the lollipop-shaped plants. He felt great. A fresh kill always sharpened his senses.

The killer stopped beyond the end of the field to listen more attentively. Hearing nothing but his own beating heart, he turned again and trudged back to camp.

I'm a frigging hero! I'm ridding the planet of miserable scum. There are too many people on it anyway. Hell, I'm performing a public service!

He laughed.

The malevolent good mood gradually changed as he carefully climbed up the rough ground toward his unit's location. Checking his watch, he was again shocked that it read 4:52 AM. He looked up at the eastern horizon. The sky was already slightly grey there. He cursed himself for losing track of time.

That's what happens when you're having fun.

Peters dropped onto his stomach about one hundred feet from the perimeter to assess activity within the camp. The recon was absolutely necessary if he had any chance of making it to his bedroll with nobody the wiser.

Scanning the encampment with his night goggles, he observed a unit member stationed behind a small bunker. The soldier peered through the night scope of a mounted machine gun, swiveling it in a 180-degree radius. Peters knew another soldier lay on the far side of the camp facing the opposite direction. He didn't need to worry about him.

Peters jerked his head down barely a second before the sentry's scan passed over his prone body. *Did he see me?* He risked look up a few long seconds later. He smiled as his battle buddy's search continued uninterrupted. All was good, at least for the time being.

I gotta create a diversion. The machine gunner has to be distracted by a perceivable threat. Then I'll make a mad dash past him before he knows it.

Eyes fixed on the sentry, his left hand probed the ground within reach. He clutched a stone. He backed down the slope a few feet and rose slowly into a crouch. *If this don't get his attention, nothing will.* When the machine gun scope was pointed to Peter's right, he hurled the stone with all his might to his left, in the opposite direction that his fellow soldier was situated.

Peters immediately crouched and waited. He heard a smack when the projectile hit a boulder and smashed into pieces. The lookout twitched slightly from the unexpected sound.

"Who goes there?" he called out, peering through the scope in the direction of the noise.

If you have a brain, you should go over and check it out.

The other sentry guarding the opposite site of the encampment appeared, looking wary. A few other members of the unit, awakened, walked or jogged out of their tents, armed and ready to fend off an assault. They spoke quietly among themselves.

Peters maneuvered to his right, angling closer to the men. He expected everybody to congregate to the extreme left corner of the camp. He intended to use that opportunity to enter from the right corner and blend in with his fellow soldiers.

Proven correct, they moved in the direction he anticipated, holding their assault rifles aimed forward, looking for targets. Powerful lights crisscrossed the rocky terrain, passing over the hit boulder without pause. Peters scrambled diagonally to the right corner, his eyes darting back and forth, willing that nobody notice him until he stood among them.

He crept on his tiptoes, leaning forward, his bloody knife in its sheaf, and rifle pointed at the ground. Shooting fellow unit members would be construed officially as friendly fire, though in reality it would really be a display of extreme hostility. He considered it for a fleeting instant, knowing it was a suicidal act.

A few harrowing seconds later, Private Peters stood behind the others. He addressed the platoon commander, Lieutenant Theodore Rosefield.

"Sir, do you want me to go and see who's out there?"

The lieutenant turned around, looking at him neutrally. Then the expression changed as the sharp eyes took in Peter's uniform, face and hands. "Are you injured, Peters?"

"No, sir."

"Then explain, private, why you're a bloody mess."

Peters, confused, looked down at the front of his outfit, noticing for the first-time evidence of his misconduct. *Crap! What do I say?* He lifted his gaze to the platoon leader. The entire unit regarded him with discernible disapproval and moved away from the disgraceful grunt.

"Private Peters?'

"Yes, sir. I don't know." He patted himself with a free hand, his hand getting bloodier from the mostly dry congealed stains. "It's not mine."

"Whose is it and how did it get there, Private Peters?"

Peters looked back at Lieutenant Rosefield glumly. "I can't say, sir."

"You better say, Private, unless you intend to intentionally disobey an order in front of witnesses. Would you prefer speaking to me in the privacy of my tent?"

"Yeah."

Rosefield moved closer to Peters, his thick moustache twitching and jaw moving. "Yeah what, Private?"

"Sir," Peters replied condescendingly, barely hiding a smirk.

Rosefield turned to a corporal. He ordered him to escort Peters to his tent and wait there with Peters. Peters intentionally failed to salute Rosefield before turning to the unit commander's quarters. The corporal vigilantly keeping pace two steps behind.

Peters fretted in the tent for thirty minutes, waiting for Rosefield, forbidden to speak, while the officer prudently had the immediate surrounding area swept for hostiles. The reconnaissance did not extend as far as the poppy field.

The lieutenant, a great grandson of war hero and President Theodore Rosefield, tried to emulate his famous ancestor whenever possible, even resorting to saying "bully" at times. He was liked and respected by all, except one.

His contempt for Peters went back to the day he had taken command of the platoon. Peters' attitude from the beginning was poor and Rosefield had been unable to improve it.

The man is untrustworthy and contemptible. Why on Earth did he enlist? Was it only to satisfy his perpetual bloodlust? He is little more than a wanton killer, though I have to admit that he has saved the life of more than a few members of my platoon.

I doubt he even loves our great nation. He thinks the country owes him everything.

What would TR have done to shape up the slouch? Beat him with a big stick? No, of course not!

Rosefield postponed his interrogation until the following morning due to the lateness of the hour. He wanted the Rangers adequately fresh the next morning.

Peters was sent back to his cot with orders to think very carefully about what he had done. Anything other than stating the full truth would be unacceptable and dealt with according to army code.

Lieutenant Rosefield rushed outside shortly after dawn when he heard the approach of a loud, sputtering vehicle. He stared narrowly at a rusty old truck weaving along on the rough terrain, navigating between large rocks.

He assessed the situation as a peaceful mission. To be on the safe side, he quickly gave orders for the thirty soldiers to be alert. All eyes were on the heavy vehicle as it screeched to a stop about fifty feet short of the perimeter.

The moment the engine was turned off, the disturbing sound of wailing filled the morning air. It came from inside the truck. Three angry men jumped out of the front cab. They appeared unarmed.

The Army Rangers alertly watched the Afghani men walk to the back of the truck. More than a few Americans wondered if some weaponry and soldiers were inside the vehicle. Possibly not, as the cries of mourning women immediately grew louder.

Some air escaped Rosefield's lungs when two women in long black robes were helped out, and then a long cloth covered parcel emerged. *What in the world?*

Another man jumped from the back of the truck. Then the four men, two on either side of the mysterious parcel, carried it solemnly up the embankment toward the military camp.

It's a damn body! There are blood stains on the cloth. Blood stains? Where is Peters?

He spun around, looking for the man. *There he is.* The private's beady eyes were locked on the six-foot-long coffin being carried up the incline by the Afghanis. Peters frowned deeply, his lips mouthing a curse that Rosefield read. Peters then turned his eyes at Rosefield and grimaced.

Rosefield kept his eyes on the private. He did not want to back down from their faceoff but keeping his back to the visitors would be taken as a sign of disrespect. That wouldn't due at all.

"Private Peters, come here on the double."

Peters hesitated, turning his eyes again on the somber procession. The visitors stopped at the camp perimeter. There, they waited for the customary formal greeting.

"You better obey my order, soldier. We do not want to ignore our visitors, do we?"

Peters stepped stiffly over to Rosefield, eyes stubbornly on the ground.

"I'm surprised but pleased you have not changed your uniform. Remain right here so that our visitors can see you front and center. We don't want them to miss viewing your bloody uniform, do we?"

Peters did not say a word.

"That's what I thought." Rosefield then called over a bilingual grunt to serve as an interpreter should the visitors not speak English. The pair advanced slowly toward the waiting civilians.

Rosefield bowed, reminding himself to keep a grave expression on his face. While introductions were made on both sides, the capable army officer decided what to do. He knew proper etiquette required him to invite the designated spokesperson into his tent and serve tea. He also understood that in the unlikelihood one or more of them carried concealed weapons, he could not risk allowing the others any closer than their present position.

He gravely looked at the draped coffin and made appropriate eye contact with ever one of the aggrieved party.

Rosefield personally brewed black tea from his private stock of aromatic leaves. Local customs dictated that business could not be conducted until the tea was consumed. He respected that tradition, believing civility was highly underrated and followed too infrequently.

At last, cups drained except for the remnants of a few soaked leaves, he listened to the story of the shrouded carcass. The smell of death leaked through the thin cloth and assaulted his nostrils. He blocked it out as much as possible, making a supreme effort to focus on the words being spoken by the interpreter.

The Afghani told Rosefield that the punishment given to a local for destruction of valuable property was cutting off of both hands of the guilty. He demanded that the guilty American be turned over to him and receive punishment for murdering his nephew.

When it was his turn to speak, the lieutenant asked several pertinent questions. "How many stab wounds are there? How deep are the wounds? "May our medic and I examine the body?" "May I have it photographed?"

I mean no respect to you or the deceased's family but I must build a case against the no good, scumbag Peters. I'll have the scoundrel bloody court-marshalled!

The Afghani was shocked and told Rosefield that he could not approve desecrating the body. He conveyed his words slowly in broken English. Although Rosefield did not need a translator, he kept his man present in the capacity of a witness. Rosefield promised that justice would be meted out to the guilty man.

Chapter 33

Reliving the end of my last tour of duty in Afghanistan is exactly what I don't need right now! Why reprimand myself for doing nothing wrong? I killed the enemy. Period.

Peters did not know why the mind played reruns of bad memories. Was it a form of self-punishment? Was that the reason for his bad dreams?

He would never stop blaming Rosefield for recommending that a dishonorable discharge be handed down by the military court. He harbored a special place in his twisted heart for his former commanding officer.

Perhaps I should move the bastard to the top of the list and allow Mary Godwin to live a little longer.

The man will pay the ultimate price for accusing me of murdering the Afghani while I was AWOL. I mean Afghanistan's been a war zone since forever. Even the Russians got more than they bargained in that hellhole. The Afgoons are pure hard asses.

Rosefield is a self-righteous son of a bitch. Just like his pathetic great granddaddy! He could have let it go, but no, he had it out for me. Most other platoon leaders probably would have thought nothing about what I did to that frigging Afgoon. Those things happen in war. Right? They say war is hell. Right?

It was the little bastard's own fault for being in the field that night. I killed him in self-defense!

Private Peters, against his wishes, was given a series of comprehensive tests at the U.S. Army headquarters near Kabul. He was diagnosed with Sadistic Personality Disorder (SPD). The mental disorder was linked to Peters' insatiable need to maim and kill. The need to inflict pain and enjoy watching suffering developed afterwards.

The sadist was prescribed medications and therapy before the court-martial. He hated both forms of treatment. The medicine dulled his reflexes and mind. He felt lethargic and useless, in other words, miserable. Having no choice, he went through the motions, even making the military believe he was being cooperative and exhibiting signs of improvement.

After realizing that he would not get an honorable discharge, he expected to be given the next best dismissal, a dishonorable discharge. Peters instead got a bad conduct discharge, thanks to the SPD diagnosis. He did not care that he was fortunate not to be given a long prison sentence for murdering the Afghani teenager.

Following Lieutenant Rosefield's damning testimony. Peters did not help himself in announcing in front of witnesses that he would make Rosefield pay for persecuting him. They were not idle words. He kept tabs on the decorated officer, waiting for the day he would avenge the disgrace that he had to endure.

If Peters had been dishonorable discharged, he would not have qualified for VA benefits. But thanks to the subsequent diagnosis of a civilian psychiatrist who determined that the U.S. Army was responsible for Peters' diagnosis, Peters would be able to receive VA benefits, including a monthly payment that covered rent and miscellaneous expenses.

Staring at his reflection in the mirror, the veteran did not see craziness and evil in his eyes. Instead, he saw himself as special. He was better than others, and deserved a tickertape parade for serving his country so valiantly.

He visualized butchering Rosefield with his favorite hunting knife. *Being promoted to major when you left the damned Army won't help you. Neither will your being a newly elected Congressman. Hell, I should be in Congress. I'm more qualified then you are by far. You're just milking that last name of yours. I bet that great grandfather of yours would turn in his grave if he knew what kind of a commander you really were.*

The bitterness and hatred made him lurch for the mirror. For a moment he could have sworn the aristocrat actually stood there looking back at him condescendingly.

His face and partially clenched hands smashed the mirror. Shattered glass imbedded in the palms of his hands and cheeks, barely missing his eyes. Rage immediately turned into disbelief.

What happened?

Peters fetched a tweezer, ran warm water from the sink and methodically removed the glass splinters and larger pieces impaling his skin. He was not worried about the blood loss. The hardened man had seen too many wounds to be squeamish. He knew from experience whether a wound was serious or not.

He deftly pulled glass from his left cheek.

Rosefield would have fainted for sure from all the blood.

He dropped the wet red shard in a nearby metal refuse container and placed the tweezers in the sink to soak.

He's not the man he claims to be. And Afghanistan sure ain't San Juan Hill which was the linchpin for his great granddaddy's fame. Now he was someone who would have appreciated me.

Peters stared at his damaged nose. He gently touched it with his bloody left hand. The nostrils were congested with blood and snot.

It's broken. Rosefield broke my nose! There's no end to his persecution of me. I should probably go to the hospital. They can deal with this. But then again, I'll be more noticeable now that I look like a monster. I'll be remembered wherever I go unless I wear a mask over my nose. Thanks, Major Shithead, for nothing.

The throbbing pain in his nose increased when he squeezed and adjusted the broken bone. He gritted his teeth and groaned much louder than the crunching sound made by his nose.

I don't have time for this shit!

He packed his nostrils with gauze and thickly dabbed the facial and hand wounds with Bacitracin. He sullenly stared at his partial reflection in the broken mirror. Next, he disposed of every piece of glass and finished cleaning up with his hurting hands. If he could endure pain, why not test others to see how they could handle it.

Peters begrudgingly understood that the accident extended Mary Godwin's life by a matter of days. It was a temporary stay of execution. He needed full use of his hands to do the deed properly.

And so he waited impatiently for the ointment to complete its work.

* * *

Mary and Gary walked arm in arm, deep in the moment, passing unnoticed storefronts and pedestrians.

Earlier, outside the restaurant, Gary had asked where she wanted to go. She had an image of making love to him. She couldn't do that at her parents' home, at least if they were there. Going to his apartment in Brooklyn would make a long, grueling day too long and tomorrow was another work day.

"I'll escort you to your parent's place. Do you mind walking?"

Mary replied with a long, sensual kiss.

"I'll take that as a yes," he replied later, trying to catch his breath.

"Smart man," Mary replied, grinning up at him. Their budding relationship had an intensity she craved and needed.

Ten blocks later, Marston's phone pinged. Annoyed by the interruption to their romantic mood, he used her free hand to read the text.

Freeing up both hands, he looked at her apologetically. "I got to take care of this. It won't be long."

Mary, ever curious, glanced at the screen but couldn't read the small print. Disappointed, she looked up and saw a frown followed by a determined look on his face. She did not know him well enough to ask who had connected with him and what it was about.

I won't pry. He'll tell me if he wants to. Perhaps it's a national security issue. If that's the case, well, that would be cool.

Marston sent his message and almost immediately received a reply. He nodded to himself and entered a few strokes on the small keyboard. Then he put the phone away and smiled at Mary.

"Sorry about that."

"Everything okay?"

"Yeah, no worries. Just an update from the office."

"Even at this hour?"

"Well yeah, potential threats evolve 24/7. We have to be ever alert."

"That makes sense."

He peered down at her searchingly. "It doesn't surprise me that you understand that."

"Most people probably understand that threats don't have a day off. Shall we continue walking or do you need to cut this short?"

"I'm all yours, Mary."

They kissed again. Then they strolled up the sidewalk, holding hands for the first time in their burgeoning relationship.

* * *

Although Peters give Mary a stay of execution, that did not imply he lost interest in the woman. Needing a distraction from the self-inflicted wound, he continued to monitor her movements from the apartment.

His heart beat faster when she turned the corner at the end of her bock. He could barely wait for the motion detector to signal her arrival at the front door. Then there she stood. He could barely contain himself. The urge to be there with her was almost too much for him to withstand.

His mood darkened significantly when a man appeared close to her.

He raised the volume control to the max and watched them kiss, her backside pressed against the door. The sight sickened him, but he could not avert his eyes from the couple on the live action video. He hoped that her father would silently open the door. Watching the couple fall head over heels inside the building would be hilarious and serve them right. Peters wondered who the man was as he faced the camera.

I'll have an image of the bastard's face after he removes his goddamned tongue out of her mouth.

His fingers drummed the desk while waiting for the two bodies to separate. When that finally occurred, the stranger stopped looking at Mary. Peters' eyes widened when the man peered over her head at the surveillance equipment, then back at Mary.

"Shit on a stick! What's the bastard doing?" he blared loudly. "I'm going to kill him, whoever the hell he is!"

* * *

Marston's instincts and perpetual alertness kicked in despite how Mary made him feel. The sensation of being watched was pervasive and ultimately ended their kiss. That was when he noticed the camera.

"What's the matter?" Mary asked, staring up at Gary's disgruntled face.

"I don't usually like being surveilled when kissing a beautiful woman," he replied, stepping closer to the mounted equipment.

"Where?" she asked, following Marston. "Huh," she muttered, noticing the device for the first time ever.

He concluded that the device was news to her, too. "You didn't know about the surveillance system?"

"No, I've never seen it before. My parents must have recently installed it. They didn't tell me."

Marston continued staring up at the device when he replied. "You know, there's no such thing as being too cautious or safe anymore. Security systems is a thriving industry, especially here in the city."

"So I gather. I wonder what made them get it installed. I'll have to ask."

Mary was aware that her parents had met Marston once before. It had been at the Freedom Tower. "Gary, do you want to come in a moment? And no, sex isn't included tonight. I thought you may want to say hi to my parents again. The lights are on so they're probably still up."

"I don't know, Mary."

"Be brave. They won't bite."

"Okay, I'll go in for a moment. I have a long trip back to Brooklyn from here"

Mary smiled encouragingly. She unlocked and opened the door. Marston followed her inside. Mary's head reappeared outside as she warily looked up and down the street. She squinted at the miniature camera's illuminated red light before returning inside and locking the door.

* * *

He began pacing back and forth, deep in thought.

That frigging eagle-eyed bastard had to mess with me. We'll see how that goes. I'll give him a free pass if nothing comes from noticing my surveillance.

Did I leave prints or did I wear latex gloves? Damn, I can't remember! I can't afford to get real sloppy. They better not call the frigging cops. The bastards will dust it for prints, DNA, the whole nine yards. What a mess!

I better stay glued to the monitor. My plans for Mary Godwin hinge heavily on what happens over there.

* * *

After exchanging pleasantries in the entrance hall with Mary's parents, Marston wasted no time asking them about the surveillance device.

William and Jane were baffled. "No, we know nothing about it," Mary's stepmother commented. William stepped to the front door.

"Wait up, sir. Please don't open the door," Marston implored.

"Why not?" Godwin asked, a hand on the doorknob.

"Whoever installed it has criminal intent. He, she or they are probably monitoring your coming and goings before actually burglarizing the house."

"Oh my God!" Mary's stepmother exclaimed, placing a hand over her mouth.

Marston continued. "I hope whoever it is hasn't seen Mary and me staring at the device. Having you and Mrs. Godwin go outside minutes later to look at it is not a good idea."

"I don't understand."

"If nobody pays any more attention to the surveillance unit, perhaps the installer will relax, thinking that he's in the clear. I want that person to think that Mary and I haven't discussed it with you both."

"That makes sense," Godwin acknowledged, moving away from the door. "Doesn't it, dear?" he asked, addressing his wife.

"I suppose it does. But now that I know it is there, the urge to look at it will be difficult to resist."

"You can do it, Mother," Mary said encouragingly. *Mind over matter. She's never even noticed it. Will she and dad overcome the irresistible urge to glance up? What would happen anyway if the installer sees either or both of them look or me for that matter?*

"What should we do?" Mary asked Marston. The romantic mood was over, replaced now with trepidation and jumping to unpleasant conclusions.

"You know, perhaps I'll have the apparatus removed and thoroughly checked for prints, but I'm not sure yet."

"But that would run counter to your advice for my parents to pretend it's not there."

"Yes, that's correct, but it's entirely probable that removing the equipment may completely disrupt their plans. They'll know NYPD is aware. And the lab may very well be able to provide the information we need to make an arrest. The bottom line is that the perps will want to avoid the building."

"So we're safe staying in the house?" William asked.

"Mr. Godwin, I see no reason why not. If it will make you feel better, I'll arrange for a squad car to park on the street the next few nights."

Marston looked at his captive audience, trying to radiate confidence and calmness that he hoped would rub off on them. He was concerned about Mary's glazed look. *I hope I didn't cause that with my bold talk. I feel badly for this on top of everything else she's been through.*

He had no way of knowing that Mary's stalker and the person observing the house were one and the same.

He gently patted her shoulder. "Mary, are you okay?"

Mary nodded vacantly.

Her parents anxiously watched.

William Godwin stepped over to Marston. "A moment of your time, please."

Marston nodded. He followed Godwin out of the room, wondering what was on his mind.

Stopping in the adjacent room, Godwin spoke in a low tone. "Mary's been through the ringer. I don't think she can withstand much more."

"Sir, I am up to speed on what has been happening to her. Mary's really special. I want her to be happy."

"That is good to hear. The sooner you get that patrol car, the better."

"I'll make the call, sir."

"Thank you."

"No problem, sir."

"Should I ask about your intentions with Mary?"

Marston laughed easily.

"I know that we come from different levels of the social strata or whatever."

"I'm not concerned about that," Godwin replied.

Marston cleared his throat. "I want to make her happy and worry free, sir."

"That's good news," Godwin replied with a grim smile and an extended hand.

Marston shook it firmly, feeling like an equal to the man. He saw himself on an upward path while Godwin was trying to hold on to what he had.

They returned to the spacious foyer. The operative observed Mary and her stepmother in a heated discussion. Marston wondered if staying overnight in the house would harm Mary's wellbeing. He didn't think that it was his place to suggest an alternative to her. Not yet anyway.

Chapter 34

When Marston stepped outside a few minutes later, he looked straight ahead. His mind kept repeating two words, *don't look, don't look don't look*. It was the only way he could stop himself from looking where he shouldn't. His gut told him that he was being watched by whomever. *Who are you?* he asked himself, moving past the monitor's range to the far sidewalk.

He called the 19th Precinct, identified himself, and asked to speak to the senior officer on duty at that late hour. He knew a few dozen lieutenants and captains around the city, but not the lieutenant who got on the line with him. By the end of their conversation, a car had been immediately dispatched and a forensics team assigned to dust and take down the surveillance equipment the next morning. Marston was promised that he would be apprised of the findings.

Now he stood across the street from the townhouse, feeling uneasy. He intended to remain there, as he promised the Godwins, until the expected police vehicle parked next to the nearby hydrant.

Marston looked across the street at a window and noticed Mary peering despondently at him. He waved and smiled at her. He got no comfort watching her suffer. Was she more upset being with her parents or knowing that some lowlife had criminal designs on the home? He figured the answer was a combination of the two.

She looks like a prisoner, not wanting to stay and afraid to leave.

Leaving Mary behind had not been easy. He wanted to take her home with him. With her family watching, their parting was a lot less romantic than he and Mary had wanted.

They scheduled a time to meet the next morning to look at footage from several downtown cameras. Mary's father had quickly agreed to the rendezvous, assuming it was only research for Mary's new project.

Godwin had not yet been told about the stalker incident downtown because Mary did not want to worry him. Marston thought differently and had told her on the walk home that confiding in her father was important. Knowing that someone was tailing and watching her would make Godwin more vigilant than normal.

Marston easily understood why Mary did not want her high-strung mother to know.

Mary watched the police car park next to the fire hydrant. Gary bent his frame to talk to the occupant, wave at her, and walk alone up the block. She unhappily turned from the window. Her phone pinged.

Gary: Are you okay?

Mary: Sure

Gary: Get some sleep. The house is secure.

Mary: Great. I'll try.

Gary: Thanks for the fun time.

Mary: I had fun too.

Gary: To be continued.

Mary: I hope so.

Gary: Goodnight Mary.

Mary: Goodnight Gary.

Mary helped herself to more wine and carried it to her favorite room, the library. The room represented comfort and escapism to Mary. She badly needed both that night.

She eased herself down on a comfortable leather chair. *Now what?* Taking a liberal sip, she looked around at the three walls of well stocked built-in bookcases. She had spent thousands of hours digging through books with her legs curled beneath her. Her voracious reading habit had enabled her to finish more than a thousand of the four thousand volumes standing upright.

What shall I read? She set the wineglass down on a coaster, stood, and stepped over to one of the shelves. A finger caressed the spine covers of three of her favorite works - Paradise *Lost* by John Milton, *Prometheus* by Lord Byron, and two books by Mary Wollstonecraft, *Mary: A Fiction* and *The Wrongs of Woman*. These four books were deeply imprinted on her psyche. None were exactly light reading. All required deep concentration and zero interruptions.

A shiver suddenly coursed through her. *I fear that none of my bound friends here will help me tonight.* She drifted back to the chair, sat, and promptly closed her eyes. Soon, she dreamt.

It was a haunting dream full of eerie and frightening shapes. She sensed there was a grave conflict between two shadows. A battle raged between good and evil. The shapes transformed into two clearly defined men. The evil one was handsome, the good one monstrous. The latter image was vaguely familiar looking to the dreamer.

The creepy dream morphed into another nightmare. She found herself being chased by a knife wielding, masked man. He herded her into a dingy dead-end alley. Frantically turning door knobs that did not open, she tried to escape the devil. With her back pressed against a hard, high wall, she waited for the inevitable. A scream rose from deep inside her when she felt a hand pressing down on one shoulder.

The next thing she knew, a comforting voice was reaching out to her.

"Wake up, Mary!"

Father?

She fought her way to the surface. But her nightmare pulled her back in.

"No you don't, missy. You stay put with me where you belong."

Mary looked past the demonic looking man for someone to help her.

"There's nobody there," the being sneered. He moved forward and sniffed her. "I smell fear." He licked a cheek with his rough tongue. "Delicious," he said, followed by derisive laughter.

The foul breath from his mouth and body was repulsive. She gasped.

"Mary, wake now!" The comforting voice seemed farther away.

Her persecutor keenly observed Mary looking around searchingly for a way to escape. There was no place to go.

Mary thought she had only chance. *I have to create an opening.* She swiftly raised a knee with all her might. The bony joint connected with the man's hard genitals.

She grimly smiled as his eyes widened and he doubled over, moaning and cursing. She followed through with a swift kick that broke his nose. Then, thinking surprising clearly, she sprinted down the passageway.

The subdued assailant screeched. "I'll be coming for you, bitch!"

Mary woke up in a cold sweat.

William Godwin had taken Marston's words about Mary's safety and well-being very seriously. He embraced the word of anyone whose job involved protecting the nation from internal and external threats. Marston came across as someone to be respected and admired.

He's the opposite of Shelley. Just thinking about Mary's former fiancé annoyed him. *He is a pompous, self-serving letch! Whatever happened to end their engagement is probably for the best.*

Jane Godwin had turned in early after taking a double dose of sleeping pills. She needed them because of the potential break-in by whoever installed the camera outside. Without the sleeping pills, she would have stayed awake most of the night worrying about every creak.

William peered out the bedroom window at the unmarked police car parked across the street. Seeing the vehicle eased his concern. But he still wanted to check every room to make sure the windows were closed and locked.

He began on the top floor and worked his way down. Every window on the second, third and fourth stories were shut, but two windows were unlocked. He remedied that. Half way down the stairs between the second and first floors, Godwin thought that he heard a disturbed human sound coming from ground level. He stood still to listen, concerned that his movement attracted the attention of a prowler.

There can't be an intruder now. Not with the police outside. Wouldn't that deterrence prevent a burglar from stealing into the house? Even an extremely brazen one? He thought it through quickly. *Mary isn't upstairs. Was it her that I heard? It must be. Go downstairs now like a brave fellow.*

Godwin quietly descended the staircase to the first floor. He rarely backed down from a challenge. But tonight, he was somewhat unnerved because of the combination of the surveillance device and the changes in his only child's temperament.

Stepping on the landing, he heard a low moan. T*hat's Mary! What's wrong with her?* He hurried in the direction of the unhappy sound. His late-night walk brought him to the library.

He stood in front of his sleeping daughter. Mary's pallor was ashen and her skin gleamed with sweat. She looked miserable.

"Wake up, Mary!"

William watched her eyelids flicker and twitch, but there was no other apparent indication that his words had any effect in awakening her. She seemed stuck in a deep nightmare from which escape was improbable without more intervention.

Is tampering with someone in the throes of a nightmare harmful or helpful? I assume that getting her awake now has to shorten her suffering. Here goes.

He bent forward and firmly gripped her shoulder. "Mary! Wake up now!"

He felt the tension in her tight shoulder ease slightly. The turmoil raging in her sub consciousness visibly decreased from crisis mode as her eyes opened blankly, closed, and thankfully opened for good.

They remained unfocused as tears ran down her cheeks followed by a wave of tremors.

Godwin quickly fetched some tissue from the first-floor powder room and squatted in front of Mary, softly patting her cheeks and eyes. Then he took her hands in his. He could not show her how shocked he really was. Mary needed to lean on his strength.

"Mary, look at me" he gently said.

She made an effort to look at him, but could not hold her gaze for more than a few seconds.

"Mary, you must look me in the eye until I tell you not to. It is for your own good."

Mary gave it another shot. With a concerted effort, she succeeded in her effort.

"Good girl. You are safe here with me. Can you acknowledge that, Mary?

"I am safe with you," she replied dully.

"Would you like some hot chocolate?" *Dosing her with hot chocolate always seemed to make her feel better when she was a child. I hope it still does the trick. I hope we have some left.*

Mary nodded. "That would be nice."

"Good then. Do you want to wait here or come to the kitchen with me?"

She looked beseechingly at her father. "Please don't leave me alone, daddy."

"No problem," Godwin replied as cheery as he could muster." *She hasn't called me daddy in ages.* "Do you need help standing?"

Mary thought that was funny in a way. "Dad, I'm not an invalid yet."

"No, you aren't. Mary, you seem better already."

"I do," she agreed almost happily. "Perhaps thinking about hot chocolate did it."

"Doesn't a cup of hot chocolate a day keeps the doctor away or is it a spoonful of sugar?"

"They're both better than an apple a day." she replied with a small grin.

They walked together to the kitchen. Sure enough, they found what they were looking for. It was Mary who located the tin in the back of a cupboard. Needing something to do, she set to work simmering milk in a saucepan, doling out two heaping tablespoons of the bittersweet cocoa powder in mugs, pouring the steamy milk, and finally stirring. William watched her closely during the entire process.

Grasping the warm mugs, they sat the kitchen table, occasionally taking sips and speaking quietly, carefully steering the conversation away from the nightmare.

"I like Marston," William declared.

"Dad!" Mary blushed slightly.

"Did I say the wrong thing?"

"Well no. I like him, too. You probably already guessed that."

"Quite clearly. He seems solid."

"Solid?" she asked, peering at her father above the half full mug.

"Reliable. Someone you can count on coming through in a pinch."

"I suppose you're right. Gary needs to be all that and more to be successful in his job. Is that what you meant?"

"Well partly. I think he could be what the doctor ordered. Good for you."

Dad, I haven't spent that much time with him. It's only been a few hours so far."

Godwin gulped down the rest of the drink, set the empty mug on the table, and looked sheepishly at Mary. "You're right of course," he managed.

She nodded cynically at him.

Chapter 35

He stood on the concrete pavement next to the townhouse, looking forward to her appearance. *I hope she'll be happily surprised to see me here.*

Waiting for Mary, Marston watched the two technicians methodically remove the surveillance equipment, bag and tag it, and place the evidence in their vehicle. A sergeant from the local precinct stood beside him, watching the proceedings and talking shop.

Although both men were usually vigilant, neither took notice of a man half way up the street, partially screened behind an elm tree, glaring at the activity. He violently shook both middle fingers, abruptly turned, and stormed off.

Mary was still out of sorts despite managing a decent night's sleep. She drowned her sorrows in the shower with cold water as long as she could be tolerate before raising the temperature fifty degrees. Keeping both eyes closed, she gradually felt better. But her brain wasn't quite functioning normally.

Don't I have to be somewhere this morning? No answer presented itself. *Not work, but something I have to do for an article.* It seemed right but she wasn't sure. After some time a name manifested itself in her memory banks. *Gary.* She visualized him. Doing so seemed to restore her brain. Yes, *I'm meeting him downtown to learn about how the police use the city's' surveillance cameras.*

Thinking about him in the shower turned into a pleasurable experience.

Mary stepped out of the shower enclosure when she was done, feeling happy and eager. After quickly drying off and dressing, she carried a basket of dirty laundry downstairs. The Godwins' cleaning lady worked in the building twice a week. She did a great job keeping the house looking immaculate and doing the laundry. Mary knew that today the bed would be freshly made and her laundered clothes would be neatly folded on top of it.

She quietly made her way to the front door, hoping not to be noticed. Last night's meltdown was an embarrassment. Although her father had been so kind and sympathetic, Mary was still reluctant to face him.

Stepping outside into sunlight, she was momentarily blinded. She donned her sunglasses and turned left.

"Hi Mary."

Gary? What's he doing here?

Mary stopped and spun around, a wondrous smile on her face. She saw him leaning against the service entrance gate, below where the camera was located. *Yay, it's gone!*

Grinning, Gary walked over to her. "Good morning."

"It is, especially with that thing gone."

Gary stopped in front of Mary and looked at her.

"I owe you," she said.

"You do?" he asked, a smile flickering.

Mary kissed him, enjoying the taste of coffee. She felt entirely awake.

"Are we even now?" Gary asked after recovering his breath.

"You are a man of your word. My parents and I will be eternally grateful."

"Thanks. I made the arrangements last night for its removal. The house will be watched until we apprehend the perp or perps."

"When will that happen?"

"Soon, I hope. Mary, there's no set timetable."

She nodded, troubled.

"Don't worry, your family will be safe."

"What about me, Gary? I had a terrifying episode last night."

"You did? What happened?

Mary told him about the livid dream. The fear returned. Her chest tightened and her stomach slightly lurched.

Marston grabbed her hands and gently yet firmly held them, until she relaxed, saying, "It's all right. I'm here for you."

Mary looked up at him hopefully. "Thanks, that makes me feel better."

"Are you feeling well enough to look at NYPD's camera footage downtown?"

"Sure, that works for me."

"Good." He paused a moment, then continued. "I don't mean to scare you further, but you have captivated my heart and that is not easily done. Are you an enchantress of sorts?"

Blocking out the city, Mary fixated on the gallant modern knight who had rescued her from oblivion. She felt light and airy for a change. "Of sorts, perhaps," she replied, her hypnotic emerald eyes shining on him.

Marston blinked at her. "That rings true. Seriously though, I know, of course, that you're not a witch."

"How can you be so sure?"

Marston opened his mouth to answer, but no words followed.

"Cat got your tongue?" Mary asked playfully.

He glanced at his watch and shook his head. "Time's a passing. We should get down to business and see if there's a face in the database that you'll recognize."

Mary wanted to prolong their light moment but agreed. Marston escorted her to the unmarked police car illegally parked in a tow away space. With Mary in the front passenger seat, he drove south on the FDR Drive. The ride was mostly quiet, each deep in thought about the other person as well as work that needed to get done.

Marston parked the car in the NYPD parking lot and escorted Mary into 1 Police Plaza.

* * *

Four miles uptown, Howard Peters angrily monitored the tracker. "What the f's she doing at goddamned police headquarters?"

He had had an interesting night, beginning with a multidimensional dream in which he cornered Mary Godwin in an alley. The dream was so intense and powerful that for a split second he actually felt her clammy skin on his fingertip. The terror in her eyes and the physical contact excited him immensely.

What does it mean when I can actually touch someone in the middle of a dream? It's never ever happened to me. Does it prove she's mine and she's under my control now? Will she give in to me without a fight or will she show some spunk? I like spunk. Makes it much more rewarding for me.

He needed to touch her again. Walking fast toward his destination, he considered the best way to get satisfied. *Perhaps brush up against her in a crowd? I bet that happens a lot to the vixen. She probably gets off on it.*

His high expectations of a close encounter of the kinky kind were dashed when he strode up the Godwin's street. One moment he was full of confidence and evil intent, and the next full of disappointment, anger, and hatred. *The damned pigs are removing my property. I gave them no permission to do that!*

He recognized one of the men. *He was with Mary last night, wasn't he? Why's he with the pigs? Unless he's one, too. Damn!*

He stood behind a tree and belligerently watched the device being placed in a NYPD van. *How dare you!!! You bastards!!!*

His eyes burned and his chest heaved with fury and self-pity. He couldn't believe how unfair life could be sometimes. He was so worked up that if an innocent pedestrian as much as glanced at him, he would have been unable to stop himself from striking the person. His hands clutched the thin tree trunk and squeezed with all his might until he could not bear the discomfort any longer. The prolonged death grip dissolved the anger but not the disappointment.

A man walked by, frowning at him in reaction to Peters' ragged breathing and black and blue face.

I got to leave now before I put my mission at risk!

Peters turned home after giving the double finger to the cops. He took long, quick steps, angry at the world for persecuting him. *Perhaps I should change my strategy, Take out a whole crowd instead of only one lousy person. How many deserve death? Dozens? Hundreds? Thousands? Yeah, that's more like it.*

But rest assured, the wench will be among them if I do adopt a new plan. She won't escape me that easily. No frigging way! She's dead either way. And Rosefield, too!

He felt much better as his steps turned into a swagger and a leer shaped his mouth.

Chapter 36

Her vision blurred slightly from viewing more than two thousand images on the screen in quick succession.

"Don't forget to blink," Marston reminded Mary. "Take it from me, it helps."

"Thanks," she replied, keeping her eyes glued to the monitor.

"Okay, now we'll scan camera 1102a14 from the time you specified earlier. Ready, Mary, or do you want to take a break?"

"Go ahead," Mary replied resolutely, glancing quickly at Gary with a forced smile.

Less than one minute later, he exclaimed, "Hey, there you are!"

Mary saw herself in a crowd of people climbing the stairs from the underground subway station toward ground level. She sucked in some air and released it in anticipation of seeing her stalker.

"There he is!" she declared a few seconds later.

Gary immediately froze the image. "Which one is he, Mary?" he asked, looking at the throng behind Mary.

Mary placed a finger on the screen directly under the image of her stalker. "That's him," she said, feeling a tremor course through her.

"Got him." Marston looked at her. "Are you okay?"

Mary pressed her lips together and nodded, remembering what happened after exiting the subway. She closed her eyes, not wanting to look at the man's image.

Marston gently told her, "Mary, it is okay not to look at him anymore. You've found him. Good going."

Mary smiled weakly at him.

"Do you want to leave?"

She did and she didn't.

"You have to face him, Mary. I know it's tough. But you can't let him win. He probably wants you to be afraid of him. I'll know more when we see him again."

"You'll see him on a bench with me advancing on him. If there's a camera covering that spot, you may get a better image of him."

She watched Gary switch camera feeds and advance the tape until they saw the image she requested. After Mary confirmed, Marston printed a fine color picture and showed it to her. She stared at it and nodded.

The photo showed the man on the bench with his head down. His eyes stared slightly upward. The shot captured Mary speaking on the phone in the background.

"The guy's a slick one. He's pretending not to be looking at the pedestrians walking past his vantage position. Obviously, he's waiting for you," Marston observed.

Marston advanced the footage.

"Okay, here I come," Mary said, comforted at hearing herself talk. They watched Mary stop in front of the man, turn to him and start talking.

"We have a lip reader here who can put the conversation on a transcript for us."

"That's good," she said dully, trying to overcome the anguish within her.

Marston captured a few screenshots of the heated discussion ending when Mary walked off toward the federal courthouse.

"Gary, what do you think? Can he be identified?"

"Yes, I'm fairly confident that the facial recognition system will ID him."

"I sure hope so."

"Sit tight, Mary. Give me a few minutes."

With some trepidation, Mary watched several more stills of her stalker being printed and saved in a thumb drive. Marston sharpened the image that had the best light and clarity and uploaded it after logging into the facial recognition system database.

"If he has a mug shot, we'll find him," Marston commented.

"What if he's a criminal but hasn't been arrested?"

"Well, then, if he has a drivers' license, the Department of Motor Vehicles will have his uploaded picture."

"That's awesome!" Mary exclaimed, retrieving a pad from her bag.

Marston grinned, watching her jot something down. "Hey, what are you writing?"

"Gary, didn't I tell you that I'm also here to do research on my next magazine piece?"

He watched her solemnly. "No, you didn't. So you're switching over now to the inquisitive investigative journalist?"

They stared at each other, each sensing that this was the first hurdle in their new relationship.

"Listen Gary, I'm sorry if I didn't tell you about the assignment. I really thought that I did. My mind's been playing tricks with everything that's been going on." *Will this wreck us almost before there was an us?*

"That's okay. No worries."

Marston faced Mary. "You're here because I want to help you get the guy off the street. He's been terrorizing you and I'm a counterterrorism professional.

"You can sit where you until I get a match, and it shouldn't take more than a few minutes. If you need more for your article, you would need to go through proper channels to get that clearance. Does that work for you?"

Wow, he's all business with me now!

"Is it okay still to call you Gary?"

He kept his voice low and glanced beyond his work station at his associates. His bond with Mary was none of their concern. He had to bite the inside of his mouth to behave cool, calm and collected around Mary.

"Of course it is," he answered, a little bit of hurt feeling in his voice.

Mary watched him write something on a piece of paper and push it toward her. It read, *I want you here and now. I must instead pretend you are a work consultant or pay hell later with my coworkers. I hope you understand.*

Mary loved the message. *Yay!* She drew a heart and pushed the paper back at Gary, and watched him smile at the image before folding and pocketing it.

"So Gary, what's next?"

The computer emitted a short beep.

"We may have a match," Gary declared.

Mary and Gary eagerly looked at the monitor. The face and background for Howard Peters was displayed. They silently read the information, including Peters' less than stellar war record, VA treatment, but not much else. There was no driver's license and no criminal record.

Marston's brain and experience told him that Peters was a dangerous man, irregardless of never being arrested. He doubted that the system was correct. *He's the type to have a long rap sheet. What with his demeanor, behavior, insubordination and love to kill, I would have expected to see a list of assaults and even attempted murders. What are his intensions toward Mary? Should I have him officially questioned or do it myself?*

Either or neither?

Mary was relieved and disappointed by the abbreviated biography on the screen and greatly disturbed by the face staring at her. *He was in my nightmare last night. I'm sure of it. But he is not a criminal. Have I been worrying needlessly? Do I really need to fear him? I'll ask Gary. He should know, at least I hope so as he's really a cop as much as anything else.*

"So," Marston began, glancing discreetly around the large office again before fixating on Mary's troubled demeanor, "Look at me now please. Mary?" He turned off the monitor to make it easier for her to comply with his request.

Slowly, she tore her glazed eyes away from the black screen and looked at Marston's concerned face.

"Now listen to me very carefully."

Her hands were clutched against her chest. Gary gently yet firmly took them in his, not caring anymore what his colleagues thought. Mary's safety was too important to be concerned about their reaction. Holding her hands, he searched her face for a sign that what he was doing was alleviating the shock of staring at her adversary in the face, albeit on a computer screen. He saw her pained grimace change into acceptance.

Gary waited until Mary seemed better. "Mary, listen to me. Are you?"

She nodded.

"Good. I have some suggestions for you. Number one, until Peters is put away, I want you to be a street savvy New Yorker. That means avoid walking alone down a deserted street. Walk close to other people when possible. Keep alert. Don't use ear buds. Keep your eyes and ears tuned sharply. If you feel being watched, stop and look around. If you see Peters, take a picture of him and immediately send it to me in a text indicating where the snapshot was taken. Most importantly, do not confront or aggravate him.

"Gary, won't taking a picture antagonize him?"

"I'm hoping that it will only scare him."

"How can you be sure of that?"

I can't, damn it! I've got to assure her somehow. He stalled by clearing his throat. "It will work 99% of the time. If your gut tells you it's wrong, then don't do it."

"Okay, that's reasonable."

"Good," he replied, giving her hands a slight squeeze.

"Anything else?" she asked.

"Yeah, can I borrow your phone a moment?"

"Why?"

"I want to upload a screenshot of Peters. Show it to your parents in case he's lurking near the house. Have your father decide if it should be shared with the magazine staff."

"Should I get a restraining order?"

"To keep him away from your proximity?"

"Yes."

"If you feel that he's a threat to your safety."

Mary watched as Marston downloaded a form, print it, and handed two pages to her.

"It's a Stalking Incident Log with instructions. Give me your email so I can send anything else that comes to mind. I'll give you the link to fill it in on your phone or computer."

Marston watched her study the papers. "You know, let me take back my suggestion that you take a picture of him. Only do it if he's not looking at you."

Mary looked up from her perusal. "So I don't provoke him."

"Exactly."

"I never want to see the creep again, let alone tick him off. Why has he picked me?"

I don't have an acceptable answer for her. Perhaps even Peters doesn't have the answer. I'll have to access his war records and details describing what exactly caused his leaving the U.S. Army.

She watched and waited while he tapped his desk with a finger, mulling over what to tell her.

"Gary, I really need an answer," Mary said with evident intensity. "How do I prevent him from following me, from harassing me?"

He nodded. "Go about your business. If you see him, try not to look him in the eye. If you ignore him, he may possibly lose interest in you and give up the chase."

"But you don't really know that as fact, do you?" she asked sharply.

"No, I don't. Not yet anyway. Mary, I'll make it a priority to look into his records. It'll give me insight into the man and help get him behind bars."

"Thanks, that means a lot to me."

Marston's landline rang. Seeing the caller's name, he glanced apologetically at Mary and took the call with one hand while pulling up a case file with the other. Noticing Mary watching, he shook his head at her. She nodded and politely looked away.

Marston spoke into the receiver. "Yes, sir. Go ahead."

Chapter 37

Members of Congress rarely went anywhere alone. There were usually one or more aides tagging along, briefing their employer about pending legislation, casework and district matters. Congressman Rosefield's district Manhattan and Washington DC offices had a combined staff of 18.

Some of Rosefield's schedule was accessible to the public on his congressional website. Internet viewers from around the world could view his biography, legislation, contact information, and much more. Most of the internet traffic lived in the district that elected him. Most of the others consisted of the media and the curious, even someone with bad intent.

Howard Peters easily logged onto http//theodorerosefield.house.gov. Now that he had granted Mary Godwin a stay of execution, he reverted his attention back to the man who had prematurely ended his short military career.

"Look at you," he growled, glaring at Rosefield's profile photograph. "How could you have been voted in? Voters are really dumb, aren't they? They believe whatever their candidate says. I mean some even think that global warming isn't fake news! The glaciers melt on sunny days and grow when it snows. Everybody who knows their shit knows that's true. You can't believe science. Science is liberal propaganda. Or is it socialism?"

The former Army combatant seethed as he browsed the site. He harbored little hope that there would be anything useful that would give him insight how to terminate Rosefield. But you never know.

The cursor stopped on a particular page of interest.

"Hell, it looks like he makes time for people from the district to visit him in his office. Huh. Will that work? Hmm? Could it be that easy? Just walk in, pop the bastard or slice his throat wide open. Say 'thank you very much' and leave?"

His suspicious mind wondered if the kill would be too easy.

There's probably a metal detector in the DC building where his main office is located, but is there one in the district office here in Manhattan? I better check it out. Has a congressman ever been killed in his office? Dot likely. I've never heard of it. Could be because nobody has my superior mental abilities, my killer instincts. I'll be the trend setter, the leader of the pack, the first of my species.

He looked at another picture of Rosefield, this time with a feeling of malicious goodwill.

He spoke quietly at first. The volume rose with each word, ending with a violent scream. "I'll wipe that confident smirk off you face pronto. In your last dying breath, you'll wish that you never crossed me, you bastard!"

* * *

Mary felt better. She attributed it to her new boyfriend. *He is so good for me. I wish that I'd met him sooner. I bet that if I had, I wouldn't have been at the Freedom Tower when I had and I'd be much happier.*

But how could I have met him before I actually did? I could have volunteered a few months ago to do an article on counterterrorism activities here in New York. Would that have led to being introduced to Gary? That's iffy at best.

And would I have been given the assignment to write about Abu Musab Ali if I hadn't been up there during the terrible incident? The article would have delved into the FBI investigation into his background. Apparently, ISIS pamphlets were discovered on his computer and his user history revealed that he was an avid follower of propaganda permeating the web about the evil that homegrown terrorists can do to the countries they lived in.

So Gary is the silver lining.

Marston ended his call and asked her to wait a few minutes while he had a short meeting in a nearby conference room. To pass the time, she continued meditating.

Can I attribute whatever happy feelings I have now all to Gary? Possibly, but he hasn't been the only person in my life that's been good for me.

Remember the time I fell from the horse at the family estate. My back was in agony. That night something happened.

I woke up in almost total blackness with a weight on my back. Strong thin fingers seemed to be digging into the most sensitive injured areas. The fingers purposefully moved up and down. I held my breath from the pain, afraid at first to say anything.

I noticed that the room seemed much cooler than it should be. For the longest time I was too afraid to do anything other than lay there taking the physical therapy by whomever or whatever. Reasoning out that the spirit was helping me feel better encouraged me to speak.

"Who are you?" I asked in a tremulous voice.

There was no reply, only a pause in the back manipulation.

I sensed that it was a benevolent spirit. "You can continue if you'd like. Thank you for making my back better."

I waited for something to happen. The temperature instantly rose a few degrees. Disappointed, I reached for the bed lamp and turned the light on. I looked around the room, observing that the bedroom door and windows were shut. More significantly, my back was vastly improved.

Unable to go back to sleep for a long time, I sat on the side of the bed and tried to relive the strange bedtime activity. A shiver surged through me.

11-year-old Mary shared the experience with the only person she trusted completely and adored more than anybody else. That was her grandmother, Beatrice.

They sat together in a sofa in a spacious living room. A crackling fire raged in the fireplace.

Beatrice was not at all surprised by the ghost story. She gazed adoringly with her large deep blue eyes at Mary. "I have my own ghost story to tell you, darling Mary. Do you want to hear it?"

"Sure, Nana. Is it scary?"

Beatrice smiled at Mary. "I don't think so. Are you ready?"

Mary nodded, believing her grandmother, but a little doubtful that there was nothing to fear.

"Mary, you know I lived in Paris off and on for many years. I rented an apartment in a building that dated back to the 1700s. The people who have lived there centuries before me witnessed the good and bad events of history.

"I was awakened one night from a sound sleep by a loud commotion outside my bedroom. Propping up the pillows, I sat up and listened to a boy and woman speaking animatedly in French from the far side of the closed bedroom door."

"Who were they, Nana?"

"I wondered that myself, my darling. Two strange things happened. A boy adorned in 18th Century clothing ran through the door into the room. I had the presence of mind to cover my naked breasts with the bed covers while staring at the child. I was flabbergasted that he had gone through the wood barrier without so much as a sound or making a whole in it.

"The boy, ignoring me, strode to a window as a woman, also wearing periodic attire, ran into the room, stopped in front of him, and grabbed his shoulders and berated him in French.

"Jean, don't ever run away from me again!"

"But it's fun, Mother," Jean replied with an impish grin.

He shook off his mother's grip then and dashed outside through the closed window.

Jean's mother turned to me with inflected hands saying, 'Il est impossible, n'est pas?' Then she chased after Jean."

"Wow, Nana, that's kind of creepy. Were you scared?"

"No, not really. I was more surprised than anything else. It is not unusual for spirits to roam the site of their execution. Thousands of men, women and even children were guillotined near my Paris home during the bloody days of The French Revolution."

"That's terrible, Nana. Do you think that Jean and his mother were guillotined?"

Beatrice, eyes misty, nodded at her.

"Did you see them again?"

"I did. I got a feeling that they got used to me and were somehow comforted that I lived in their old home. It made us kindred spirits in a way. But thankfully I did not see them every night or I would have died from exhaustion."

Mary desperately embraced her dear grandmother at the thought of ever losing her. The gesture was wholeheartedly returned.

"What is it, my darling girl?"

"You must never die!" Mary cried.

"Nana, why did you have to die?" Mary whispered inaudibly, staring down at the ring on her finger. It had bequeathed by Beatrice to her and was her most prized possession.

I need to be with you now.

She imagined a reply from wherever her grandmother lived on. *I am with you, my darling Mary. You must be brave and strong as I tried to be during my life.*

Yes, you were both of those, Nana. I will do my best to emulate you, but it is not easy.

Mary waited in vain for a response.

Marston, at his insistence, made arrangements for a car to be waiting for Mary outside police headquarters. He had a valid reason for minimizing her time walking alone on the mean streets of the big city.

He escorted Mary to the car with the excuse of needing some fresh air.

"You didn't have to do this," Mary said, stepping beside him.

Marston chuckled. "It gives me a chance to be with you longer."

They kissed near the waiting vehicle as people in police and civilian attire strode quickly past them. Marston thought that some passionate heat could go a long way to reassure Mary and put her in at ease. Unfortunately, the forced smile on her face revealed that the kiss was not as beneficial as he had hoped.

Upon returning to his desk, Marston set to work requesting access to Peters' military files. He had received implicit approval from the section leader to pursue the endeavor even though it was considered beyond the parameters of his regular duties. Both men concurred that Peters could be construed a threat to the well-being of the city and removing him from circulation was a reasonable and desired objective.

Near day's end, Marston received the link to the Army files. He carefully read every word in them over the next four hours. By the time the demanding mental exercise was complete, his brain was full of useful knowledge about the disgraced former army private.

He condensed the salient highlights into a report, and submitted it to the in-house profiler. Preparing to leave work, he hoped that profiler's evaluation would be sent to him the next morning. The profile and recent photos of the offender would ultimately be uploaded by Marston onto NYPD platform and circulated to every precinct. For now, Marston was only considered a person of interest. There were no grounds to arrest him.

Chapter 38

The congressman had enough battle smarts to know when he was being targeted by the enemy. Rosefield was enjoying an invigorating early morning walk in double time through Central Park when he felt that uncomfortable feeling in the middle of his back. His body tensed. *Not now!*

He spun around, lowering himself almost to a squatting position to minimize his exposure, expecting to see somebody aiming a high-calibre pistol or rifle at him. Ready to roll out, he saw with deep regret that it was too late to implement the evasive tactic.

Standing with feet spread apart in the middle of the narrow path was his least favorite army subordinate, PFC Howard Peters, dressed in fatigues.

Rosefield looked from the man's eyes to the pistol and back at the eyes. *The eyes will tell me when his decision has been made. I see hatred, insanity and triumph in those orbs.*

"You've gotten slow, Lieutenant."

Rosefield ignored the insult of being called a lieutenant instead of a major. He warily observed the gun being tauntingly waved at him. "How so, Peters?"

"I've been on your trail the better part of five minutes."

Rosefield did not want to set off the man anymore, but couldn't stop his reply. "I doubt that."

"Are you calling me a liar, you bastard!?" Peters hissed, the gun aimed with a steady hand at Rosefield's heart.

"No," Rosefield whispered almost inaudibly, carefully watching Peters struggle to hear him. "Doing this is wrong," he added a little louder. "It's dishonorable."

"Dishonorable, you say? You ended my glorious military service too early. Now it's my turn to return the favor by ending your political career. You've heard the saying, 'payback's a bitch?'"

Rosefield quietly mulled over the implication of Peters' words. Was there a way out? "What happened to your face, Private?"

Peters squinted. "Nothing that concerns the likes of you. Stop trying to distract me.

While Peters intensely regarded him, Rosefield calculated his survival chances. He was actually surprised to be still alive. Being a veteran and a survivor of a number of skirmishes with the enemy gave him invaluable experience in knowing his odds. This was a first. He never had to face the prolonged taunts of a single deadly foe.

The man's calmed down. Do I have a reasonable chance to persuade him not to kill me? Will he begrudgingly obey an order from me one last time?

"What's in that little mind of yours, Rosefield?"

"That's a fair question," Rosefield replied, fending off the terror of death as much as possible. He hoped that Peters would recognize a compliment when he heard one. "I wonder what you would accept in lieu of my death."

Peters looked down at him with contempt and astonishment. It was his turn to refrain from a quick response.

Rosefield knew that his question gave him a chance. It created the semblance of an alternative course of action, although slight. *He's never considered anything other than killing me. Has my question done anything other than postpone the inevitable?*

"Tell me now, Peters. What will you do if I walk away now?"

"You mean other than putting a bullet hole in you?"

"That's right," Rosefield replied.

"Why would I not end your miserable life here and now?"

"Because that would be rather bully of you if you didn't. I will be grateful, of course."

Peters scowled at him. "If you use that goddamn word again, I'll gut shoot you without hesitation. You have no right to use the great man's words against me. You understand me?"

What word is so offensive to this maniac? "Can you clue me in?"

"You are totally unbelievable" Peters said, back to wagging the pistol again. "Is it possible that you say it without trying to sound like you're better than everyone?" He glared at his adversary with his mouth open, gun aimed now in the air, and shrugged. "It's the damn word that begins with the letter 'b.' Your granpappy or whoever used it in every lousy sentence. If you can't figure out the word, you don't deserve to live, let alone be in Congress."

Bully? He opened his mouth to say the word out loud, but stopped when he saw Peters aim the service revolver at him with the attached silencer. He noticed a finger on the trigger. He closed his mouth immediately, reluctant to say anything. He watched Peters scan the surrounding empty wooded area, wishing he had permitted his private bodyguard to accompany him on his jaunt in the park.

"Bully this!" Peters snarled, squeezing the trigger.

He jerked up in bed, the dream jolting him completely awake. There was no chance of falling asleep again. He looked at his wife to make sure his abrupt movement had not disturbed her slumber. Thankfully, it had not. Wondering what time it was, he glanced at the clock radio on the night table. 4:58 AM. Only thirty-two minutes before the alarm was preset to sound.

He got up, walked quietly to a window, pushed the heavy drape aside, and peered outside to clear his thoughts.

Why should I waste my time thinking about the scoundrel? Just because I recently ran into him in the street shouldn't be a reason for losing any sleep? That's preposterous. I have nothing to worry about. I can take care of myself, even against the likes of him. In any case I have Thompson to cover me.

He peered down at the street and noticed a dark form standing there. Rosefield's heart beat a few ticks faster as the form remained immobile. *What the hell? Is that him? Too bad I can't see his face. We'll see about this!*

He quickly exited the bedroom, considering but ruling against retrieving his trusty Army pistol from the gun safe. Less than a minute later, he turned off the sensor for the front door, and stepped outside in his silk pajamas.

Uproarious laughter from the man across the street greeted him as he stopped just beyond the open doorway.

"Nice jammies, Rosefield. They ain't military issue, are they?" the all-to-familiar voice snidely said.

"What the hell are you doing standing vigil outside my home?"

"Oh, I can come inside if you want to invite me in, Lieutenant," Peters jeered, followed by a snicker.

Angered by the bad dream, the intrusion, and now a taunt, Rosefield briefly considered crossing the street to teach Peters a lesson with his respectable boxing skills. But news of an altercation on the street would probably end his young political career. He looked away then back again at Peters but could not make him out anymore.

Where is he? Is he trying to maneuver to my side?

Wishing he had his night goggles and sidearm, he peered carefully from left to right and

back again. *Blast him, he's gone!*

Mocking laughter pierced the predawn from the end of the street.

* * *

Peters had heard the tension in Rosefield's voice. *I think I've gotten to the arrogant bastard. He's afraid of me as he should be. The man's seen better times. But he won't see any more unless it is on my terms.*

Was he even armed? I could have simply marched across the street, grabbed him, forced him inside, and taken him down right there. What a fool to face me unarmed.

His useless bodyguard won't arrive until 6. He's no deterrent from what I remember about him. Yeah, it should be easy with or without him.

He contemplated turning back and getting the job done now instead of waiting. But with dawn brightening the sky, he realized that wasn't such a clever idea.

"Tonight!" he whispered hoarsely, striding along the deserted sidewalk.

Visualizing Rosefield in the bright pajamas crossed his mind. He laughed. "What an appropriate color, my friend. It'll blend nice with your flowing blood."

He laughed again until his eyes watered.

Chapter 39

Mary had the most restful night since her ordeal high above the Manhattan skyline of week ago. She practically leapt out of bed, stretched, and threw on her jogging outfit.

She cheerfully greeted her parents before going outside. They were pleasantly surprised by her high spirits.

Her route took her by the Rosefield's home. Mary noticed the congressman and his burly bodyguard speaking animatedly. She wondered what concerned them.

As she jogged past them, Rosefield called out to her with a hand up.

"Mary!"

Is that hand signal commanding me to stop? Well, he is a distinguished war hero.

Mary abruptly stopped as Rosefield left his nonplused New York City security detail and stepped smartly over to her. She absorbed the enigmatic smile and kisses on both cheeks.

"Mary, it is bully weather we're having. You're taking advantage of it the way I should be doing."

"I know you jog in the park, sir."

"Mary, you know better than to call me that," he said.

She observed that the man looked tired and slightly strung out. *It must be his congressional work load,* she thought. "Theodore," she acknowledged.

"Thank you, Mary. Almost everyone calls me Teddy, like my distinguished forefather was fondly called. He disliked that nickname as much as me."

"I know that. I always refer to you and him as Theodore or TR."

"Thank you for that Mary," he replied, solemnly looking down.

"Is there something I can do for you?" Mary asked, noticing the uncharacteristic downturn of his mood.

"Aren't you kind?" he replied with a weak smile. "I'm involved in some ugly business that only I can handle. But I appreciate your offer just like I appreciate your helping me win the congressional seat."

The compliment, coming from a rising star who she respected, made her blush. She did not know what to say other than thank him.

"By all means, Mary. If there is anything I can do to repay you, say the word." He glanced at the impatient-looking bodyguard. "I better cut this pleasant interlude short and return to my shadow."

"Nice to see you, Theodore."

He bowed and strode toward the frowning man. Mary continued the interrupted jog, wondering about the encounter and intrigued by the bodyguard's demeanor. She deduced that there was an issue regarding the congressman's safety. It was something that had already occurred or anticipated.

It is probably nothing more than my imagination on overdrive.

She entered the park as Rosefield and his bodyguard, a veteran who had served with Peters under Rosefield, wrapped up their disagreement how to handle the threat.

* * *

The most important bondage device in the room was the retrofitted horse bit and harness gag leather mouth restraint. Although the room was soundproofed, Peters did not want to risk any loud agonizing sounds being overheard by neighbors. Controlling the inability of the wearer to make much more than muted sounds through the mouth was crucial to a prolonged undisturbed torture session with his visitor.

He got the idea from watching a number of S & M films that permeated the marketplace. Most of what he saw was far too tame for his particular needs and desires. He needed to ramp up the pain and incorporate his version of a final solution, climaxing in death.

* * *

Her apparent restoration carried over to a productive day at the office. Mary worked on the street surveillance system, using what she learned from Gary Marston. She really got in the zone; managing to write nearly thirteen hundred words before she had a quick late lunch at her desk. She spent the afternoon editing the piece.

Everybody knew not to disturb her when she wore earplugs. It implied that she was in her beat the deadline mode. Mary had them on now, not because of time constraints, but because she needed an uninterrupted work session. It produced an endorphin-like high in her.

Mary removed the plugs from her sore ears and set them down on the horizontal surface. She sat as erectly as possible, stretched, and studied her surroundings.

Something was up. People were huddled in small groups, looking at something on their screens. She gazed at the publisher's office. It was packed with people doing the same thing. She got a bad feeling.

Has there been another school shooting? How do we make sure that psychotic, violent people aren't permitted to buy a gun?

She stood and walked over to the nearest group. A few greeted her with half smiles and nods before returning their attention back to the news story on CNN. There had been a shooting, but not at a school. It happened in New York City. She recognized the facial image of the victim.

* * *

Former Corporal Vic Thompson ran into a headwind with the stubborn Rosefield in determining the best way of discouraging Peters. Congressional bodyguards usually got their way with their charges. As security professionals, they dictated what precautions should be taken to safeguard a specific member of Congress. Thompson's situation differed in two important ways. Rosefield was his former unit commander and he was currently employed directly by Rosefield as his private bodyguard. These valid reasons shed light why his advice was not always accepted.

Thompson believed that the best way to protect his employer was a direct approach with Peters. He knew Peter's capabilities as well as anybody, having served with him for two years. He expected that Peters' abilities had diminished since becoming a civilian while his own had remained close to military caliber.

He and Rosefield had been debating the best approach when the pretty young woman whose name eluded him got the congressman's attention. He stewed until Rosefield returned to continue their discussion.

"Give me an hour, sir."

"That sounds reasonable, but you don't know where Peters resides."

"Oh, I have the address, sir."

Rosefield's eyebrows arched for a few moments. "Thompson, you never cease to surprise me. I knew there was a reason why I took you on to protect me whenever I'm here in the city. You stand up well to my DC protective detail."

"Thank you, sir," Thompson replied, beaming. He almost saluted.

"Very well, permission granted. Be smart about it, do you understand me?"

"Yes, sir." *Smart about it? What's he talking about?*

Thompson texted him Peters' address before setting out. When he departed, he was too fixated on his mission to be aware of the concern on Rosefield's face.

Licensed to carry, Thompson was armed with a holstered pistol. He wore a loose-fitting jacket over the secured weapon. The jacket was kept zipped up whenever he was outdoors to ensure that a wind gust would not expose the pistol to public scrutiny. The last thing he needed was some citizen, thinking he was a criminal, reporting him to the police.

He used the time during the walk to Peters' residence, to plot out a strategy how to handling the man. It would largely depend on how Peters perceived him.

We got along okay in Afghanistan, although he made a bad habit of challenging my orders. He even told me once that an experienced private knew more than most corporals. He always acted like he knew more than me. I had to put my foot down multiple times to make the bastard obey me. I always hated that smug look on his face.

The more he considered their history together, the less confident he became of inducing the former private to stay away from Rosefield.

I've committed myself to the major. I must carry out the mission and not return to him shamefaced. That'll lower his opinion of me and maybe get me fired. That's total unacceptable!

Approaching the small apartment building, he glanced at the windows to ascertain if he was being watched. He didn't see anybody. He walked up the front steps, noticing a wireless camera mounted on a column. *It's the superintendent's camera, of course.*

He unzipped the jacket while examining the tenants' names posted by the front door. Then he pressed the assigned button once, long and hard, and waited. Feeling observed, he looked up at the camera. He was surprised that it had rotated, with the lens now pointed at him.

That's strange. I rang Peters, not the super.

"Hello?" Peter's tinny sounding voice said.

"Peters, Vic Thompson."

"Thompson."

"That's right, Howard."

Silence.

"Don't tell me you've forgotten me." *Is that possible? Is his brain fried or is he playing dumb?*

"Corporal."

"That's right. You want to come out and chat?"

"What for?"

Unfriendly bastard. He's not making it easy.

"Come on in then."

The buzzer sounded.

Preferring to speak out in the open to the devious and potentially dangerous man, he reluctantly opened the door and stepped inside. The door closed loudly behind him. He felt the pistol against his tight stomach. It provided some comfort and self-assurance but not enough to make him feel relaxed.

He heard a door at the rear of the first floor open and saw Peters standing there, peering without any emotion at him. *Let's do this!*

"Hey," he said, taking the first stride forward. *Easy does it.*

"Hey yourself," Peters replied. His eyes moved from Thompson's face to his jacket and back again.

Thompson kept his eyes trained on Peters, forcing a weak smile. Peters did not bother to return it.

Stopping within an arm's range, he looking into Peter's disquieting eyes and extended a hand. He didn't like what he saw there, but had to keep up the charade. Peters kept one hand on the open-door knob, and the other hanging down at his side.

"You want to talk here?" Thompson quietly asked. He didn't want to attract the attention of neighbors as voices could amplify in the hallways and stairwell of buildings. The conversation was none of their business.

"Well, well. Why, after all these years, are you here now? Serving together doesn't mean we're pals," Peters gruffly declared.

"I'll leave then." He turned around and walked toward the building exit, silently urging Peters to tell him to stop.

"I'd hate for you to go back to Rosefield feeling like a sore loser," Peters said contemptuously.

Thompson stopped half way to the door. *He knows, damn it!*

"Yeah." Peters laughed mockingly at him.

The bodyguard inserted a hand inside the open jacket. He was indecisive about grabbing the revolver as he didn't want to escalate the confrontation any more than necessary. He turned around and froze when he saw his adversary holding a knife. Thompson remembered that Peters' marksmanship with a blade was first rate. At thirty feet, he was a dead man. *Unless I'm real lucky.*

"Come on in if you have the balls," Peters said, waving the blade.

Rosefield had followed Thompson to Peters' residence. He wanted to make sure his bodyguard was safe. Having one's back went both ways. He considered Thompson a capable soldier on the battlefield and a worthy bodyguard. But Peters was second to none in stealth and had the highest body count in the unit.

Rosefield wore a wig, beard and mustache, and a New York Yankees cap pulled low. He did not want to be recognized by anybody, especially Thompson and Peters.

He stood, peering at the window of a barber shop, looking at the distant reflection of Thompson entering the building.

He ignored a comment from inside the establishment as he turned away to leave. "You could use a haircut, pal."

You are no pal of mine.

Rosefield imagined himself back in Afghanistan as he cautiously advanced on the enemy position.

Thompson risked close quarters again with Peters as he advanced toward the apartment doorway. He would have to react instantaneously to any threatening moves. Would that be good enough? Trying to being alert to his host's body language, he moved past him sideways, never giving him his back.

"You uptight or something?" Peters asked with a smirk.

"Something," Thompson replied, backing a few steps into the living room. He did not like Peters remained by the door, blocking his escape.

"So what do you want with me?"

"I want you to stay away from the major."

"The major," Peters said tauntingly. "Is he your hero?"

"I have a lot of respect for him. He was an exceptional commander for all of us."

Eyes glaring, Peters laughed.

"We are brothers in arms."

"Brothers!" Peters exclaimed mockingly.

"Sure. The major was our big brother."

Peters gaped at him.

Thompson continued expounding the attributes of their former unit's senior officer, hopeful that would make Peters stop harassing Rosefield. If that didn't work, he was prepared to warn the former private that Rosefield was considering obtaining a restraining order from a judge. It would require Peters to maintain a certain minimum distance at all times from the congressman. Thompson hoped it would not come to that. That course of action could escalate the tension and probably end badly.

I can't believe this asshole is trying to make Rosefield sound like a mother effing hero. He sure knows how to kiss ass, and perhaps he really is doing that. Are they in love with each other? Have they gone down and dirty on each other?

I don't want to get one of those diseases from the faggot. He's outta here! What has he touched in here? I better get him out now!

Movement outside the living room window diverted his attention from Thompson. "Who the fuck is that?"

"You trying to trick me into turning my back on you?" Thompson inquired, his hand inching toward the holster.

"Look for yourself. Aw shit, he's gone!"

"Who?"

"Some bum. Probably hoping to steal something to support his drug habit. You know, I think I've seen him before some place."

"Yeah?"

"You accusing me of lying?"

Thompson smiled.

"Thompson, I'll give you a free pass because of our time served together. Get out of here while you can before I change my mind!"

"I won't leave until you promise to leave the major alone. Do I have your word?"

"Sure."

Thompson looked hard at Peters.

"What, you don't believe me?" Peters said, feigning emotional pain.

They each carefully took the measure of the other. Peters calculated how many seconds it would take for Thompson to pull out the service revolver, and aim and fire it.   He liked his chances. A knife against a gun at close quarters could go either way and depended on several factors. Time and accuracy were two of them. Being a moving target could make the gunshot less of a sure thing. He wasn't concerned about missing his own target, moving or not moving.

"Thompson, you have ten seconds," Peters warned.

"You going to stay by the door or move aside?"

Peters grinned at him. "Two seconds." Then he reached with lightning speed for his knife and lunged at Thompson. The bodyguard, not expecting a frontal attack, was caught by surprise. He barely had enough time to reach for his gun and get off a wild shot.

Rosefield had caught a quick glimpse inside the ground floor window at the rear of the building. The scouting confirmed his suspicions. *It will not go well for Vic and to top it off, Peters saw me. The question is, has he made me or has my disguise fooled him?*

He quickly moved to the front of the building. Time was of the essence. He had to get inside. *Hopefully I'll catch a resident arriving or leaving.* Reaching the front entrance, he saw that his hope was dashed. That still left one possibility of getting inside.

Rosefield impatiently rang the buzzer for the building superintendent and checked the time. He was due in the office in less than an hour for a strategy meeting. *If I'm late, I'm late. This is more important than a meeting.*

"Yeah, what is it?" a heavily accented voice said.

"I have a life-and-death emergency. Come to the front door."

He waited for thirty seconds. Agitated, he pressed the buzzer again long and hard. He refused to let go until the super showed his face. With his free hand, he removed the wig and cap and dropped them on the ground.

The superintendent opened the door almost immediately. He glared at the congressman.

Rosefield was not wearing the standard lapel pin worn by active members of the House of Representatives but he did have his photo ID, which he held directly in front of the greasy man's face. The plastic card was issued by U.S. Government and specifically indicated that Theodore Rosefield IV served in the House of Representative for the 11th District.

The emotion on the man's face quickly changed from anger to shock and surprise.

Rosefield was extremely aware that time could be working against his bodyguard. He hoped that it wasn't too late to save him. He quickly explained why he was there, his intent, and warned the superintendent not to call the police unless the man heard a gunshot.

"A gunshot?" the super repeated, horrified.

"I hope it won't come to that. Now if you will excuse me, time is of the essence. I only ask that you make sure nobody loiters in the hallway adjacent to Peters' apartment. You should not either."

Moments later, he tiptoed quietly down the first-floor corridor. The walls were plaster, not sheetrock, providing better than average sound insulation. He would only be able to hear raised voices. He did, but they were muffled sounding. He removed his shoes, left them in an upright position against the wall, and inched closer to the door.

He had not used stealth since Afghanistan. Making an effort to stem memories of the everlasting war, he recognized with irony that Peters had unknowingly returned him to the battlefield.

Although Rosefield was a reasonably perceptive person, the honorable discharged veteran failed to notice the motion detector. If

Peters was alive and well, he could very well be aware that somebody was inches away from the apartment door.

Rosefield gripped the door knob, turned it, and slowly opened the door.

A loud gunshot rang out inside the apartment. The projectile tore through the air and lodged in Rosefield's chest. He fell backward and crashed on the corridor floor, unpleasantly surprised about being the victim of friendly fire. Then he blacked out.

Peters heard the sensor's beep but was in no position to find out who was in the hallway. He was too busy trying to get the upper hand with his guest. The bullet missed him by a fraction of an inch. He heard it whistle past him as he continued his forward momentum toward his adversary. He saw the knife bounce off the man's chest. *What the hell! He's wearing a damn bulletproof vest?*

Looking into Thompson's eyes, he heard a groan and saw a drastic change come over the man.

Thompson dropped the fired gun on the floor and knelt there, staring past his attacker.

Peters managed to stop before tripping over Thompson. Then, deciding to follow the man's despondent gaze, he turned his head toward the apartment entrance. Congressman Theodore Rosefield, lay there holding a bloody hand over his chest.

Am I dreaming? Is life good or what?

As Thompson rushed past him to his benefactor's side, sudden knowledge dawned on him. Thompson had accidently shot Rosefield. It was too funny for words.

Chapter 40

The building superintendent anxiously called 911 immediately after hearing gunfire. An ambulance and multiple NYPD vehicles arrived at the scene five minutes later. While two Emergency Medical Technicians worked to compress the chest wound and get Rosefield on the portable stretcher, the police cordoned off the crime scene around the perimeter of the building and tried to determine what had happened.

Thompson, miserable, had been forcibly moved away from Rosefield and stood inside the living room quietly answering a barrage of questions by a first responders from the local precinct. He felt like a failure in not only not keeping his employer safe, but possibly being his unintentional killer. Head hung low, he complacently allowed the police to put him in handcuffs, eyeing a team of paramedics worked on Rosefield.

Rosefield, awake, and in severe pain, whispered to the technicians preparing to evacuate him. "It was an accident."

"Don't worry, the police will handle it."

"Get me the officer in charge," Rosefield demanded, followed by agonized coughing.

"Sir, no more talking."

"Now or I'll sue you!" Rosefield managed between gritted teeth.

A tall woman overheard the congressman's words. She rushed over and identified herself as Lieutenant Laura Moseby.

"Congressman Rosefield, what is it?" she said, leaning low so that the stricken man didn't have to raise his voice.

Rosefield was barely able to speak now. Grimacing and fighting dizziness, he got off a few short words at a time. "Thompson's my loyal bodyguard. No charges against him. Unshackle him now. Friendly fire."

"What about Peters?" she asked.

She received no response because Rosefield had blacked out again. He was quickly wheeled out of the building to the double-parked EMS vehicle.

While the handcuffs were removed from Thompson's wrists, he entreated Moseby for permission to accompany Rosefield to the hospital.

"Tell you what, you can go in the police escort leaving shortly. But this is with the understanding you will be available by 4:00 PM today to be interviewed.

"Yes, you have my word," Thompson said.

She led him outside, ordering the two cops in the lead squad car to give Thompson a ride. She firmly placed a hand on his arm and looking at him intensely said, "I will be getting the details of what you told the officer in Peters' apartment. Describe Peters to me in one word."

"Killer."

Moseby regarded him sharply. After a slight pause, she added, "Thanks."

Thompson nodded and got in the back seat of the cruiser.

Moments later, the ambulance, sirens blaring and lights flashing, motored away, led by the NYPD escort.

News that the congressman had been shot went viral. It was national news because it involved a member of Congress. His relationship to a popular former president from a century ago, added another dimension to the story. Network historians and political analysts declared that if Rosefield recovered completely, he would be the new favorite in the next Senate race.

When Marston learned that Howard Peters was involved, although not the shooter, the operative knew that he must go to the scene of the crime. *If Peters is involved, then he must be somehow responsible for the shooting because of his connection with the congressman.*

He received permission to go to the site in a liaison role.

Marston hurried to the crime scene, appreciative that his section chief' called ahead to the precinct commander on his behalf to apprise him that Marston had a special unspecified jurisdiction in the matter. Marston would be able to interrogate Peters directly. Most importantly, Peters' actions would have a ripple effect on Mary. Speeding uptown, he expected that she was fully aware of her stalker's role in the shooting.

She must know what had happened. There's always someone at the media listening to police chatter. Mary will find out from some news source.

Should he call her? *Is it better that she hears about from me first? And that the shooting happened at Peters' place? How will that knowledge affect her? God damn it, she'll be pissed that I didn't tell her! But look, I'm here already. I'll call after I'm back in the car.*

Marston jumped out of the NYPD vehicle and walked quickly to the entrance, passing and nodding at fellow police officers. He ignored the phalanx of news media. He expected that a much larger contingent was probably already staking out the hospital.

Showing his badge, he stepped past the yellow crime scene tape. A policewoman studied his badge and directed him down the hall. He noticed nervous tenants huddled in a small group. He nodded empathetically at them. *They must know now that there's a monster living in the building. Some or all of them are thinking about moving out. I would!*

He approached the apartment at the end of the hall. The door was wide open. A CSI technician was measuring the bullet hole in the solid-core material. Passing through the door jamb, he made a mental note that the door had the standard peep hole, heavy duty latch, deadbolt, and chain. He nodded at the two uniformed police officers standing vigil there.

The ongoing conversation stopped when he entered the living room. The two plainclothes cops and one uniformed officer assembled there regarded him with interest. His eyes alertly scanned them, calculating their respective roles in the melodrama. He obviously recognized Peters from the surveillance video and profile image that he and Mary examined yesterday. He could not afford to let Peters know that he knew Mary.

Marston did not at all like the smirk Peters gave him. The unexpected reaction momentarily distracted him. Shrugging it off, Marston looked at the others.

"Come with me please," Moseby requested. He followed her down a short hall to Peters' bedroom. He found himself staring at her familiar black ponytail while stepping close behind her.

As Moseby quietly watched, Marston studied the bedroom. He noticed the tidiness and cleanliness, the combat photos, and the closet door. Marston opened the door and peered in. He noted that the clothes were assorted by color and the boots and shoes were even shinier than when they were new. Seeing nothing that struck further investigation, he turned around and faced his old acquaintance from the Police Academy.

"Thank you, Laura, for allowing me to be here."

"Don't credit me, Gary. I am only following orders."

"I'll try not to step on any toes, but I must interrogate Peters."

"Why?" Moseby inquired with raised eyebrows.

"He's a person of interest in a case I'm involved with," Marston honestly said, meeting her probing gaze.

"You're telling me that he may be a terrorist, a national security threat?"

Here we go. "Laura, I really can't say anymore now. I'm sorry."

The lieutenant shook her head disdainfully. "Politics," she murmured." More audibly, she said, "Okay, I'll bring you up-to-date."

"Thanks, I appreciate that," he replied, smiling graciously.

"Based on our preliminary questioning of Congressman Rosefield's bodyguard, Vic Thompson, and more extensively questioning Howard Peters, it seems that Peters and Thompson were involved in an altercation. Peters had a nasty looking knife and Thompson had his licensed pistol. Both men allege that the other started it and they used their weapon in self-defense. Thompson, fearing that Peter's was about to stab him in the chest, got off a shot that went through the open apartment door.

"Thompson alleged that he had no knowledge that the congressman followed him here, and more importantly, that he had opened the apartment door an instant before Thompson got off the shot."

"Wow, talking about being in the wrong place at the wrong time!"

Moseby frowned at him.

"Have you heard anything about Congressman Rosefield's condition?"

"The bullet entered his chest. He's in surgery as we speak."

"Do you know if it lodged close to his heart?"

"I'm not sure. I arrived on scene a couple of minutes before the ambulance left. The congressman made it a point for me to release Thompson, saying that he was accidently shot. He mentioned something about friendly fire."

"Yeah," Marston commented, knowing that Thompson and Rosefield had served together.

"Yeah what?" Moseby suspiciously replied.

"I hope the congressman's luck holds out."

Moseby looked at him inquisitively.

"He's a hardened Afghanistan veteran is all I'm saying. He survived that hostile environment and hopefully will make it through what happened here, too."

"I hope he does, too. I'd hate to have a member of Congress die from a bullet wound in my precinct."

Marston agreed wholeheartedly. "I don't want that to happen anywhere. Right now, there's no way to prevent guns from getting into the hands of unstable and sadistic people."

Moseby probed him with her eyes. "You sound like a combination of a politician and a concerned citizen."

He laughed. "Of course I'm concerned, Laura. That's a reason for working as hard as I do. There seems to be an infinite number malevolent people who want to destroy our nation." He looked around the room again before locking on the precinct lieutenant. "So what has Peters told you so far?"

"Peters has said very little."

"Do you mind if I have a stab at it?"

"Go ahead, Gary, although I can't see why he would open up to you more than the rest of us. One thing though."

"What?"

"The surveillance camera out front was installed by him."

"Interesting. Okay, good to know."

They returned to the living room. As the pair entered, everyone watched them expectantly, especially Peters.

Marston observed Peters watched them both with slightly different telling facial expressions. *He looks like he wants to do something terrible to Laura. His gaze at me, on the other hand. is inscrutable one second and a smirk the next. I'll have to wipe that off his face in a legal manner.*

Moseby introduced Gary to the other attendees and announced that he would take over the questioning.

Marston promptly ruffled feathers by rearranging the seating. When that was accomplished, Peters sat alone, fidgeting slightly, facing the others. Marston sat in the center, eight feet away but directly in front of him.

He'd prefer Moseby in my seat. I'll have to keep his attention on me and spare her as much discomfort as possible.

* * *

I wanna kill them all! Save the cop bitch for last.

Peters had immediately recognized Marston when he entered the apartment. *Not him! He was the one with Mary Godwin the night before my camera was taken down. It was his doing, wasn't it? I will make him pay for today and that night.*

He watched the man head to his bedroom with the hot looking policewoman. *They better not get my sheets all dirty. And they better stay out of the closet. I don't want them snooping around in there and finding the access panel to my den of iniquity downstairs.*

He's a marked man for sure. He's next in line right after Mary Godwin or do I do him first? When he's lying incapacitated on the table, I'll tell him in detail all about my plans for Mary just before ripping out his heart. It'll make my top ten list of accomplishments. Too bad that David Letterman's show ended. He would have been surprised by what's on my top ten list.

God is delivering my enemies to me.

* * *

Marston was an experienced interrogator. He put on his poker face, hoping it would remain there throughout the proceedings, and focused intently on Peters. *What's he thinking about? Couldn't be anything good. Let's see how he reacts to some verbal jabs and feints! Here goes.*

"Howard, how are you doing?"

"I'd be better if you and the other pigs get the hell out of here."

"I bet," Marston replied agreeably.

"Why are you all still here if I'm not being arrested?"

"I want to go over what happened here this morning."

"I already told all that."

"I wasn't here to hear you."

"That's not my problem, is it?"

"No. Rather than hear it secondhand, I want you to tell me directly. Are you afraid to?"

"Peters leaned forward. "I ain't afraid of you or nobody."

"Excellent. So let's get started. Are you ready, Howard? It's all right to call you that or do you prefer Howie?"

"Whatever," Peters answered, struggling to a less aggressive posture.

"Excellent," Marston replied with another fake smile. He wanted to annoy Peters with an inordinate number of smiles and repeating certain key words. A little bit of psychology could go a long way to extracting what he required from the man. He already knew that Peters disliked him. That was a good start.

The others glanced judgmentally at Marston. He didn't particularly care as long as they didn't interfere.

"Tell me what you were doing when Vic Thompson arrived."

"That's none of your business. Why does it matter?"

"Are you afraid to answer the question, Howard?"

"Hell no! Let me think here. What was I doing when he rang the bell?"

"Is that when you first became aware that he was here to see you?"

"I haven't answered your earlier question, have I? If you're a guest in my home, and an unwelcome on at that, I insist you use some frigging manners."

"Excellent point, Howard. So sorry." Marston was not sorry at all. He gave Peters a big smile. "Go ahead."

"I don't know why he came here. You'll have to ask him. When did I know he was here? When he knocked, of course."

"Oh really? You didn't monitor his arrival on the surveillance camera you installed near the building's front entrance?"

Peters blinked. His glare intensified.

Could Peters have set up the device I discovered at the Godwins? It makes sense for somebody wanting to monitor Mary's movements. It's a shame his prints weren't evident. Only a few smudges were discovered.

"How do you know Thompson? You work together?"

"One frigging question at a time or I'm kicking you out of here. So far, I'm cooperating with you. I'm going beyond the call of duty."

"You sound military, Howard. Did you serve?"

"You betcha, I served. I'm a damn hero!"

"Private Peters, let me commend you on behalf of all of us here."

"You know my rank," Peters commented unhappily.

"You saw Sergeant Thompson arrive outside the front of the building and you knew when he was at your front door."

"Marston, you are a know-it-all just like Rosefield, well never mind. You tell me what happened!"

"It's you turn, thank you," Marston replied calmly.

Peters glaring angrily, stood. "Yeah, asshole?"

Marston, slightly unnerved, readjusted his face again. He learned long ago never to show fear to criminals and deviants. If Peters took more than a step forward, he would move to protect himself, even subdue the aggressor. He noticed from his peripheral vision that two of his cohorts were also standing. He motioned for them to sit.

"Let's all be seated. We're not done."

"I'm not sitting until you're gone."

"Sit down private. That's an order."

Peters face reddened. He glared at his antagonist, visibly trying to control himself. Chest heaving, he slowly lowered himself on his chair.

Okay then, tell me what happened next. What did do and Sergeant Thompson do?"

"Thompson's no damned sergeant. He was only a corporal. You know that, don't you?"

Marston refused to give Peters the benefit of an answer. He probed further. "What was his explanation for the visit?"

"I told you I don't know. Don't you remember? The first thing I know was him pulling out his piece and trying to shoot me."

"You'll say that in a lie detector test?"

"Lie detector test?"

Marston hid his amusement at the nervous twitch on Peters' face. He continued the questioning.

"What is your opinion of Thompson's marksmanship in Afghanistan? Was he a good shot?"

"What kind of stupid question is that? Everyone there could handle himself okay."

"Why is it, if he came here to shoot you, he missed hitting you completely? Was it because he barely had time to defend himself from you?"

"That's complete bullshit, you shithead!"

"I think not." With little hesitation, he went to the next question. "Describe your relationship with Congressman Rosefield."

A look of pure hatred flickered across Peters' face.

"We are all waiting your answer," Marston declared with open arms.

Peters looked from his inquisitor to the others. He huffed. "Rosefield was the unit commander. I haven't seen or thought about him since Afghanistan. I have no clue why his bodyguard forced himself on me. I should press charges against both of those scumbags."

Let's see how he likes this. "I understand that Congressman Rosefield was an exemplary unit commander. You are very fortunate to have served under him."

Peters' mouth opened agape as he processed the statement. Then he yelled, "You don't know a damned thing about Rosefield and me!"

"You are wrong about that, Howard. I've examined your military record."

"That's an invasion of privacy! I'll sue you!" He looked up and down the line. "I'll add all of you to the damned list! You'll end up broke and jobless! I'll get a key from the city!"

"Why did Major Rosefield have you discharged, Private? Tell us, Private. Tell us now."

"I'll tell you jack shit! Go to hell!" Peters sprung from his seat and hurled himself at Marston.

The intelligence operative was prepared for the attack. He leaned backward and raised his feet. When Peters drove into them, Marston bent his knees, propelling the man over him onto the hard floor beyond. He crashed backwards on top of Peters without injuring himself badly. He quickly rolled off the man.

Marston's colleagues made sure that Peters remained on the floor. That was easy, especially as the wind had been knocked out of him. Moseby had the honors; she cuffed him.

Marston got up slowly. His quads were understandably sore. He thought that was totally worthwhile. At the very least, Peters was guilty of assaulting a police officer, a Class C felony. *That should keep him away from Mary for at least a year.*

He did not reveal the contentment inside him as he did not want the others to think that baiting Peters into attacking him was premeditated. Because the interrogation wasn't over, he was not completely satisfied. He really wanted was to manipulate Peters into admitting the extent of his grudge against Congressman Rosefield.

"That was exciting," Moseby told Marston. "Do you have any more questions for him before I have him Mirandaed?"

Peters stood, a police offer at both sides holding an arm, glaring at Marston. "You broke my favorite chair. That means you owe me. Don't forget."

Marston looked down at the chair. A leg was cracked. "Send me the bill, Peters!"

"I'll make sure you pay. That's for sure," he said menacingly.

Marston looked back at him with a hard stare. *Is that a threat? He'll be behind bars soon enough so it doesn't matter.* Turning to Moseby, he said, "No more questions for now. You can tell him his rights. Then, when he's out of here, I need to fill you in on our cuffed friend here."

"Don't talk about me like I'm not here," Peters warned.

Smiling, Marston folded his arms across his chest while watching Peters' reaction to being Mirandaed.

Chapter 41

With a few exceptions, the next year was a happy and productive time for Mary. Knowing that Peters was securely behind bars did wonders to restore her mental and physical health. And speaking of prison, she gave testimony at the trial of Abu Musab Ali, playing a pivotal role in putting him away for thirty years.

Mary enjoyed a shorter than usual summer vacation at the family's island property in Maine where she enjoyed sailing on the chilly azure waters of scenic Penobscot Bay and hanging out with childhood friends.

Her least enjoyable moments there occurred when she saw her former fiancé, Percy Shelley, at parties they were both invited to. Seeming to have accepted the permanent end of their relationship, he complained to Mary about being overwhelmed by the constant flow of overindulgent houseguests.

Mary ruminated. *Why's he telling me? Is he trying to make me feel sorry for him? If we were married, then I'd have to entertain those Broadway types. Better him than me. Besides, it is his choice whether to invite them or allow them in his house.*

She was annoyed with herself for still feeling a trace of anguish about the abrupt ending of their engagement. Old wounds sometimes never completed healed.

Gary surprised her by flying up for a long weekend. Mary wanted him to stay in her bedroom but her mother insisted he stay in a guest room instead. They managed to make up for lost time anyway. They squeezed in nine holes at the golf club. A few golfers raised their eyebrows when Gary helped Mary with her swing with the front of his body pressed against backside.

Mary was a little nervous when she took him to a dinner also attended by Shelley. After introducing them she noticed Gary was confident and at ease. Shelley, on the other hand, flaunted his songwriting successes and tried to insult Gary. Was he jealous? Mary and Gary left the dinner party early for a romantic walk along the shoreline.

Returning to the city a week later, she immediately invited Gary over to the townhouse. They planned to spend the next month at their island Shangri-La. She hoped Gary would stay with her until then. If he needed some coaxing, well, she would use her wiles to do whatever it took.

Greeting him wearing a bath towel helped.

"Nice outfit," he said huskily, pushing himself against her.

Breathing heavily, she pushed him away, intending to hold out a while. against her lover until they were on her bed. They didn't make it that far. Neither of them could wait that long.

She allowed him to take her on the landing of a staircase. It was rough, intense, and what they needed. Afterwards, he carried her up to her bedroom, where they spent the next hours enjoying each other in between serious interludes of serious discussions.

"Mary, what's wrong?" he tenderly asked.

"Nothing."

"You're keeping something from me?"

"A woman is allowed her private thoughts even with her lover and you're surely that, Gary Marston."

"Yes, we are that," Gary said, smiling intensely.

"You are the best thing that's ever happened to me. Does that scare you off?"

He smiled. "Not at all, but are you saying you prefer me to the songwriter?"

"I do."

Gary pushed Mary on her back and kissed her tenderly. Then Gary inched away so that he could take her hand and clutch it over his heart.

Mary sighed contentedly.

* * *

Rosefield had seen his share of bullet wounds in Afghanistan. Witnessing medics compressing the injured area to stem the loss of blood stuck with him over time. After he was unexpectedly shot by Thompson, he helped ensure his own survival by pressing a hand against the hole in his chest.

The four-hour surgery went well. A quick healer, he was released from the hospital one week later. Ignoring his doctor's orders and overriding the concerns of his wife, he decided to put in a few hours of work at his district office.

Carefully lowering himself in his comfortable desk chair after fending off well-wishers, he devoted a few minutes to studying the correspondence and reports deposited there by one of his aides.

He discovered a sealed envelope marked "Personal and Confidential" from V Thompson. Grimacing, he sent for the bodyguard. Waiting, he sat back and reflected. His loyal employee had visited him several times in the hospital. Although he was sedated with pain killers, Rosefield was sufficiently alert to discern Thompson's guilt-ridden demeanor.

When Thompson entered the office, he nodded, bowed slightly, and stood at attention in front of Rosefield's desk.

Rosefield made a show of breaking the seal of the envelope. He had a good idea what lay inside. He cleared his throat, read the letter of resignation, and tossed it in a trash receptacle.

The bodyguard opened his mouth to protest, but Rosefield raised a hand to stop him.

"Vic, your request is denied. You have been at my side for three years now and I intend that will continue for some time to come. It is my own bloody fault that I was shot. I should never have followed you to Peters' residence. Now please have a seat."

Thompson, visibly relieved, obeyed.

"Shall we celebrate you're staying?"

Rosefield rose slowly from the desk, stepped over to an armoire, grasped the two brass knobs, and let the tall panels swing open.

Thompson watched him return a short time later holding two glasses of cognac. Thompson gratefully grabbed the offered glass. "Sir, your doctor will not approve mixing meds and alcohol."

"Please stand."

Thompson stood, drink in hand.

"To hell with him." Rosefield raised his glass. "To your good health and mine. God bless our great nation."

They clicked their full glasses and downed the strong brown liquor in one long swallow.

They both sat, feeling the satisfying warmth glide down.

"Sir, what will you do when Peters is a free man?"

"Do?"

"I think he'll go on the offensive, sir. He's one to carry a grudge to his grave and I'm sure it's festering in prison."

"I expect that you're spot on. In fact, I'm counting on it, Vic."

"You are, sir? Why?"

"I'm confident you will figure out in due course. You have the better part of a year to do so. In any case, Peters is the least of my concerns right now."

* * *

Howard Peters sulked and agitated in the Metropolitan Correctional Center, located only a few miles south of his apartment. He got into scuffles with other prisoners during the first week of his incarceration. His ability to savagely defend himself and fight back earned the grudging respect of the prison population.

With help from the prison psychologist, he made an effort to control his anger. His objective was being released at the earliest possible date. He had unfinished business to take care of. Gary Marston and Mary Godwin would pay for his time served. Moseby and Rosefield's turn would follow.

When he learned Rosefield hadn't died, he took out his disappointment and fury on the heavy barbells. He pressed iron until his aching muscles wouldn't let him lift anymore. By the time he lay panting, a decision had been made to let Rosefield stay alive. By his reasoning, Rosefield's miraculous recovery meant that the man was ordained to live out his life.

Peters hung onto the apartment with all of its secrets. Electronic payments covering his rent and utilities were automatically withdrawn from his checking account as the Veterans Administration continued to remit income payments to him. He suspected that the Feds and NYPD monitored the activity. Although he resented being scrutinized, it was more acceptable than allowing someone else to lease the apartment.

He had a recurring daydream. It began with a guard informing him that he had a visitor. He pictured himself having a face-to-face with Lieutenant Moseby.

Moseby: "How's it going, Howie?"

Peters: "I didn't know we're on a first name basis."

Moseby: "Well, I've gotten to know you much better."

Peters: "How can that be with me locked away in a federal prison?"

Moseby: "We can't let that stop us. So I have some good news for you."

Peters: "I doubt it, but tell me."

Moseby: "I've searched your chamber of horrors."

Peters: "What!!!!"

Moseby: "That's right. I've been down to the basement with half of NYPD and the FBI."

Peters: Silence.

Moseby: You won't be getting out of here for a very long time. And if you ever make it out of here alive, you won't have a place to go to."

Peters: "I'm going to kill you!!!"

* * *

Time passed a little slower every month as the date of Peter's release inevitably approached. Mary's mood took a hit despite Gary's daily reassurances that steps had been taken to protect her. He promised to give her the details over drinks at one of their watering holes.

They huddled in a corner booth. With food and drinks in hand, Gary looked at her in anticipation. She looked back, overcome with dread.

"Gary, I feel like the good times are about done. Am I wrong?"

"Yes, you are. I'll tell you why now.

"The Court has issued a restraining order. It mandates that Peters maintain a distance of no less than 1,000 feet from you 24/7. Furthermore, he must wear an electronic monitoring bracelet around his ankles at all times. Any infraction would be immediately investigated by NYPD personnel and subject to more time in prison."

"Thank you for telling me."

"Mary, I plan to tell your parents."

"Even though I don't live there anymore?"

"Yes, even so. Don't they deserve to know?"

"You're right. After all, Peters did rig the camera outside their home. Thanks, Gary, for being here for me. I also don't know what I'd do without you."

"I'm not going anywhere except to work of course. You're stuck with me." He grinned at her.

"That's what I wanted to hear. I feel better knowing what you have done to make me safe," Mary replied, loading a modest forkful of buffalo chicken salad in her mouth.

Eating gave Marston an opportunity to reflect on the texts he exchanged that morning with Vic Thompson about measures to protect the congressman when he was in New York City. Neither man expected Peters would be a risk to Rosefield in Washington DC as there was no evidence to support that he traveled much.

THOMPSON: *No decision yet to add to Rep Rosefield's NY security detail. It is still only me.*

MARSTON: *Not sure if that's good enough. Peters is a dangerous man.*

THOMPSON: *No need to tell me. I know that firsthand. The Congressman is stubborn. I cannot guarantee his safety in NYC without his cooperation.*

MARSTON: *Will let you know if I think of something to help.*

Marston considered recommending that an NYPD detail be attached to Rosefield whenever he was in town. It was a matter beyond of his jurisdiction. But as Peters was a common threat to Mary and the congressman, he felt a need to find out what protective measures the precinct commander covering the Rosefield home was considering, if any.

Immediately after texting, Marston called Laura Moseby. They had been in touch a few times since Peters' arrest. He asked if it was okay to swing by the station. She sounded pleased about the prospect of seeing him.

After grabbing a quick lunch at a favorite deli, Marston headed uptown. He sat in the lieutenant's cramped office.

"Laura, obviously you're aware that Peters will be released on the 29th." He went on to brief her about his communication with Thompson.

"Gary, listen, I know that you have a vested interest in making sure that his movements will be monitored. I will personally make sure that he doesn't pose a threat to Mary Godwin or anybody else whenever he's here in the precinct and that should be most of the time. I'm very sensitive about everything that occurs in my turf, especially the criminal element."

He smelled the air. *She's wearing a nice perfume. Should I ask what it is and suggest to Mary that she buys some?* "What if Peters does something in another precinct?"

Moseby grinned at him briefly before answering with a serious face. "Gary, have you forgotten about the tracker on his person?"

Did she see me sniffing? Did I do something inappropriate?

"Do you think Peters is planning to do something for when he's released?" she asked, looking at Marston with interest.

"Well, he may try to finish off Rosefield. Have you considered that?"

"Sure, the topic has been discussed. The Commissioner wants a patrol car at his home when he's in town."

That's good to hear. "What about his midtown office?"

"Unnecessary. The building has in-house guards around the clock."

"I see." Marston didn't think that wannabe cops would pose much of a deterrent to someone as dangerous as Peters.

Moseby frowned at Marston. "You don't think that's sufficient?"

"No, I don't."

"I think your concerns are unjustified. Despite the accidental shooting, Thompson is competent and experienced plus he knows as well as anybody what Peters is capable of doing."

"Yeah, you're right, Laura. You'll track the ankle monitor 24/7. That should do it, right?"

Marston stood, signaling the meeting was over. Moseby looked disappointed. That was not lost on him. He liked her, though not as much as she did him. He knew that she was still attracted to him years after their short-lived affair. If it wasn't for his relationship with Mary, he would have been tempted to ask her out.

He watched Moseby step around her desk to him, a wistful smile on her face.

"Anytime you want a change, let me know," she said, showing him a small dose of her provocative bedroom look.

"Thanks, Laura. I'll remember that."

He walked away, feeling her hot eyes on him.

Chapter 42

"It's Discharge Day!!!" Peters exclaimed, stepping outside into the land of the free for the first time in a year. The meds prescribed by the prison doctor made him euphoric, happy enough to celebrate his release with dear friends.

I should have a party. Invite some close friends like Mary Godwin, Gary Marston, Vic Thompson, Teddy Rosefield, and perhaps even Laura Moseby. Do they even know I'm out? Where's my welcoming committee?

And they love me so much that they gave me jewelry to permanently wear around my ankle. I can wear it forever! So thoughtful! How do I thank you all in person? No worries. I will find a way very soon. Oh look, one of you came to see me, perhaps give me a ride home. I will show you to your special guest room. You won't mind the basement. At least I won't.

Marston exited the maximum-security prison, a familiar structure as it was located only a block from his office. He was there for two reasons. He wanted to speak to the psychotherapist who treated Peters and then speak to the ex-con himself.

He watched the bulked-up man stroll out of the prison in apparent bliss. Peters stopped outside the gate, grinning idiotically, and taking a few deep breaths as though he had never before smelled the city air. The man looked around like he was expecting somebody. Marston was curious who it might be.

Should I wait and see who shows? It could be someone of interest that my NYPD brothers and sisters of a different mother would want to know about. But then again, he could simply be waiting for a taxi.

Marston decided to wait a few more minutes. To bide his time, he examined the notes that he'd hastily scribbled in the facility's mental health professional's uninviting office. He went through a list of meaningful single words and phrases on the note pad - "rehabilitated" "docile" "reasonable adjustment disorder" "misunderstood" and "unrequited hero worship."

They read like descriptions of some other convict. Can Peters have changed that much? Improbable at best. I don't believe he's the type that can be rehabilitated. Definitely not! Speaking of which, nobody's shown up. Time to find out his plans.

Marston pocketed the pad and strolled over to the ex-con, approaching him from behind. Treading as lightly as possible, he caught the convict by surprise.

"Howard, you're looking well," he exclaimed pleasantly, standing a foot behind Peters' left shoulder. Marston's composure was enhanced by the knowledge that they were visible on the prison's vid screens. If he could coerce Peters to take a swing at him, he would be behind bars again in short order.

Peters froze instead.

A huge disadvantage of standing behind Peters was the inability to look at his face. Marston didn't know if there was anger, lunacy or something else there. With no time to lose, Marston stepped around Peters and stood there, up close and person.

He was positive that the facial expression on Peters' face had just changed, but Marston wasn't positive about that. *Was that a scowl? I wish the prison shrink could have seen that!*

Peters smiled serenely at him briefly before looking down at his shoes.

Is he shy now? That's a switch. A year ago, he assaulted me for provoking him. Has he really reformed?

* * *

When that bastard Marston snuck up on him, Peters wanted to ram an elbow in his windpipe.

Does he think I'm an idiot? Did he think I was scared? He has a lot to learn about fear. Just wait. I'm no fool. I know where the enemy is. I know the frigging guards are probably staring at me right now. I can't let Marston get to me. I can't look at him or the hatred will show for sure. Perhaps another time. Yeah, back at my place.

"Good to see you, Howard. It's like old times. So what's up?"

I'll show him what's up! Easy does it. Play along with him like I did with that idiot prison doctor. Yeah!

"Marston," Peters said, purposefully glancing at the top of his head.

"Ah, you remember me."

"And you remember me. I appreciate your coming to see me. You here to give me a ride home, Gary Marston?"

"Call me Sergeant Marston. And yes, I'm here to see how life treats you. A ride? Are you a comedian?"

"I refuse to call you by your rank. My time doing that ended when I became a civilian." *Maybe I should suck up to him if that's what it'll take to get what I want.* "But bygones being bygones, I'll make an exception to the rule if that's the price of getting a ride home from you, Sergeant Marston."

* * *

Marston appraised the ex-con. *Do I want my girlfriend's stalker in the car? That makes zero sense. Yet perhaps I can use the time to my advantage. The bottom line is credibility. Can I believe what he has to say and trust him not to try to assault me in the car?*

I'm responsible for his prison time. I can't understand why he's not being an asshole around me. He's not the same anymore. He must have reformed, improbable as that sounds.

Marston watched Peters looking up at the city skyline while he contemplated what to do. Peters seemed patient, agreeable, and docile.

"Okay, listen. I'll take you home."

"Will you really?" Peters replied, both pleased and surprised.

* * *

Peters was actually ecstatic. He bit down on a lip to curb his excitement. *How good is this! I was about to walk home when the jerk actually came up to me and, slap me dead, is my new chauffeur driver.*

"Sure, that's good of you," he said amiably. He considered goodness a human weakness. He had no problem taking advantage of whatever came his way.

"This way," Marston said, leading him to his car.

He didn't know where the cop wanted him to sit. The back seat was where perps sat. It was where people who employed chauffeurs sat, too. Marston surprised him again when he was invited to sit in the front passenger seat. *Is he my new best friend? Does that mean that I'm now supposed to let him live?*

Peters continued the masquerade. He smiled like an idiot even though his cheeks began to ache. He could easily tolerate it though. He wondered if that's how Mr. Hyde felt when he reverted to Dr. Jekyll.

He willingly slid into the passenger seat, duly noting the proximity of the police radio console near his left leg. He also noticed Marston placing his phone on the dashboard holder.

Peters stared straight ahead at the cityscape visible through the front windshield. He would do his damnedest not to ask Marston about Mary Godwin. It was a tall order, ready to spill out of his mouth at the slightest lack of resolve.

The vehicle pulled out of the parking space, merging into uptown bound traffic. Peters was mindful that he wasn't asked his address. It was a sore reminder of Marston's cunning interrogation of him in his apartment. *I can't wait to repay the favor and interrogate him in my special room. I hope he appreciates my style. I damn well will!*

The car stopped at a red light. Marston turned to look at his passenger. "What are your plans?"

"What business is that of yours anyway?" Peters queried mildly, again avoiding looking directly at Marston.

"Let's stop the bullshit, Peters. You and I both know that you have to report to your probation officer and report your activities. I also know about the ankle bracelet and the restrictions on where you cannot be," Marston declared, giving him a prolonged meaningful look.

A honk from the car behind them alerted Marston that the light had changed to green. His foot pressed down on the accelerator. His phone rang as the car kept pace with the traffic ahead.

Peters' eyes bulged when he read the name on the screen.

Marston saw Peters glancing at him with a frown as the ringing continued.

"You should take the call. Pretend I'm not here."

"You'd like that, wouldn't you?" Marston replied. "I won't give you that satisfaction."

Glaring out the passenger window, Peters muttered something that Marston couldn't understand. He heard a mixture of bitterness, anger, and disappointment.

The call ended with Mary leaving a muted message. *Terrible timing. I shouldn't be giving Peters a ride.*

The growing tension from Peters was palpable. *This is a bad idea.* He grimly parked next to a fire hydrant and looked again at Peters. "Get out," he commanded.

Peters turned his head fast to Marston. "Sergeant, listen. I'm sorry," offering a slight shrug. The gesture was better than nothing, but not by much.

They looked hard at one another. Marston could not be certain if Peters lied or not. *Is he manipulating me? I usually know when that's happening. Either he's a master at disguising his manner or I'm a fool. Should I evict him now or relent?*

* * *

Gary had told her that he was swinging by the prison right around the time of Peter's release and that he would call her. When that time came and went, she grew uneasy. She tried to work through it, but kept glancing at the computer clock.

I know that Gary can take care of himself. He has faced terrorists in the eye and his police friends have told me that he always has their back. So why should I worry just because he hasn't called or texted me. Will he think I'm neurotic if I call him?

Unable to curb her nerves and fears, she couldn't wait any longer. Her anxiety ramped up when Gary did not answer. *Something's wrong!* Trying to sound calm but not quite managing it, she left a message. "Hi, it's me. Just wondering how things went. Is he out? Call me. Love you, babe."

Her phone rang a minute later. She took the call without seeing who was on the end of the line. "That was fast!"

"I'm clearly not who you were expecting," her father began. "Mary, can you see me in my office?"

"Sure, I'll be right there."

She sat in the publisher's office, blinds drawn, a tissue dabbing teary eyes. William Godwin sat on a loveseat next to Mary.

"Honey, do you want me to call Gary?"

"No, dad. What's he going to think if you're running interference for me?"

Godwin looked intently and affectionately at her. "He's a busy man, you know. He'll probably call you soon."

"You think so?" Mary asked imploringly.

"Without a doubt, Mary, but to make you feel better, I'll call Lieutenant Moseby to ascertain Peters' whereabouts. He may be home now."

"Dad, I hope you're right. And I would love to know what Gary's doing right now."

Chapter 43

Marston did not exactly know how it happened. He had allowed Peters to persuade him into dropping off the man off at his apartment building. The rest was hazy. Using poor judgment, he had agreed to go inside Peters' apartment instead of adhering to his plan of returning Mary's phone call. *Oh yeah, I needed to use the bathroom. It seemed harmless enough. But he was waiting for me. When I came out, um, he, uh.*

Marston found himself bound and gagged in a blinding white light. He couldn't close his eyes, let alone blink. They seemed to be held open. He was unable to turn his head, too.

A figure appeared overhead. Peters. Leering, he stared down at the captive.

"Gary, you should know that you have a chance here to save Mary Godwin's life. I will do to her what I will do to you if you don't cooperate. Let me demonstrate before I rip the tape off your damn lips."

Marston saw Peters move away and return a few heartbeats later holding a scalpel in a raised hand. *The bastard's showing it to me on purpose. He wants to frighten me. Does he dare harm on an officer of the law?*

"I see that you don't think I'll use this lovely little blade," Marston seethed, holding the scalpel closer to Marston's eyes. "Just wait and see," Peters warned, moving it out of sight.

Marston's pulse quickened as he wondered where the incision would be made. He now had little hope that it was only a threat. *Don't!*

A searing pain emasculated him when the surgical instrument carved a line in the sole of his right foot. Severely arching his back, he screamed in agony through the seal over his mouth. The pain lessened a little when the cutting stopped.

He held his breath until Peters reappeared over him holding the scalpel. A drop of blood fell on his face. "You've got about 7,000 nerve endings in the bottom of each feet. I've severed a few of them," Peters gloated, "so far," he added tauntingly. "You get the point, right? Or do you want me to continue?"

Marston shook his head repeatedly, silently urging the torturer to be merciful.

"What's that you're saying? Here, let me help." Peters ripped the duct tape off his mouth, taking some tissue with it.

Marston yelled again, much louder. He hoped the hellacious sound would carry through the walls.

"If you don't shut up, you'll be sorry. Get me?"

Marston understood immediately. He quieted down, emitting only a faint groan.

"Do you want to talk or would you like to be carved like a pumpkin?"

"Talk," Marston croaked. "Can I have some water first?"

Squinting in the blinding light, he watched Peters consider the humanitarian request. "Talk first, water second. Understand?" He paused for his captive's acknowledgement which came in a small nod. "Okay then. I will get to the bottom line now without any more fun and games. I will spare you further pain if you call Mary Godwin and invite her over. Only when she's taken your place on my special sacrificial table, will I spare you."

"Not on your life!"

Peters furiously slammed a fist on Marston's stomach.

The abdominal pain was nothing compared to his foot. Recovering his breath, he contemplated his options.

"That was very noble and stupid of you, unless of course you happen to be masochistic like me. Perhaps that is a special quality we share. Is it, Gary?"

Will it do any good to play along with the monster? Will he go easier on me? Not unless I give him what he wants and even then, he probably will want to work both of us over before killing us. I won't put Mary through that. I'll be tortured to death first. But I'll test him now.

"I'm not at all like you but I must admit there may be one or two things about you that I respect."

"Oh yeah, what are they?" Peters said, waving the scalpel in the air.

"Well, you did serve our country. That is commendable."

"What else?" Peters demanded.

Hell if I know. That's all I can come up with. Anything else will be bullshit just to buy time.

"I'm waiting, pig!" Peters threateningly lowered the scalpel toward his victim's face.

"Okay," Marston replied, grimacing. He noticed then that his captor's head blocked the blinding light, creating a halo effect. He considered it ironic as Peters was a devil, not a saint.

His brain rescued him while the blade hovered only inches from his face. "Most people never follow their destiny or have a job that they enjoy. It seems that you have solved the mystery and are good at it." *Will he believe that crock?*

"That's very interesting, Gary. It really is. I'll probably have to think about what you told me long after you're done and gone."

Done and gone? What about Mary? He's going to go after her, ankle monitor or no ankle monitor. I sure hope he dies trying. But I won't be alive to stop him.

A tear drop rolled down his face.

* * *

Godwin got off the phone with Moseby. Mary sat across the desk from him. She asked him to repeat what the lieutenant had told him.

"Peters is home," according to the electronic readout on the ankle bracelet."

"Okay," she said, feeling a knot in her stomach. "So where is Gary?"

"Moseby promised to contact Gary's office. She said that there's nothing to be concerned about. But when I told her he was going to the prison and was probably going to see Peters there, Moseby sounded surprised. She asked me why he would do something like that. She promised to get back to me with any news."

"Okay." She fought off a convulsion.

Godwin began to grow alarmed about her. He thought her boyfriend was safe and sound doing something work related not in his office as calls to his work number went straight to voicemail.

Godwin nodded gravely. His hands were interlocked on the desktop. He didn't want to tell her about his most recent conversation with Gary in the study at home.

"Listen, Mr. Godwin. I don't know how much you know about Peters. He may be incurably sadistic. There are no guarantees that the prison shrink has changed him. All we can do is hope for the best and make sure he doesn't violate his restraining order. Keep your exterior doors locked and be alert. If you or Mrs. Godwin see him, let me know immediately."

"You actually expect he'll risk breaking the terms of his release?"

"I don't know the answer. Peters is a savage and they don't usually obey rules or orders. Driven by an inner fury, they do whatever it takes to get they want."

"God help us!"

* * *

Peters took a break from the torture session to use the bathroom. Sitting on the throne, he reflected on what a glorious day it was. *This is without a doubt one of the best days of my life. First, getting out of that shithole of a prison. That alone would have made the top three of the greatest days ever. And then, to top it off I got the hotshot Gary downstairs.*

How easy was it to get him to take me home? And the imbecile thought he was safe using this very bathroom. He's nothing more than an overconfident pig. He gave me plenty of time to sneak downstairs to get the hypodermic needle. I couldn't stop laughing at the look on his astonished face when I jabbed the needle deep in his neck.

Mary deserves better. She deserves yours truly.

I hope he didn't piss on the toilet seat. Well it's too late to worry about that, I guess.

Did he really think that prison made me a goody two shoes? Idiot!

Marston laughed long and hard when he visualized the cop falling on the floor in the hallway, a surprised look on his face.

Heaving the unconscious body into the bedroom, then through the opening in the closet wall and down the staircase to the basement was a challenge but not difficult at all thanks to his intense regimen pumping iron during the past year.

Let the good times continue. It's up to me to make them great. I've got to motivate him to get Mary here. That will make the past year worthwhile. He owes me big time, whether he knows that or not.

He flushed the toilet, scrubbed his hand clean with scalding water, and rejoined Marston downstairs.

The floor around the base of the long table was covered with plastic sheets to contain blood and body fragments. Peters wore a long green surgical gown and booties to keep his clothes and shoes spatter free.

Peters looked down with great satisfaction at his helpless and suffering victim. He waved at the camera that had been set up to record the goings-on down there. The recording would supplement viewings of the *Saw* movies. He turned back to Marston, hoping that the man would have enough stamina not to pass out for some hours. Marston glared up at him. *That's good. Keep up the fight while you still can. Play the hero. It's all for me!*

"Are you ready now to call your green-eyed girlfriend?"

"No way, Peters!"

"It's a win-win for me whether you cooperate or not. Do you understand that, Gary?"

Marston, mystified, shook his head.

"Come now, you're supposed to be an intelligent man. I had plenty of time in prison to learn all about you. I know you have profiled misunderstood heroes."

"You mean terrorists?" Marston snarled.

Peters laughed. "Terrorists and heroes are much the same, depending on one's point of view. Surely, you know that. Or are you even dumber than I thought you are?"

"I must be."

"I agree with you there. You're the one laying there and I'm the one who is not," Peters replied, grinning widely. His demeanor rapidly changed to frown followed by menace and finally fury.

"You are a disgrace to the frigging police department!" Peters screamed, spittle flying.

Marston looked away.

"That's right, you moron. Think how easy it was to manipulate you today. I should send a video to your superior but I won't. Maybe instead, I'll send it to Mary Godwin. Now look at the camera and say goodbye to her!"

* * *

Mary, like her father, called Laura Moseby. They had become friends even though she knew that the police lieutenant was into Gary. Mary did not mind it as long as Gary behaved himself.

"I'm sending a team over to Peters' apartment. He's not answering his phone and neither is Gary.

"Are you worried, Laura?"

"I'm concerned. But perhaps Peters went out. He could be grocery shopping for all we know. I'll check the GPS on his ankle monitor."

"You have no idea where Gary is?"

"We only know that he was last seeing driving away from the prison with Peters."

"What!!! He's with Peters? I feel nauseous. Tell me it's a sick joke, Laura. Tell me that's not true. Why would he do that?"

"Mary, perhaps I shouldn't have told you. I'm sorry. We both know Gary can handle himself, don't we?"

Mary was too afraid and sick to reply.

"Mary, are you okay?"

She fought against her defeatist attitude. *Gary needs me to be strong now. I owe it to him to be that way.* "No, I'm not. Please find him, Laura, and find him safe."

"I will. Got to go."

After the call ended, Mary quickly left the office. Her father tried to get her attention, but Mary didn't notice. She was hell-bent on seeing for herself who if anyone was at Howard Peters' home.

* * *

Peters was distracted by the ringing telephone. Three incoming calls in the past ten minutes was totally unacceptable and excessive. He did not appreciate being interrupted from his favorite pastime and having to listen to the messages on the basement speaker.

One call was from his probation officer who announced their first meeting was scheduled for tomorrow morning at 9:00 AM sharp.

Fuck you! You don't know the meaning of the word sharp!

The next call grabbed his attention much more. Lieutenant Moseby demanded he pick up the phone and speak to her immediately.

"You don't want to ignore her," Marston warned through clenched teeth.

Peters looked down at him. "Oh you bet! I do hope to see her down here very soon. After you comes your little girlfriend. Then I'll play the good host of the lieutenant."

"You have my word that you won't get away with this."

"I'm getting tired of listening to you. I may have to remove your insolent tongue."

That shut up Marston.

* * *

Mary never thought that she would arrive before the police. She had expected to see Peters locked up surrounded by armored police wilding high power rifles.

Seeing Gary's car double-parked in front of the building mystified and worried her. *Why hasn't he responded to my calls and texts? Is it because he has left his phone in the car? Is that why?*

Trying to suppress bad thoughts, she stepped to the car and peered at the front seats and the dashboard. Sure enough, it was propped in the dashboard mount in plain sight. *No wonder. Should I notify the police that he's in the monster's lair with no way to communicate?*

Dread consumed her as she instead turned to the building entrance.

Why the hell did Gary go in there? I know I can't do that. God, give me a sign.

Noticing an elderly couple approach the door, she nodded to herself. *Is this what God wants me to do?*

Jogging toward the door, she called out, asking the pair to hold the door for her. One of them warily looked over a shoulder at Mary while the other inserted a key. They hurriedly opened the door as Mary approached.

"Please don't close the door. I have an emergency involving someone who lives here," Mary exclaimed. "Do you know Howard Peters?"

"What are the likes of you doing visiting that monster? Isn't he in prison?"

"He was released today."

The woman nervously crossed herself.

"He's a sneaky one," the man said, turning for a moment toward Peters' apartment at the end of the hallway." Frowning, he looked back at Mary. "You sure you want to see him?"

"I must. I think my boyfriend's in there with him."

The woman shivered. "Miss, I'm sorry for your boyfriend."

This is difficult enough without being discouraged by the neighbors. "That's his apartment door down there?" she asked, pointing.

"Yup."

Mary noticed that the man wore a watch. "Can you keep an eye out for the police? They're supposed to be here now."

"We don't want any trouble."

"Please, it could be a matter of life and death."

"All the more reason not to get involved with that awful man."

Fed up by their attitude and unwillingness to help her, Mary lit into them. "What's wrong with you? Don't you know that your apathy can be construed as being accessories to whatever crimes Peters may be committing in there right now?"

The old-timers looked at each other questioningly. Then the man looked at Mary. "Okay, when the cops show up, I'll tell them where Peters' apartment is." To his wife, he said, "Time to move."

"Thank you so much!" Mary exclaimed, hands clasped over her heart.

"Don't mention it," the man replied as his wife regarded him stonily.

The relief and appreciation Mary felt immediately evaporated when she strode past them into the hallway. Time seemed to slow as she took the scariest walk of her life toward the distant door. It seemed like an out of body experience. Her pulsating heart beat in her ears, her legs were wooden, there was a huge pit in her stomach, and there was a debilitating pressure in her head.

I am crazy to be doing this. It is just what he wants, perhaps even more than he could hope for. Me going to him. What will he do when he sees me? Gary would do this for me in a heartbeat. Is that why I'm here? He had better be in there, safe and sound.

Mary stopped at the door, too afraid to ring the bell.

She was shocked when the door suddenly swung open and there stood Peters in a bloody surgeon's gown. Too shocked to move, she made it easy for the man to insert the hypodermic needle.

Her eyes flickered open a few minutes later. She was disoriented by the glaring light. *Where am I?* Mary attempted to sit. *I can't move!* Screaming for help, she discovered her mouth was gagged.

She fought against the bindings. Uproarious laughter made her stop struggling. When the merriment ended, Mary angrily renewed her efforts. She heard approaching footsteps. *Don't,* she silently urged to no avail. When a finger meandered over her body, she went berserk.

"Mary, Mary, Mary. It's real nice of you to welcome me home with this surprise visit. I will make the most of it, now that you are actually here," Peters said with maliciously glee.

No, no, no. I'm alone here with the madman? Where's Gary? Her mind was still clouded by the fluid Peters had injected into her blood stream, but she was well aware that something very bad was happening to her. Mary stretched her neck from side to side in an effort to look around her while Peters grinned at her. She couldn't see much beyond the brightness enveloping her.

"I'll make it a little easier for you if you behave." Not waiting for a response, Peters stepped over to a light switch and flicked it off. The room was still moderately lit with a ceiling fixture. He returned to her side promptly.

Mary looked up at her abductor. She conveyed her appreciation of the gesture with a nod. He seemed satisfied with that acknowledgement.

The temporary détente ended when a moan broke the silence. Mary turned her head toward the sound. Sure enough, there lay Gary, leaning against a wall, bound, bloodied and gagged. *Oh Gary, what has the monster done to you?*

"That's right, Gary's not going to come to your rescue and you sure as hell didn't rescue him. He's in for a real teat. But first, he has a ringside seat to what I'm going to do to you." Peters turned to Marston. "Isn't that right?"

Marston glared at him. Peters thought that was hilarious. The sadist turned back to Mary.

Mary, now clearheaded, devised a plan. She began by murmuring repeatedly at Peters. He looked down at her quizzically. Shrugging, he removed the gag from her mouth somewhat more gently than he had with Marston. Marston watched from his uncomfortable position.

Although her lips hurt, Mary didn't complain. There was no point in antagonizing Peters. Nothing good would come from that.

"You're about to return to prison, possibly for life or worse."

"Yeah? How so?"

"The police will be here any minute now." She looked at Gary, nodding slightly to confirm that she spoke the truth.

"Stop looking at him!" Peters viciously slapped her face.

Marston seethed, helpless to do anything more.

Severe pain seared Mary's head. Her nose was broken. She couldn't breathe and see as tears flooded her eyes. Beginning to feel asphyxiated, she opened her mouth to suck in air. Ironically, that would have been impossible a minute earlier. She would have passed out and died a slow death with her mouth and nose both blocked.

"Look what you made me do," Peters bitterly complained.

Dizziness and pain overcame Mary's ability to speak and think coherently.

* * *

Moseby stood in position alongside the hostage rescue team. The elite cops worked at NYPD's Emergency Service Unit. They all knew Marston as he had trained periodically with them. They respected their brother officer. A few had met Mary after hours at social gatherings.

Moseby spoke to the building superintendent. Get something to cover up Peters' surveillance camera. It better be done in less than on minute. Now step on it!"

Waiting impatiently, she hoped that Peters hadn't been observing the monitor feed from inside his apartment. The element of surprise in recovering Marston was important. She glanced at his car.

Less than a minute later, the lens was painted over, impeding Peters' view of who stood in front of the building.

Using her sharp memory, Moseby briefed the team on the apartment layout and reviewed the assault plan one more time. They planned to storm in, hot and heavy, hoping the shock and awe would force Peters to give up immediately. That assumed the one hostage they knew about was still alive and unharmed, at least the former.

Moseby was present in a backup capacity only, not part of the assault team. That did not sit well with her. She was itching to go in with them for two reasons. She wanted to witness her friend's rescue and if possible, make sure that Peters did not survive. *He's way beyond redemption and doesn't deserve to live. If justice would be done, Peters' cold body will be at the morgue by day's end.*

Donning a spare bullet proof vest, she felt her adrenaline flow and nerves spike a bit. But her hands were steady and resolve strong. She was ready to be a warrior if need be

Moseby quickly surveilled the street, satisfied that it was closed to pedestrian and vehicular traffic. Then, given the go ahead signal by the unit leader, they moved through the open front doorway into the corridor, assault weapons pointed ahead.

* * *

Peters' battle smarts told him that something was wrong. *I think that I'd better see what's happening upstairs and outside. A quick glance at the monitors will do it.*

The hated abandoning his houseguests. A good host shouldn't leave his guests alone. So, after bounding Mary's mouth again, he dowsed her head and body with a pail of ice-cold water. He stood for a brief moment enjoying the shock on her face and seeing her body was responding. Then he dashed upstairs and turned off the basement lighting, leaving it in virtual darkness.

Mary's body convulsed and her teeth chattered. Her clogged nostrils barely functioned well enough to inhale enough air. The heavy congestion was tough on the brain. On top of that, she was dehydrated, sore, and frightened. She was certain that that her life would end very soon. The only good news was that she was not alone. Gary was nearby.

Mary moaned through the gag to remind him she was there. She heard him reply in the same manner. The sound soon changed to a grunt. *What is he doing?*

* * *

Peters peered through the open closet into his bedroom. All was silent. The coast was clear. *Is this a false alarm? Or does danger actually lurk nearby.*

His war years honed his ability to intuit that death loomed not far away. It hadn't happened yet, but was imminent. Feeling excitement build inside his beefy chest, he stealthily moved forward, carrying a sawed off semi-automatic in his steady right hand. He missed his old trusty knife. It had been seized one year ago to the day.

Leaving the portal to the basement open, just in case he needed a hasty retreat, he tiptoed into his bedroom. He crouched forward in combat mode and stepped firmed into the hallway.

Up until that instant, he hadn't considered the possibility that he might not have the luxury of any more time with his captives. He now considered whether it was prudent to use them as hostages. It was a viable option that might come into play.

It's a last resort. But do I really want to do that? The damn cops will probably nab me no matter what happens. I'd rather die than go to prison again.

He stopped just past the kitchen and listened. *What was that?*

* * *

Marston managed to bite through the tape, shredding his lips more in the process. That did not matter to him. What did matter was getting Mary loose and somehow getting her out of the hellhole.

"Mary," he whispered hoarsely. "I'm working on getting out of these bonds. Then I'll come right over and set you free. Hang in there, babe!"

He was relieved to hear her mumble an acknowledgement but distressed by the tone of the sound. Hearing her suffering was almost more than he could withstand.

Don't give up! Her duress made him redouble his efforts to tear apart the strong duct tape around his wrists with his teeth. He ignored his own aches and pains.

A short time later, he was free. He had an easier time undoing the foot restraints.

Marston painfully limped over to Mary, trying to keep pressure off the festering, sliced foot. He arrived at Mary's side as a crash upstairs reverberated through the basement ceiling.

* * *

The police rammed through the dead bolted and latched door, guns and eyes in search of Howard Peters and Gary Marston. They were unaware about Mary's presence.

They went room to room, saying "clear" when a room was deemed empty. The frustrated cops congregated back in the living room after completing what looked like a clean sweep.

"I don't get it," Moseby irritably said, glaring around the room. "What have we missed?"

"Nothing, Lieutenant. We got bad intel. They're simply not here," the ESU squad commander replied harshly.

"They have to be here," she countered, watching the man's nostrils flare. "Marston's car is parked outside." That gave her an idea. "We need a dog in here ASAP!"

The ESU sergeant frowned at her a moment before nodding. "I don't think that will do any good but I'll get on it right away."

* * *

Peters peered through the hallway monitor at the heavily armed squad striding toward the apartment door. "Shit!" Knowing he had little time, he made two fast decisions. *I can take out three or four before they gun me down or I can beat a hasty retreat. They don't even know that my hideaway exists.*

He was not afraid to die. But then again, if the police couldn't find him, he would have more fun with Mary and Gary. That's the reason why he backed toward his bedroom. He barely made it across the threshold into the bedroom closet when he heard the front door being smashed and the home invaders announcing themselves.

He was again tempted to make a stand. *Retreating is for sissies! But I'm not actually doing that. I'm just repositioning myself.*

He slid the closet door shut and backed into the dark empty space beyond. He left the panel partially open to better hear what the police were doing. It was a calculated risk but necessary.

Ten seconds later, he heard someone sharply say "clear" followed by footsteps in his bedroom. He aimed his gun straight ahead and held his breathe when as the closet door was opened. *Nobody's here. Walk away now or you're a dead man!* Anybody noticing him would have seen the fiercest look on his face. The cop left the door open, proclaimed the room clear, and exited.

Peters relaxed then. He wanted to know what the cops would do once their search was completed. *I wish I was a fly on the wall and could hear what their plans are. They'll be totally bamboozled not to have found me or Gary Marston or Mary Godwin. Will they leave?*

Peters turned around, facing the dark staircase and void below. "What do you guys think? Should I use you as human shields and leave now or should I continue showing you my hospitality?" He didn't expect an answer because his victims were bound and gagged. But hearing himself talk helped with the decision-making like it usually did.

He crept through the closet and the bedroom until his ears could pick up the thread of conversation coming from the living room. When he heard the word "dog" his hoped evaporated. He knew then that he had minutes left before his scent would be traced to the closet and basement. When the time came, he would not let himself be captured alive.

I'll go down like a hero in a fiery blaze of glory!!!

Marston and Mary were ecstatic that their rescuers were almost within reach. Marston sat down on the table next to Mary, to rest the bad foot and comfort each other. They silently gazed up, listening to footsteps moving across the apartment.

Marston expected to hear gunfire break out any second. He grew uneasy when the search seeming ended without any sounds of violence or raised voices.

"What's going on up there, Gary?"

"I think Peters has somehow managed to evade capture," he said, squeezing her hand.

"Are you serious? I mean how is that possible?"

"I'm not sure. I was unconscious when he brought me down here. I know you were, too, because I was here watching him carry you down the steps."

"You're right. I never saw the layout. I don't know about the basement entrance."

"Wait a minute. A year ago, I did a walk through. It was the day I was here to interrogate him."

"So you saw a basement door?" she asked hopefully.

"No, I didn't. I would remember that and I probably would have checked it out. Damn if I know where it is!"

They silently looked up at the ceiling again, wondering what the police were doing and also curious about Peters' position. They feared the police were preparing to abandon them.

Marston had an idea. He had to let the police know where they were.

"Listen, we have to make a lot of noise that they can hear. That should be enough to keep them from leaving and it could help them locate the access to the basement. Do you agree?"

"Won't that bring Peters back here and hurt us even more?"

"Mary, it's a risk I think we have to take. Otherwise we're as good as dead."

Mary loathed the idea of seeing Peters again. But she understood Gary's reasoning.

"Okay," she whispered.

A floorboard creaked close to where they expected the top of the stairs to be situated.

"Peters might be able to hear us," Marston whispered.

"God help us!" Mary moaned softly.

Although his eyes had adjusted to the darkness, he couldn't see well enough to identify what was in the room. *I've got to find something long that I can use as a weapon and for banging the ceiling. Peters will be down here in a flash with murderous intent. I can't let him do anything more to Mary than he's already done. What if I attack him? If I subdue the bastard, that'll save her. The good guys upstairs should hear a scuffle.*

"Wait here,' he whispered.

Mary grabbed his wrist tightly. "Where are you going?" she asked in desperation and panic. to move.

He activated the flashlight on his watch. A swath of light illuminated the immediate area. He bent his wrist to display the floor and limped around in search of something useful. All he found was a broom. *It's better than nothing.*

An overhead floorboard creaked and he thought he heard voices. He turned off the small LED light and quietly made his way toward the bottom of the stairs. He looked up. The bend in the stairway made it impossible to see the top landing. But some greyness emanated from beyond his line of sight.

Do I dare venture up to the where the 90-degree turn is and peak up? Will he hear me? There better not be a creak or I'm a dead man! Will he see me if he looks down? No, I don't think so because I'm literally in the dark. Here goes!

Marston took a step and stopped. Then he moved onto the next step, not putting all of his weight on it to make sure it wouldn't make a noise. So far, so good. He made it up to the quarter-turn, stopped, and listened. He risked moving his head around the bend and peered up at Peters.

Ah oh! He's looking right at me!

* * *

I swear I'm being watched. How can that be?

Peters pivoted and stared down the stairs, seeing nothing but gloom. He was prepared to go downstairs to confirm that his captives were still tied up when his ears picked up footsteps again entering his bedroom. He turned around to face the closet door and prepared to fire.

He listened to two guys talking.

"This is kind of a shithole isn't it?"

What an asshole!

"It's kind of creepy with all the photos of these wounded women."

I'll be more than happy to make you feel what's that's like!

"Yeah, Moseby said the guy's a real sicko!"

That's enough!

Stepping forward, he fired two head shots, killing both cops instantly, and enjoying the surprised expressions on their faces as the bullets penetrated their brains

* * *

Marston observed Peters turn away from him. He heard distinct voices from beyond Peters' position. Seconds later, Peters advanced forward, followed by two quick gunshots and laughter.

Now!

He hobbled up the stairs holding the handle end of the broom forward. He was full of fear and determination. Taking each step with his good foot, he approached the top landing. He saw a light switch and turned it on. *At least Mary won't be suffering in the darkness.* Then he continued on.

Not wanting to fully expose himself to Peters, he stopped inside a closet and chanced poking his head forward at the room beyond. Two armored cops with holes in their foreheads lay on the floor. *Goddam it!* Shaking his head, he dropped the broom on the floor and grasped a holstered pistol.

Deafening gunfire from the open bedroom door burst out. He felt helpless just standing idly by and listening. *I can't just wait and see what happens. I've got to help my people get him.*

He dashed through the bedroom to the open doorway.

"Give it up Peters now!" a man shouted from some distance away.

"Fuck all of yous!" Peters bellowed from much closer. "It's last man standing. I've taken down at least three of you so far. Who's next?"

"Where's Marston?" Mosely demanded.

"Wouldn't you like to know? Don't leave out poor little Mary Godwin" Peters taunted.

"She's here, too?" Moseby asked.

"Come see for yourself, bitch!"

Marston craned his head into the hallway, hoping to see Peters' back facing him.   The only person he saw was Laura Moseby, crouched behind a couch in the living room about forty feet away. They nodded silently. She pointed her pistol at the right side of the hall. Marston understood Peters was in the room off the hallway. He nodded and moved in that direction, ignoring her demonstrative head shakes that Marston should hold his position.

Marston trod slowly and methodically, trying to overcome the resilient pain in his foot. He closed to within two feet of the room. The next step landed loudly on the floor. Marston, holding the gun in front of him, aiming the gun at the open doorway, silently cursed himself as he correctly guessed that Peters heard him. His finger pushed down slightly on the trigger to save a fraction of a second. It could make a difference.

Deranged whooping and hollering came from the room. Then rapid-fire bullets strafed the hallway walls, hitting Marston twice. He fell down on his back, his heart pumping once, twice, three times before it stopped beating.

* * *

Mary had asked Gary not to leave her alone. "Why not let the SWAT team do their job?", she had whispered, before he left her side.

She was unable to prevent him from going upstairs. He was simply being true to himself.

She appreciated his turning on the light. As her eyes adjusted, gunfire erupted overhead, Whimpering, she hugged herself and prayed. "Please protect Gary from that devil incarnate. Thank you, Lord."

The gunfight, starting and stopping sporadically, seemed to go on for a long time. Fear slowed down time. At one point, shortly before it finally ended, she heard shouting and a body fall on the floor.

I can't stay down here another minute! She stood, swaying on her feet.

Gary then appeared in front of her, smiling sadly. Mary reached out to him desperately. They embraced. Mary couldn't understand why she couldn't feel his body.

"I will love you forever. Farewell," he said.

Then he vanished.

* * *

Peters heard somebody in the hallway go down. He, himself, had sustained two wounds, none mortal, but serious enough to impair him. Usually one to enjoy pain, his shattered right elbow and left shoulder were agonizing, especially when raising the rifle to shoot.

Ugh, I'm hurt real bad. I'm going to die here on my own terms. They've got the superior numbers and have infinite reserves. Who the hell was in the hall? The bastard seemed to have been near the bedroom. How could that be? I killed the coppers there. Pure head shots. Did I miss somebody? No, it can't be! He's tied up downstairs. I gotta check this out myself.

Arms hung low, he approached the open doorway.

"Peters, are you ready to surrender?"

"Not on your life, pig!"

Despite the possibility of being seen from the kitchen entry, he risked satisfying his morbid curiosity by sticking his head into the hall. He recognized Marston an instant before the bullet lodged into his skull. He died with a look of bliss on his face.

Chapter 44

Mary heard footsteps descending the stairs. If Gary was okay, he'd be the first to go to her. Laura Moseby gravely approached her from the foot of the stairs. *Nooooo!*

"Gary?" she croaked.

"I'm sorry, Mary. I really am," Laura replied, stopping in front of her.

Two paramedics rushed down the stairs, carrying a foldup portable stretcher, an IV, and an emergency medical kit. They were followed by two detectives from the precinct. The man-woman tandem and the soon to arrive CSI crew would examine every inch of the room and collect DNA. Moseby wanted to know if there was evidence of missing people there.

"Please wait," Mary demanded when the EMS techs began questioning and examining her. Can I see him?" Mary asked Moseby.

"Mary, I don't think that's appropriate, at least not the way he looks now."

"I've got to. Please, Laura."

Moseby pressed her lips together as she looked doubtfully and compassionately at her. "He has a bullet wound on his face."

"I need to look at him," Mary pleaded.

"Okay, but not until the paramedics here have completed their preliminary and taken you upstairs. No arguments there." Moseby nodded at them and then went over to speak quietly with the detectives.

"I really don't need the stretcher or need to go to the hospital," Mary advised, shaking.

The paramedics patiently recorded her blood pressure and fluid levels. Mary's vein was injected with the IV and told her there was no alternative to hospitalization. A few minutes later, she was happy to finally leave the basement, although embarrassed to have to lay on the portable stretcher. She avoided looking at faces.

She attempted to prepare herself to look at her lover's face for the last time. *Should I really be doing this? Would Gary want me to? Probably not. Definitely not!*

Moseby led the paramedics and Mary to the living room, where Marston's body now lay. More than a dozen of Marston's ESU buddies were assembled, all watching her sadly. More than one of them shed tears upon seeing her. She could not bear to be laying prone on the stretcher a second longer.

"Put me down now!" she ordered the stretcher bearers. They gently set the stretcher down. Unseen hands helped her to her feet. Trembling, she peered down at her favorite person in the world. Tears flowed freely as she looked down at his face. Her eyes were glued to the ugly head wound for longer than she wanted. Turning her wet eyes to his closed eyes, she spoke.

"You're the love of my life." She bent down over him and kissed a bloody cheek. Raising herself to an erect posture she said, "You protected me until the very end."

Mary forced herself to look into the eyes of the men and women around her. Their presence strengthened her. Before allowing herself to lay down again and be carried out, Mary embraced Laura Mosely. She felt a return squeeze.

"Thank you," Mary whispered.

Laura nodded, fighting back tears of her own.

Then Mary lay down on the stretcher, emotionally devastated and physically spent, and was carried out of Howard Peters' apartment.

Afterward

"How are you?" asked the psychiatrist.

Mary, avoiding his direct gaze, glanced around Sidney Barrett's well-appointed office, trying to buy time. She hated the question that began each session. *Dr. Barrett's been asking me the same damn question week in, week out for two months now. He's like a broken record. What does he want from me?*

She risked looking at the 43-year-old therapist, realizing that the session was off to yet another poor start. "I'm sorry, Dr. Barrett. I guess you can see for yourself how I am. Why don't you tell me?" she demanded angrily.

Barrett sat erectly in the arm chair, a pad and pen on his lap. He nodded agreeably at his patient, whom he was treating for severe depression. Recovering from the disease was a slow, arduous process.

"Mary, you know better than to have me answer my own question. However, I'll make an exception just this once. First, have you been taking your meds as prescribed?"

"You're asking me another question?"

"Humor me, Mary. You have a sharp mind and your profession requires analytical questioning. So pretend that I am you, conducting an interview for an essay in *Manhattan Magazine*." He paused a beat. "Are you with me so far?"

Very clever.

"Yes, I understand, even in my condition." She continued after sighing. "Well, to be honest, I've been trying to wean myself off the Venlafaxine."

"Mary, you should not do that without my permission. Tell me the reason for cutting the dosage. Is it your weight loss?"

"Well yes. The meds make me nauseous and I have trouble sleeping."

"This is the first time you've told me this. You should know that Venlafaxine is not the only solution. I'll give you a new prescription." He jotted on the pad.

"Can't I just go a week med free?"

"That's highly irregular." Barrett looked at her contemplatively.

"I'll call you if I feel a need for something before then."

"Yes, please do that. Okay then. Getting at least seven hours of sleep is important for your recovery as is eating nutritionally. You need to have your strength and energy back before I reduce your sessions."

"I understand that, Dr. Barrett."

"That's good."

Mary began to cry, something that she did a lot of during the past two months. She had been a mess at Gary's funeral and internment. The church overflowed with members of NYPD, friends, and family. The haunting bagpipes released whatever tears were left in her at the time.

She still deeply mourned losing her man and continued to be tormented by Peters in her sleep. The medication and the comfort of her parents helped, but she was not sure how much. Gwen came down from Boston almost every weekend to visit. Mary thought that her friend helped her cope more than anybody or anything.

Barrett kept a box of tissue handy on the side table next to the patient's chair. He watched Mary pull out a tissue and wipe her eyes.

"Tell me what you're thinking," he gently demanded.

"Have I told you that I saw Gary in that awful room in Peters' apartment after he died?"

Barrett, an unreadable look on his face, shook his head.

"Gary appeared out of nowhere in that horrible room. He told me that he loves me. He disappeared before I could say anything back. I didn't tell him how much I love him. Isn't that terrible?"

"You're being too hard on yourself, Mary."

"It's my fault he's dead."

"No Mary, it isn't. Look at me, please."

Mary wiped her eyes again and gazed despondently at the psychiatrist. She had been comforted by his words many times. But so far, she had not altered her conviction that Gary would still be alive and well if they had never fallen in love.

"Mary, are you ready to listen to me?"

She scolded herself for not being stronger.

"Mary."

Mary, inhaling, nodded at the therapist.

""Exhale now, Mary. You know the routine," Barrett said reassuringly. After watching her breathing stabilize, he added, "You are a strong woman, Mary. Stronger than most. Are you ready to proceed?"

"I think so," she said tentatively.

"Good. Now listen to me. You must believe what I tell you or else I won't be able to help you completely recover. I can help, the meds help, rest helps, healthy food and exercise helps. Trust me when I state that most of the heavy lifting is done by you.

"You have faced more than your share of misfortune. Your experience in the Observatory, followed by the stressful ending of your engagement to Shelley, and the episodes with Howard Peters can be considered a trauma trifecta. The abundant inner strength you had before these events began has enabled you to persevere more than you realize.

"As for Gary Marston, I have examined his record and can tell you the man had sound judgment and was highly respected. I do not believe that to his dying breath he ever regretted knowing you or how he felt about you. You did not make him go to Peters' apartment. That was Gary's decision and his alone."

Barrett stopped speaking and attentively observed his patient deliberate on his words.

Mary agreed with Barrett. It made sense. She had never interfered with Gary's work nor had he with hers. They respected and cared for each other too much for that. *He'd be horrified what's become of me. He'd say encouraging words and cheer me with a long hug that would lift me up from this funk. I must do better, for him and for me. I will beat this thing and enjoy life again!*

Barrett's message and her own thoughts were cathartic. Had she gotten over the hurdle? Mary thought that she did.

"I feel better now. Thanks."

"My pleasure, Mary." Barrett smiled, happy to see her eyes sparkle ever so slightly. The positive emotional display was a first in their many sessions. It was a clear sign to him that the improvements he had been patiently waiting for in her wellbeing were finally happening.

THE END?

Mary's story is not over. Read more about her in my first novel, *Son of Terror: Frankenstein Continued* and my next book, tentatively titled *Staying Alive*. Please feel free to follow me on Facebook and Instagram: https://www.facebook.com/AuthorWilliamAChanler and https://www.instagram.com/william.a.chanler/

CPSIA information can be obtained
at www.ICGtesting.com
Printed in the USA
FSHW011609200121
77746FS